Stuart White was born in Lancashire, and has lived in London, Hong Kong and Los Angeles. As a journalist he has travelled widely in Europe, Africa, Asia, the Middle East, North and South America.

He covered the drug wars in Colombia, the Iraqi Scud attacks on Israel, and the civil war in Yugoslavia.

He lives in Teddington, Middlesex. This is his fifth book.

Also by Stuart White

FICTION
Death Game
Operation Raven
'Til The Fat Lady Sings

NON-FICTION
Zeebrugge: A Hero's Story (with Stephen Homewood)

The Shamrock Boy

Stuart White

BLAKE

Published by Blake Publishing Ltd,
98-100 Great North Road, London N2 0NL, England

This edition first published in Great Britain in 1993
Previously published by The Bodley Head Ltd. (1990)

ISBN 1 85782 048 7

British Library Cataloguing-in-Publication Data: A catalogue
record for this book is available from the British Library.

Typeset by BMD Graphics, Hemel Hempstead

Printed by Cox & Wyman, Reading, Berkshire

1 3 5 7 9 10 8 6 4 2

"Turning and turning in the widening gyre, the falcon cannot hear the falconer; things fall apart; the centre cannot hold, mere anarchy is loosed on the world, the blood-dimmed tide is loosed, and everywhere the ceremony of innocence is drowned."

W. B. Yeats, *The Second Coming*, 1921

CHAPTER

1

The inside of the van stank of male sweat, pine needles and gun oil. Sweat from the two men concealed on the floor, the out-of-place Alpine scent from the Christmas trees in which they lay, and gun oil from the heavy, polished weapon that nestled between them like an intruding bedfellow.

The sweat was new and old; corruption past, corruption yet to come. It seeped through them like acid from their pores, through the old and never-cleaned cheap and shoddy clothes. Dermot took it into his nostrils, down past his throat, raw and parched, down deep into his lungs.

The foulness of his body's stink, and that of Seamus, mingling with the heady, breezy smell of the trees with their reawakening of Christmases past, and the lovely deep oil and wood smell of the machine-gun.

All Dermot could think of was Guinness – a long, dark pint of the stuff with a top like Irish cream. He was thirsty beyond speaking of it, was cold, was scared to his core.

And God, he had never felt so alive.

He nestled the heavy wooden stock further into his shoulder, feeling that overpowering physical sensation of oneness with the weapon. His fingers were waxen even

1

in the cut-off woollen gloves, but he knew they'd function when the moment came.

Outside the two of them could hear the voices of the shoppers, distant, as though heard from beneath the ocean, and above it all the tinny crackle of an amplified carol: 'O come, all ye faithful'.

A hollow bang on the van, fat slap of an open palm striking the thin metal roof. That meant the patrol was at the far end of the market square.

Dermot said in a hissed whisper, 'Ready?'

'Aye.' There was a quaver in Seamus's voice.

A couple of minutes at the most, that was all.

'Birnam Wood to Dunsinane come, eh, Seamus?'

But Seamus hadn't read Shakespeare, Seamus was not one of your Provo intellectuals. Seamus just hated the British.

Now was always the worst time. The bowels turned to water, the throat was parched. The moment when at last it was all real.

The gun firing, the noise it would make. Imagining the return fire from the heavy army SLRs, the awful, pounding hurt if you were hit. The thought of dying slowly, bathing in your own blood, or being captured and spending a lifetime in the Kesh.

This was the moment you wanted to throw down the Armalite and be away, away anywhere but the awful place that time and fate and history had put you.

But they'd trusted him with the big gun, and damn the bowels, damn the ice in the fingers, the belly dropping

2

away like a man over a precipice. He'd stay and do the job. And if that meant the end of him, so be it.

Dermot calmed himself, going through the specifications of the gun he was about to use. Only two of them in the whole of Ireland, smuggled in from Libya in a cargo boat.

A 7.62-millimetre PK machine-gun. Standard Soviet infantry weapon since the mid-sixties, made by the world's leading small-arms designer, Kalashnikov, who made the famous assault rifle. The PK was bigger fish. It took a 250-round belt, though today they were using a 200-round one for convenience. Muzzle velocity, 2,700 feet per second. They could fire the whole belt in 20 seconds.

Dermot went on with his assassin's catechism.

Weight 19.8 pounds, total length 47.2 inches, barrel length 25.9 inches, gas automatic operation system. Today its front barrel would rest on the elevated bi-pod. It was a formidable weapon.

The first time in the North, Dermot lad, the first time the Brits have had a taste of this, and you won't mess it. You won't.

He noticed the carol change: 'Away in a manger'.

He checked the weapon again. Belt clear, held by Seamus, ready to feed the rounds through. Weapon cocked, first finger through the trigger guard.

The front door of the old Morris van was opened and Billy settled in the cracked leather seat. There was a click of a key and the whirr of a starter motor.

3

Then the bag o'nails engine sound of the old Morris coughed into life, still warm from the trip up from Dundalk.

Could only be thirty seconds now, maybe less. The patrol would be crossing the square now.

Dermot was ice-cold but sweating, like a fever victim.

His armpits, crutch, back and chest were hot-souped with his sweat, yet his face, hands and feet were dry and arctic.

A clunk as first gear was selected on the non-synchromesh box. Billy'd have the clutch in, ready for a quick getaway.

They'll be here, Dermot, always are. Might be late, the Brits, but they'll come eventually. Reliable, they are.

Carols, the engine sound, Seamus's breathing, that heady cocktail of pine and sweat and oil.

Two slaps, sharp.

'Go!'

Seamus kicking open the rear doors, the van roaring away, tyres slipping on the wet stone, all light suddenly flooding in, a moving amoeba-blob of people and faces, a large Christmas tree lit up, the sound of the carol suddenly louder.

And there, like miniature toy soldiers, the patrol. Camouflage smocks, rifles at the ready, red hackles dancing on their black berets like the plumes of circus horses.

Dermot fired.

The indescribable din, blinding red and yellow flames

erupting before his eyes. One man down, another tumbling, a third jerking up and back, pounded by the heavy bullets.

For a micro-second Dermot got a glimpse of the soldier's face, white and spotted, and had the simultaneous thought, He's just a boy. And – he's dead.

Then the van was off the market square and into the road, the tyres squealing. Dermot stopped the burst, and tapped the barrel back; it was already very hot.

The market place was a stampede. He heard screams, cries of terror made faint by his temporary deafness from the roar of the big gun. Stalls going over, produce scattered, parcels falling as the shoppers scrambled and fought, trampling on each other, anything to be away from this killing thing that had suddenly come among them.

Not for you, loves, thought Dermot fiercely, for the Brits, just the Brits. He sighted again, the van still moving. The patrol was down, the soldiers flat on their bellies, those that could still move cocking the SLRs, hard to hit.

There was a flash, and a punch-whack-bang as the round impacted into the van, and ricocheted with a maddening clank and whirr. Instinctively Dermot ducked, and brought his head up quickly, ashamed at his cowardice. They were good, these bastards.

Seamus screamed a good two seconds after the round hit him, as though only then could the terror of it communicate itself.

Dermot bit his lip. Remember the bloody job.

The van was moving; he brought the barrel round, feeling the fir branches scratch him and the taste of a pine needle in his dry mouth.

Two soldiers were kneeling now, two more flashes, one metal punch and a whistle as the round went through the van and popped the windscreen like sugar-crystal.

He heard Billy shout in panic, and Seamus screamed again.

You're messing it, Dermot.

He pulled the trigger, no aim now, wildly, feeling the gun kick and buck like a mustang under him, saw the bullets hose into the square.

Then the frozen moment of horror as he saw the big bullets plough into the woman with the child in her arms, saw the doll-figure torn away and dashed to the cobblestones.

Saw the woman arching back, tumbling like something caught in the wind, leaving splashes of red as she slithered to a halt on the wet stone.

Then the van was off, tyres biting, past the post office on their left, past the pillar box with its sign GR – George Rex, an out-of-date, wrong-country relic.

Out on to the pot-holed mine-pitted road, towards the comprehensive school and the safety of the Irish Republic.

Seamus tried to speak and there was a bubbling sound. He said wetly, 'Christ, Dermot. I'm hit, man, I'm bloody hit.'

Dermot shouted through the foliage to the driver, 'Move it, Billy, put yer bloody foot down, man. If they've got a chopper up we could be in trouble.'

He felt the little van pick up speed, then searched through the entrapping pine branches for Seamus. He felt a warm spray on his face, tasted blood, gagged and spat.

He found Seamus and saw his face, purple-white in the darkness.

'I'm bleeding, Dermot. It's pouring out of me. That fuckin' bullet come down through the roof, my neck's all numb. I need a priest, help me.'

'Come on, lad, you'll be OK. We'll be in Dundalk in the half hour and Dr O'Neill will have you right as rain.'

But Seamus was sodden in his own lifeblood, thick and red, coming in timed spurts from his neck, taking the man rhythmically by the beat of his heart towards his funeral.

He'll be lucky to see the border, Dermot thought. He put his arm around the man, and felt his wrist grabbed, heard the terrified sobbing whisper, 'You've got to help me.'

'You'll be OK, I'm *telling* you.' The blood was hitting Dermot's face, warm and sticky.

There was mortal fear in the grip now, sheer terror in the washed out and ready-for-death face.

'I'll not make it . . . leave me, for God's sake. Please leave me. Please! Maybe the Brits'll help me.'

'The Brits'll blow yer fucking head off after what we just did.'

'Please, Dermot, I'm dying, I know I am. Hail Mary Mother of God, Blessed art Thou among women.'

Dermot shouted, 'Billy, pull over.'

'Are yer mad, or what? They'll be after us. Maybe have a chopper up.'

'Stop the bloody van!'

The van stopped in a shower of mud and gravel, and Dermot pulled Seamus out, a stubby Christmas tree coming with the injured man, snagged in his blood-wet clothes. Dermot propped him against a grassy bank, took the man's hand, curled it into a fist and thrust the fist into the wound, against the severed vein smashed by the bullet.

'Hold it like that. Keep the blood in 'til the Brits come and they'll give you a transfusion.'

Off to their right, set back from the country road, was the glass and brick of the comprehensive school where Seamus the local lad had been a pupil.

Seamus saw it with his dying eyes, and said weakly, 'They said I'd come to no good.'

'You'll be OK. After you're out of the Kesh and we kick the Brits out of the Six Counties you can go back for speech day.'

'Aye, I will that.'

His face was dirty pastry, and Dermot knew it was just the cemetery for Seamus. The cemetery and the procession first. The oratory, then the boys in the black berets stepping from the mourners to fire the salute. And all the while the Brit helicopters chattering above, the cameras picking out the faces of as many Volunteers as they could.

But not the face of Seamus, because Seamus would be in the box. Killed on active service. A martyr for the cause of a united Ireland.

'I'll be off.'

'Have a pint for me.'

'I'll do that.'

He touched the man's face and felt the cold of death approaching like winter.

'See you, Seamus.'

'See you.'

The slam of a door and the van was gone.

The patrol found Seamus squatting in a pool of blood like a man incontinent with his life.

The corporal said, 'Is he a stiff?'

One of the young Fusiliers, white-faced and shaking, cradled his rifle and knelt over the sitting man.

'No. His fucking eyes are still open, and he's breathing.'

He stepped back and kicked the man in the leg. There was a low groan.

The corporal looked carefully both ways up the country lane. Then he turned to the other soldiers.

'Get back in the vehicle and face the other way. You didn't see anything and you didn't fucking hear anything.'

The soldiers climbed back into the Land-Rover.

The corporal took his SLR and crouched down next to the dying man, who still lay snagged to the Christmas tree.

Seamus was trying to say something, and the corporal moved his ear close to the man's mouth.

'Medical attention? What, like you gave my lads and that woman and kid back in the square?'

Seamus formed his last words, 'Get out of Ireland.'

The corporal stepped back and levelled his rifle.

'Sooner the better. Merry Christmas, Paddy.'

He fired a single shot.

CHAPTER

2

The man strapped in the chair in front of him was dark-bearded, hollow-cheeked, and his eyes burned with the deep, furious fire of the true fanatic.

Joe Biddle said again, 'All I need to know is the name and address of your contact in Bahrain.'

The Iranian stared straight ahead, unblinking.

Joe ran a hand through the stubble of his hair, cropped down to disguise the thinning crown and the baldness that crept in at the sides of his head like tidal rivulets.

'Just the two of you, right? Laurel and Hardy in a rubber dinghy, nothing larger than a pistol between you. Hardly enough to start a revolution, eh?'

The dark eyes burned fiercely.

'No bombs, nothing to make them with. So why are you here? To start bother, get the local Shiites going a bit, bring them a pep talk from Uncle Khomeini?'

He moved behind the Iranian. 'When the patrol got you, you were half way across Muharraq and heading for the airfield. Damn few Shiites there, but plenty of big 747s. Is that what you were planning, Ayatollah? To pot a Jumbo for Islam?'

He came back round to face the Iranian commando. 'And if so, where was the RPG or the SAM? Because you couldn't shoot down a 747 with a pistol, could you?'

The silence had a deepness to it, almost a sound, like rushing water, and a smell, a fierce body smell. The Iranian was strong, strong in his mind and in his body.

Joe was depressed. His sunburn itched. He didn't much care for the sun now. He had when he was younger, but now he was a cold-weather man, loved the damp and the drizzle, the mean, narrow streets, cobbles shining with the rain. That was his territory, he could operate there.

'So where were you heading to pick up the rocket launcher? Just a name or number, that's all.'

The Iranian sat perfectly still in his bonds, the poise and the breathed fanaticism an unnerving combination.

Joe grabbed the man's shirt collar with both hands. 'Listen you stupid bastard, I'm your last chance. I'm British, right? Civilised. Those buggers out there are just itching to take you out, cut your balls off and dump you in the sea with your hands tied. You do know that, don't you?'

Iranian kids of twelve and thirteen had charged through minefields and Iraqi machine-gun fire, clutching pictures of the Ayatollah for protection. How did you frighten a race like that? But they had to be stopped from exporting their craziness.

The Iranian said softly in perfect English, 'I am ready to be a martyr for the Islamic Revolution.'

Something flared in Joe, and he took out his Browning service pistol, pulled the slide back and pressed it against the Iranian's temple. 'I'll count to five, chum, then that is exactly what you will be. One. Two. Three. Four . . .'

He put the pistol away. It wasn't on, he knew it and the Iranian did too, either that or he genuinely didn't care. Joe had lost face, and that was bad. It was down to Sainsburys now. It was a gamble, but it was all he had left.

He said, 'I'll be back,' went out and closed the door behind him.

He took the small, brown-paper package, noticing the dark stain on the wrapping and the high, sweet smell. It had come in from RAF Lyneham two days before and he'd left it out of the refrigerator for twelve hours. It smelled awful.

He went back into the room, the package held behind him. He moved out of the prisoner's vision, ripping off the brown paper and the clear cellophane wrapper. He said, 'You're a Muslim – right?'

'I am Muslim.'

'And Muslims don't eat pork?'

'I am devout. I keep the Koran. Pork is forbidden to those of the Faith.'

Joe stayed behind the prisoner, and glanced down at the pork chop that sat wetly in his hand. The meat had a turquoise tint to it, and an unhealthy sheen like the scales of a long-dead fish.

'You hungry?' The prisoner had been allowed no food since his capture three days before. The man gave no reply.

Joe came round to face him, the pork chop still hidden. Then he brought the decaying meat out slowly and held it up so the Iranian could see it. Fear registered immediately in the coal-black eyes.

'Exactly right, Ayatollah – pork. And you are going to eat every last bit of it.'

'You cannot, this is a Muslim land, too, even these people would not let you.'

'*Let* me? They don't have any bloody choice in the matter, mate. The door is locked, they haven't the faintest idea what's in the package and they have strict instructions not to come in here no matter *what* noises they hear.'

The man's eyes were on the putrefying meat, his nostrils flaring at the ghastly smell. Joe jabbed the pork chop with his finger.

'Best Sainsbury's, that. Bought in London last Tuesday. Of course, it being Friday now and the fridge having gone on the blink in the Mess, well, it's kind've lost its original condition.'

The man looked on the point of nausea. From his back pocket Joe took out a penknife and began to saw off a fatty portion of the meat.

The Iranian said through gritted teeth, 'No . . . pork is *unclean*.'

'Not to me, mate, I'm C. of E. We eat anything . . .' He held out the slice on the blade of the penknife. 'And so will you.'

'No! '

'Yes, you're going to eat every last scrap of it.'

'Please, I beg of you . . .'

'Don't beg me anything, 'cause you'll get nothing. There's somebody out on Muharraq with a couple of RPG 2s, or maybe a SAM, and they can't use 'em, but you and your mate can. And if we hadn't caught you, you'd have sat on the roof of some mud hut until a 747 presented its big, fat belly, and you'd have spread three hundred-and-odd men, women and kids in bits over the tarmac, wouldn't you?'

He pushed the slice of luminous pork closer to the Iranian's lips, and the man strained backwards to be away from it. Through gritted teeth, he said grimly, 'You are the Great Satan, the Islamic Revolution will triumph.'

'Will it . . . ?' The pork was a fraction away from the man's lips.

'Please . . . please . . .' The Iranian could smell the evil smell. The forbidden, unclean meat invaded his soul.

'We've had it; had it up to here with your lot; Gadaffi, the Red Brigades, Black September, the IRA, all of them. You talk lofty but the reality is corpses and kids with their legs blown off, funerals and fucking cripples . . . EAT IT!'

'No!' the Iranian screamed, high-pitch.

Joe said, 'Just the street and the number, or you get the whole bloody lot, and then your mate, too. You're expendable, but next week there'll be another two like you who know where the rockets are and how to use

15

them, and maybe we won't catch those two. TELL ME!'

'No, in Allah's name, please no.'

'The number and the street.'

The man whispered something and Joe strained to listen, his head bent close to the man's mouth.

'It'd better be right or you get half this and your mate gets the other half. Sorry it had to be this way, but it's the name of the game now. You people changed it all with your car bombs and Kalashnikovs at check-in counters. But we're learning, we're learning fast.'

Joe put the meat back in its paper and went out.

Two hours later he was back.

As he came in the room the Iranian lifted his head from his chest and looked up dully, fire gone from his eyes now, just the grey paste of ashes left.

Joe said, 'I owe you. I'll make sure you're not harmed. Way I see it, they'll repatriate you within a couple of months. Nobody really wants to admit you're here, it'll all be done through the Red Cross on the qui vive.'

The Iranian said, 'It's impossible. Do you understand?'

Joe read the man's face. He understood, but said, 'Don't be a prat, you're a young man. Blame the people who sent you.'

'Please. Allow me the redemption.'

Joe breathed heavily in the musty room, taking in the still faintly lingering odour of the fetid meat. Then he took his penknife and severed the leather straps that bound the man to the chair.

The Iranian got shakily to his feet, massaging his cramped limbs. He said, 'Please leave me now.'

Joe went out of the room and locked the door. He said to the Bahraini sergeant, 'Siddiq, let's take a walk.'

'What about the prisoner?'

'He isn't going anywhere.'

There was a clatter of furniture from the locked room and the Arab said, 'He's harming himself!'

Joe grabbed his arm. 'We've got the information . . . *Leave him*. What can he do, go back to Iran with them knowing he told us? And how long would he have lasted in one of your jails, if he'd got that far? LEAVE HIM.'

They left it ten full minutes, sitting out on the step in the warm night air, then Joe went back in. The Iranian commando was hanging by a leather strap from one of the window bars.

What a game of choices it has become, Joe thought. One dead fanatic, his religion and his morals outraged, now dead by his own hand? Or a plane-load of innocents shot out of the sky in a pyre of metal and blazing jet fuel?

He cut the man down, laid his body on the floor, then walked back out into the night air. An Arab orderly handed him a telegram, and said, 'This came from London for you. Oh, and Merry Christmas . . .' The man was grinning.

Joe took the telegram and looked at his watch. It was 12.02.

'Oh yeah, Merry Christmas.'

He ripped open the telegram and started to read.

CHAPTER

3

Kathleen spotted her father immediately, a head taller than most of the greeters huddled around the arrival gate.

'Dad! Hi, Dad!'

He saw her and eased through the crush, gently, not pushing, aware as ever of his image and his responsibility.

'Kathleen.' She felt that familiar, remembered bear-hug embrace as if she was a ten-year-old again, safe in his arms. 'Merry Christmas, honey.'

He held her out by the shoulders. 'Beautiful as ever.'

'Handsome as ever.'

'You should be a politician. God, but it's good to see you. Let's get to the car.'

She linked her arm in his, and as they came through the automatic door she took the Boston air into her lungs. 'Wow, that is c-o-o-o-old.'

It was snowing as he drove, thick story-book flakes that drifted into the deep walls already cleared by the plough, and she felt snug and secure there in the car with him.

Just the two of them, the way it had been until Margot.

She said neutrally, 'How *is* Margot?'

Margot was apprehensive as she looked out of the window at the deepening snow. Thank God, she thought, that the car has snow chains.

Soon the Senator would be back with Kathleen, and that was when the ordeal would begin. Once, accidentally, she had picked up an extension telephone to make a call and heard Kathleen and her father talking. At that precise moment Margot heard Kathleen say, 'How is the new wife?'

Not even *your* new wife, but the insulting definite article like *the* new car or *the* new refrigerator. Margot had replaced the receiver gently, feeling unspeakably hurt.

It was clear that Patrick's daughter had resented her at the beginning, but after four years Margot had hoped that would fade. Her last visit, in the summer, had proved that the resentment was still alive and strong.

Perhaps if it had not been his house, *their* house – and of course, Kathleen's mother's house too. The girl had only been ten when her mother died, and then, with the exception of the housekeeper, she and her father had lived there together, bonded by their sorrow and specific sadness.

But then Patrick had met Margot, and she had become the mistress of the house. And Kathleen hated it, hated the thought of it, hated seeing her climb the steep stairs with Patrick, hated her face at the breakfast table.

Perhaps if she had not been so different from Kathleen's mother. Patrick Minihan, senior Democratic

Senator for Massachusetts, was a son of Ireland, a first generation American, and the most outspoken voice on Ireland – all of it, North, South, East and West – the Senate had ever known.

Mary Minihan had been a raven-haired girl from Boston's south side with a family tree planted in the soil of old Erin. Margot was a Virginian who could trace her line back to the first settlements: English stock, supporters of the Confederacy, Protestants with a streak of Calvinism, a dislike of rhetoric, and a wedge of common sense. And Patrick had loved Margot for it, loved the contrast to his fiery emotional self. Adored the caustic wit, the lack of respect for his views, the sobering sensible realism that doused his wilder Irish fantasies.

He and Mary had been like a pair of wild, harnessed horses, pulling together with abandoned passion for what they believed. Margot nudged him, calmed him, led him, teaching him to think before speaking, teaching him the art of reflection and the value of moderation.

They had met and married within five months, he a widower for ten years, she a widow for seven, and all their friends and the gossip columnists said this crazy combination couldn't last.

And they were blissfully happy . . . Kathleen was the only cloud in the blue sky. She was her father's girl, raised at his knee on tales of old Ireland: of Aunt Kathleen, for whom she was named; of Uncle Michael, another family success story; of all the Donals and Kevins and Seans across the water.

Shamrock tales and patriot games, the Dublin Post Office at the Easter Rising, Black and Tans, ambushes, ships hove to in the dead of night, Branch spies and tarring and feathering. With Patrick it was all tempered by age, political reality and now the sobering effect of Margot's hand and political savvy.

But young Kathleen took it neat, like strong Irish whiskey, and Margot knew it was a potent draught. Sometimes she felt her stepdaughter was drunk on it and the sobering would be bitter and painful.

Margot pulled the curtain closed and went into the kitchen. Perhaps the last six months had changed her stepdaughter. Instead of the Hibernian society perhaps there were boyfriends who took her to Westwood cinemas. Instead of the 'armed struggle' perhaps there was something else to occupy her mind; maybe one of the half-dozen boyfriends of the last couple of years had stuck.

Then it might be love and marriage and babies they'd be talking. At the least, please God, a job with a good law firm. And Margot, hating herself for it, hoped it would be 3,000 miles away in California. She heard the toot of a horn, took a deep breath and prepared for the fray.

Kathleen had known her mother was ill. She had seen the prolonged 'lie-downs' become weeks in bed with a nurse in attendance, had seen her body wasting away.

As a child she had resented it; the lack of attention, the lack of interest on her mother's painracked face. Then one morning Kathleen had woken, aware somehow that the house was different, quiet and spooky. But definitely different.

She had cried out, for her mother, for her father, and then Dad had come into the room, scooping her up, lifting her from the polished wood floor and tucking her back into bed.

And he held her tight, unable to speak, until she glimpsed the big tears gliding down his face. And she knew then, without words, that her mother had died.

She said, 'Is Mummy dead?' And her father had nodded dumbly, choking on his tears. 'I'll look after you. Just you and me together now.'

And it had been the two of them, for ten years, long wonderful years. Until Margot.

Senator Minihan stopped the car, killed the engine and turned to his daughter. 'I'll make it quick and easy. It's Christmas, she's my wife and I love her. As I love you. You're entitled to your views, she to hers – and me to mine. There'll be a ceasefire for the festivities. OK?'

'*Our* views, Dad, yours and mine . . .'

'. . . a ceasefire, a *truce*, or so help me I'll paddle your behind with a hurley stick.'

'So much for the season of peace and goodwill.'

'Promise me, Kathleen. It's her home too, remember?'

She looked up at him in the darkness of the car's interior. 'Are you happy with her, Dad, *really* I mean?'

'Yes,' he said, 'I am. I never thought I could love again after your mother died –'

'But she's so – different.'

'Yes, she is, and why not? I was lonely and cold inside and I was hitting out at everything, including in my politics.'

She said doggedly, 'You said what you believed, what you still believe. Don't let her put out your fire.'

'The fire is still there, it's just more *directed* now.'

'Good old Dad.'

'Not so much of the old. You'll be nice to her? For me.'

'It's a promise.'

And it went better than each of them could have expected. They exchanged gifts and Kathleen seemed genuinely impressed with, and grateful for, the antique brooch Margot had chosen.

Then they ate by candlelight, making inconsequential talk, gossip, anecdotal politics, until the Senator said casually, 'Any thoughts about what you're going to do now? I presume this post-college community law centre thing has run its course?'

Kathleen nodded. 'Yes to that, it was only for three months. As to the first . . .' She shrugged. 'I don't really know. I gave up my apartment, so . . . goodbye L.A.'

'You can stay here,' her father said, 'long as you like. It's still your home, right, Margot?'

'Yes,' said Margot, with all the warmth she could muster, 'if it's anyone's home it's yours.' Patrick squeezed her hand, knowing what that had cost. 'A law firm perhaps?' Margot added, 'Boston is a good place to practise law.'

'Mmmm . . .' Kathleen moued indecision, chewing a mouthful of food. Then, 'I thought I might travel. I met this medical student who's going to Guatemala. There's a jungle clinic there, maybe I could, you know, head down there . . .'

'Guatemala? For Christ's sake, Kathleen!'

'Patrick, it is Christmas Eve . . .'

'I'm sorry, Margot, but *Guatemala*! Kathleen, you are twenty-four years old and you possess a law degree from UCLA and you tell me you want to go and work in a jungle *clinic*. Perhaps all that money I spent on fees should have gone towards you studying *medicine*?'

Kathleen speared a succulent vegetable, and toyed with it in front of her mouth. 'I did say, *maybe*.'

'Then keep it at maybe. If you want to travel you can go to Mexico, or Hawaii, or Europe, for God's sake. Guatemala.' He shook his head. 'Let me tell you, one of these days we're going to have another Vietnam down there. That place is dangerous.'

Margot said carefully, 'I don't know, Patrick. I think working with under-privileged people could give Kathleen a valuable insight –'

'Into what – diphtheria, yellow fever? She has a *law* degree, can't either of you grasp the contradiction here?'

'I'm sure we both can, Patrick, but life is full of contradictions. Kathleen, I think it's an excellent idea, don't let your father bully you.'

'I said,' Kathleen spoke slowly, locking eyes with Margot, 'maybe. And maybe I might just go and live on a commune in the Aleutians.'

The telephone rang; long, clear, persistent rings, and everyone raised their eyebrows. The Senator looked at his watch. 'At ten o'clock on Christmas Eve?' He got up from the table and lifted the receiver.

'Senator Minihan.'

The two women watched him, and then each other, unsure of the other, and wary. Kathleen had made one decision. She was damned if she was going to Guatemala, not if Margot approved of it.

The Senator gave a My God, then several yeses, more yeses and a not sure. After a brisk Merry Christmas he hung up and returned to the table, pushing his plate away from him.

'Serious?' Margot asked.

'Dad?'

The Senator shook himself like a dog, as though trying to rid himself of something, then exhaled. 'Gerry, my assistant. There's been a bad shooting in the North of Ireland. The IRA opened fire with a machine-gun near to the border with the Republic . . .' He stopped, closed his eyes and then opened them again. '. . . It was a market place. They killed three British soldiers and a woman and her young daughter.'

Margot said, 'My God – on Christmas Eve?'

Kathleen glared, then pushed her chair back and went round to her father, encircling him with her arms. 'It's not your fault, Dad. It will go on and on, and *on*, just as you've always said, until the British get out of Ireland.'

'Really?' said Margot evenly, 'and that justifies the death of a child? Killed by mistake, a regrettable error, isn't that what these people always say?'

'Please, Margot.' Senator Minihan waved a limp arm of protest.

'Is that what you believe, Patrick?'

'You used to, Dad. Has it changed for you now?'

'It's complex; a complex problem, you can't condemn and you can't condone, it's not a question of that.'

'Dad . . .' she hugged him closer, resting her chin on the top of his head . . . 'No one wanted that child to die, or the mother, or the soldiers. No more than they wanted Bloody Sunday – thirteen innocents shot by British paratroops, houses wrecked, women blinded by rubber bullets, the farce of a trial without jury.'

'No,' the Senator said, 'you're right. No one wanted any of that. Poor old Ireland, will it ever be at peace?'

'Yes,' Kathleen said, 'when the British go, when the Irish men and women are left to solve their own problems.'

Margot stared at them both icily. 'It's what *you* think, Kathleen, and it's what you want your father to think –'

'Shut up.' The Senator's words lashed across the table like a whip, cutting off Margot in mid-sentence. 'I've been a supporter of a united Ireland all my life. I hate the goddamned British for what they've done to my country.'

'*This* is your country, Patrick,' Margot said softly. 'You're an American.'

He stuck his chin out. 'Yes, and I'm a son of Ireland,

and the two are a powerful mix. Don't tell me what I think – *either* of you.'

He looked at Margot. 'If it takes the IRA to get Britain out of Ireland, then so be it.' He unwound his daughter's arm from around him, took her hands and got up to face her. 'But it doesn't mean I have to support the deaths of children.'

He left the room, and the two rivals for his love.

She found him in the library watching the TV news. The Crossmaglen killings were the lead item. The camera closed on an overturned stall, debris and a long mis-shapen bloodstain on the cobbles.

Shots of a road, another, larger bloodstain, soldiers squinting in the glare of the arc and TV lights, and two men in dark mackintoshes loading a cheap wood coffin into the back of a windowless black van. The newsreader said the Pope had appealed in a special message for both sides to keep a truce over the period of Christmas.

When the item ended Senator Minihan's hand touched the remote and switched off the TV. He turned and saw his daughter.

'I dreaded this – you and Margot.'

She ignored it. 'Will you make a statement?'

He shook his head. 'No,' he said flatly, 'not at Christmas, not on this – it wouldn't be . . .' he searched for the word 'appropriate.'

'Dad, Margot isn't your conscience, she's your wife. Don't be swayed by what she said. Say something.

You can couch it in the right terms, but say *something*.'

'She isn't, but you are, is that it, Kathleen? Have you become my conscience where Ireland is concerned? Is that what the Hibernian Society has made you, another long-distance expert on the subject?'

She felt the tears prick her eyes at the bitterness of the rebuke.

'Because you don't know, can't know, can't *feel* . . .' he clenched his fingers into a fist . . . 'what it's like, not from here. It's my struggle and it's every Irishman's struggle. It's in our blood, like whiskey or a bad sickness. But it's not your fight.'

'It is . . .' she said sullenly.

'Because I've poisoned you with it, that's why, and I wish to God I hadn't, telling the tales I told to a young girl.' He shook his head with regret and suddenly he looked terribly old.

'Whatever you say, Dad, you're wrong. It's my struggle. *Mine*.'

No one spoke of it again over the holiday. They were restrained and formal, correct and polite until it hurt. Then, the day before New Year's Eve, as they were eating dinner, Kathleen said casually, 'I thought you'd like to know, Margot – Dad – that I've made my decision about the law and Guatemala.'

'And . . .?' Margot asked.

'You're damn well not going to Central America, Kathleen –'

'I know, Dad. And I'm not going into the law either, just yet anyway.'

'So what do you intend doing, Kathleen?' Margot asked, mentally placing her bet.

'I'm going to Ireland,' Kathleen said, a shade too triumphantly.

The Senator just looked at his daughter, thoughtfully, as Margot carefully collected her winnings and placed it double or quits.

'The North part as well?'

'Yes, the *occupied*,' she stressed the word, 'part as well. I can see for myself, instead of being a *long-distance* expert, right, Dad? I can see Aunt Kathleen and your cousin Michael.'

'Patrick.' Margot looked at her husband, quizzically. 'Do you have an opinion on this?'

'Yes I do . . .' He pushed his chair back from the table. 'You're not going, Kathleen. If you want to get yourself killed, *go* to goddamned Guatemala.'

'You're being ridiculous, Dad. You can't stop me and you know it.'

'She's right, Patrick, and besides, I think she should see for herself.'

'Thank you, Margot,' the Senator said bitterly. 'Thanks for your support. Will you both excuse me?'

Kathleen caught him in the hall, turned him and saw with shock the big tears coursing down his cheeks. 'Dad, oh Dad, I'm sorry.'

'I love you both and you tear me apart.'

'She's against everything you believe.'

'And you're a fool – she's a realist.'

'Perhaps after Ireland *I'll* be a realist, enough to be acceptable to you again.'

'In God's name, Kathleen.'

'I'm going, Dad.' And he saw the stubborn jut of her jaw, the defiant, fighting Irish in her eyes.

'Are you, by God? Then go with my blessing and my love. It's in your blood too. But be careful. If anyone harmed you I'd never forgive myself, nor would Margot.'

They embraced and she felt the salt tears on her forehead. 'Dad, Dad, I love you so . . . I just . . . I just . . .'

'That's us Irish, dangerous and sentimental; that can be a lethal combination.'

'You're the best man who ever lived.'

'I'm an old fool.'

Later, she thought of what he had said. She mulled it over as she dozed in the comfortable bed, in the warm house; a world away from Ireland, the damp and the violence. Was that what Ireland was, dangerous and sentimental?

She would soon know.

CHAPTER

4

The battered Cortina dropped him at the corner, hard under the edge of the flats. Treacle-black, only the tiny, distant remaining street lamps like sickly fruit in stout-rich cake.

'Yer a bloody fool, Dermot.'

'I am that.'

'Be careful. Pick up at five, and get you the hell out before first light.'

'I'll be here.'

He scrunched across the carpet of broken glass, kicking aside the jagged half-bricks and dented cans, the scorched bottle necks, legacy of the most recent riot.

Into the dank entrance perfumed with the familiar scent of his childhood: dampness and faeces, animal and human piss, the deep gut-turning stench of poverty. He inhaled it as a reminder, savouring it as a man will linger over a long-forgotten, much-hated picture of himself. Then he heard a sound of scuffing feet, threadbare trainers slithering on the concrete stairs.

Dermot pushed himself back into the deep darkness and waited.

First the lad saw just the figure and he started with fright. Then when Dermot spoke, the soft voice registered with the boy like a trademark, and real fear grabbed at his vocal cords.

The Man.

'Mr McGarvey?'

'Danny.'

'You've come back.'

'You'll know to be quiet, lad.'

'On my life.'

Dermot let the silence hang, one, two, three seconds, time falling like globules from a dripping tap.

It was then he smelled it, and moved closer. In the darkness he couldn't see the glazed eyes, or glimpse the deathly pallor, but there was something in the way the boy moved in that closed space, feet shifting on the stained floor, fluttering like some captured bird, the chemical unease destabilising his poise.

'Danny, if you've been for the glue you know it's a bad thing.'

Deep breathing, fear, and the smell again, unmistakable, seeping from the mouth and pores.

'Jesus, Mr McGarvey, I swear it was only the once. I'm for the Volunteers when I'm old enough.'

Dermot reached out in the darkness, found the boy's arm, followed it to the wrist and the palsied hand, closing his own around it.

'You'll be joining no one if you keep taking that stuff, or putting the other lads around here on it, d'you understand me?'

'Yes, yes.'

'It'll just be a ride, a pistol at the back of your leg and a spell in the Victoria. You want a walking stick and a plastic knee-cap, Danny?'

'No, sir.'

He could hear that the boy was crying now, and squeezed his hand with appalling gentleness.

'Then remember what I said. And Danny, I was never here.'

'On my life, sir.'

'It will be, Danny.'

And he was gone, silently like a ghost until the boy realised he was standing alone, weeping to himself in the dark night.

The power of fear, the awesome power of the fear he could instil with a look. Not just boys either, but grown men. Even the RUC detectives, the Branch men who'd kicked him around the bare room at Castlereagh, grunting and puffing with the effort of their blows as the fists and boots did their work. Even then, as he just rolled, curling with the blows, eyes open and focused on them, silent, the deep fear was in them.

They couldn't finish him for good, that was against the rules in there. Maybe he was for the Kesh, but the fear was that one day he'd come back.

A knock on the door, an innocent Sunday tea destroyed, a single bullet, surprise and death; or the kick of a starter motor, white light, perhaps some faint seconds or minutes of dawning realisation as they sat in the burning wreckage, the lifeblood flowing out of them.

For he was the one they called the Man, and they knew it and feared him. The Man never missed, never failed, and there was no pity in him. And now he carried that knowledge like a flak jacket around him. He was being foolish, sentimental even. Risking his life and his liberty.

He stabbed optimistically at the lift button, the scarred stainless-steel doors patterned with familiar graffiti. Support the H-Block, Provos Rule, a spray drawing of a man in a black balaclava. He jabbed the button again but there was no answering whine from above, so he took to the stairs.

What a place for a home. Sixth floor, Mam with the shopping, Dad with his hernia, and no power on earth could make a Prod lift engineer come in here among our kind.

So the lifts stayed broken and the casualties of war had to climb. The old ones stayed stuck for weeks like lone birds in a tall nest, high in their prison eyrie, fed only by the kindness of those fitter than themselves who shopped and fetched errands for them; the weekly pension and the Social Security allowance.

An orange light glowed on a landing as he paused for breath. A door opened, the figure of a woman putting out a bag of rubbish, with a child behind her, tugging at her skirt.

The widow Rosie, wife of Donal McConnelly, Belfast Brigade, ambushed and shot down by an SAS murder squad in Andytown, buried now in the Milltown cemetery.

She saw him immediately, and came out on to the landing.

'Rosie.' He touched a finger to an imaginary cap.

'Dermot.' Her face was set. 'I heard you was down South. It's a big risk you're taking.'

'Aye.'

'We heard about you on the telly. The bairn was just two, Mam gone and two more left without a mother.'

'I'm at a loss, Rosie.'

'No you're not, Dermot.'

'You're talking about the action in Cross?'

'Aye, Crossmaglen.' The little red-headed girl with a white Irish face pulled at her mother's leg . . . 'Wait, Roisin! We heard how it was you.'

'I was in Dublin. Dreadful business, and regrettable. They were mixing with legitimate targets; casualties of the armed struggle. They died for Ireland.'

The woman's face was twisted and strange in the luminous glow. She gave him a smile of sweet and honest hatred that genuinely shocked Dermot.

'Don't worry, brave man. No Peelers here, or touts, you don't have to watch your mouth in these flats. The Man. That was the word here. They trusted you with the big gun and you messed it.'

He felt a sting of anger, and worse, shame, an acid bile he had been keeping down since that night. And now it seeped back, sour in his stomach.

'Don't believe all you read in the Brit press, Rosie. They like to spread these horror stories about us. It gives them an excuse to let their death squads loose.'

She laughed, cynically, and then a young boy, not more than seven or eight, pushed past her to peer at the stranger.

'My daddy died for the Cause.'

The woman slapped him. Quickly. Hard. The sound of the blow echoed in the bare hall. His head jerked, he cried out, his face a mask of surprise and hurt. Then he tore away, tiny feet padding down the hall, the sobs coming. The little girl Roisin broke free and ran after her brother, scared and confused.

'What the hell was that for?'

He found he was breathing heavily, angry and off-balance, disturbed by this woman, and the way she spoke.

She thrust her face six inches from him, defiant, no sign of the fear of which he was so proud. 'Because I don't want him spouting that garbage at eight, that's for why, Dermot McGarvey. Because I don't want him growing up to be like his dad – or you!'

He resisted the temptation to strike her, to crash his fist into her angry face and send her reeling back into her prison flat.

Instead he spoke, slowly, measuring the words. 'The boy's father was a hero. Shot by British occupation forces while fighting for the freedom of all Ireland, and the lad has a right to be proud of him.'

'Donal was a bloody fool!' She spat the words. 'Never worked a day in his life, and when he wasn't talking about Ireland he was drinking to it with *my* kids' family allowance.'

'He loved you, Rosie, and the kids. But he loved his country too, and that's why he ended up with three SLR rounds through his guts, his jaw blown away and some Brit fucker from Hereford giving him the *coup de grâce* with a Magnum.'

She pushed him with the heel of her palm directly into his shoulder, and he could feel the blood coming to his face, his head pounding with it.

'Rosie.'

'Don't, Dermot . . . don't. Maybe you're right about Donal. I just wish he'd loved Ireland less, and me and the kids more. Maybe then they'd have a father instead of a stone in the Milltown and a myth to play with.'

The little girl returned, crying and pulling at her mother.

'I'm coming, love, promise.

'Maybe you did kill that bairn and her mam and the Brit soldiers down in Cross over Christmas, and maybe you didn't. But one day they'll get you, Dermot, sure as eggs are eggs, just like they got Donal, and then it'll be either Milltown or the Kesh.'

'It won't happen.' Then he dared say it, stung to it by her insolence and her lack of fear. 'I'm the Man, and they never get the Man.'

She put her palm out, gentle this time, laying it on his shoulder. He suddenly realised he was a full ten years younger than her.

'No, Dermot, you're not the Man. You're just another bloody Shamrock Boy. And we're sick of you, the whole of Ireland's sick of you. Just bloody Shamrock Boys from the Easter Rising down, playing their patriot games.'

'Games, is it?'

'Games, my lad, bloody terrible games. And no one wants to play any more. We want peace, and we want jobs, and decent homes to live in, and streets that we can walk down, and washing machines and two weeks in the bloody sun.'

'Ah well, sure and we all want those things. But perhaps a thirty-two counties united Ireland first.'

She said, 'God save you, Shamrock Boy,' and closed the door in his face.

He could smell cabbage seeping under the front door, and rapped on the glass panel with his knuckles.

An hour later it was as though he had never left. As though he had never been gone these twelve months, never been back just sixty short minutes.

His father sat in the battered plastic armchair facing the TV. It was switched on, burning bright and colourful, pulling in the human moths with its never-diminishing flame.

Dermot could not recall a moment in his conscious life when the TV had not been switched on, it and his father linked by some invisible umbilical cord, a phenomenon of symbiosis that ended only when one was forced to rest for the night. Then it seemed that both lay silent and dark, only waiting for that moment when they could be reunited. His father talked, smoked, ate, snoozed – probably had mated – under the gaze of the TV.

It rewarded his devotion with an endless platter of sweetmeats to delight, stimulate, flatter but ultimately to drug him.

Dermot's mother was in the tiny kitchen, her bony bird-like figure darting from pan to stove, cupboard to shelf, shouting occasionally over the waterfall roar of the TV.

Colm, his elder brother, sat, feet curled up beneath him, on the black plastic sofa which matched his father's chair. He was reading the *Sporting Life*, marking it off with the working half of a fractured ballpoint pen.

Sixty minutes. For the first thirty he had been treated like a hero. They were exultant, then scared, then resigned. He was a stone dropped in a pond, the ripples of their surprise and welcome radiating outwards, then vanishing as the water surface of their life settled into its familiar pattern.

But at first it was God be praised. How was he? The rumours they heard. The Peelers and army had been, seven PIG loads, plus armoured cars, on Christmas morning too, the Lord's birthday, God, had they no respect?

They'd lifted Da and Colm, kept them two days, and Dad with his hernia too. The boyos had got a little riot going, stones mostly, one petrol bomb, a soldier hit in the face by a stone from a catapult, a few plastic bullets fired.

And on Christmas Day. But the Brits had not been back, and Da and Colm were out the day after Boxing Day so they'd had the dinner then, and sod the Brits.

'Quiet since then?'

His father broke away from the smart stranger in the box. 'What?'

'Quiet, since then? No Branch men?'

'No.'

One hour and ten minutes. The meagre meal eaten, Colm picking the winners.

How old is he now? thought Dermot. I'm twenty-six, they had Colm when Mam was eighteen, Dad twenty Christ, Dad isn't fifty yet and looks seventy – Colm'd be thirty.

Dad cast him a glance. Teeth gone, their replacements wallowing around in the shrunken gums, the puckered mouth clenching and sucking at itself. Thin arms, emaciated almost, yet the curved hump of a small pot belly, and rounded shoulders from his hunched sitting position.

'D'yer manage to find work, Colm?'

His brother looked up, eyes uneasy, over the rim of the *Sporting Life*.

'That a joke or what? You being my brother, who the hell'd employ me?'

'Was it rough when they lifted you?'

'No picnic.' Dermot heard a voice, but saw only a racehorse and predictions.

'I'm sorry.'

'Not your fault.'

A mug was thrust into his hand. 'Watch out, it's hot.'

'Ow, I know.'

She was happy, he could see it in his mother's thin, prematurely lined face. Her lad was home, whatever he might have done. The family was complete.

'What time d'you say Fionulla'd be back?'

'I said eleven, at the latest, that's my strict rule.'

A key turned in the lock and she came in the door, long hair, dark and wild, framing her oval face.

'Dermot!'

He grabbed her and swung her round.

'You look gorgeous. Good enough to eat.'

'Dermot, I don't believe it . . . God, it's bloody fantastic . . .' Her face suddenly clouded. 'You shouldn't be here. The Brits have been, and the police, they say – after Crossmaglen . . .'

'Liars, all of them. I'll be gone by five.'

The *Sporting Life* moved. 'Nulla.'

'Hallo, Colm. Oh, Dermot, I can't believe it, I can't, you've lost weight, your cheeks – oh God, it's great you're here.'

Their mother looked on beaming. Brother and sister together again. Forget the Troubles, forget the squalor of the Divis, forget the agony of bringing up kids over nearly twenty years of nightmare.

Forget that your middle child was a Provo, and a top gunman if what they said was true, and if he never spoke of it. Forget that he may have the blood of children on his hands.

Forget all that, because he was her son. And he loved his sister, and she loved him, and even if Colm seemed to love no one but himself and the betting shop, that didn't matter either.

They were a family again.

'Too beautiful to be in school.'

'Sixth form, no uniforms, no silly discipline.'

'No fooling around with boys.'

'As if I'd ever . . .' Her eyes sparkled.

He gave her an extra squeeze. 'I've really missed you, Nulla.'

'Same here. Will you ever come back, permanent I mean?'

He shrugged. 'Probably not.'

She brightened. 'Then we'll all have to move somewhere, Canada, Australia–'

Colm's face jerked up from behind the *Sporting Life*. 'What's the time?'

'Twenty past. Why?'

''Cause I'll still get a pint down at Paddy's, and I'm fair parched.' He slipped on a nylon windcheater that had been draped over the couch, folded his *Sporting Life* and brushed past them.

'Hey, Colm.'

His brother turned.

'Careful what you say. I'm not here.'

'I wasn't planning to drink in the Shankhill, Dermot.'

Dermot put out his hand, palm inwards for a handshake. 'I know that, it's just that it's a big risk I'm taking.'

Colm took his brother's hand, his own palm cold and damp.

'Oh, ignore him, Dermot. He's funny sometimes, aren't you, Colm?'

'Sorry about Christmas, honest,' Dermot said.

Colm's face was set. 'Not your fault. Like you said earlier, you weren't anywhere near Cross, were you?'

'No, I wasn't, but have a care, Colm, remember what the Brits used to say in the Second World War, careless talk costs lives.'

'I'll have a care, Dermot. See you, Nulla.' The door closed behind him.

Dermot said, 'He's changed.'

'He lives in your shadow.'

'He had his choice.'

'And you?'

Her dark brown eyes were fierce and deep, penetrating his soul. Probably above all other human beings he loved his sister, respected her, would die for her.

'Yes, I made mine.'

She held both his hands in hers, face cloudy and serious.

'They say you were down at Crossmaglen on Christmas Eve, when the little girl was killed. They said you fired the machine-gun.'

'Do they? And who's "they"?'

'People . . . People who usually know. Tell me you didn't, Dermot. Christ, I know you're with the boys, I support you, we all do. If you've sniped a Brit soldier or an RUC man . . . well, so be it . . . they shouldn't be here, and it's our country, and they should get out . . .'

He squeezed her hand, as just over an hour before he had squeezed the frightened boy's. One squeeze for fear, another for love.

'No. But killing kids, little girls, even if it was a mistake, you wouldn't have, would you, Dermot? Not you, I know it.' There were tears glistening on the wet coals of her eyes. 'Would you?'

'Kill bairns? Never. Not even for Ireland.'

Just lie for it, Nulla, lie for it when a lie is all that is left to me.

'On the word of the Mother of God?'

'On the word of Mary.'

'God, Dermot, I knew they were lying.'

And she hugged him, tight and close.

A lie all right, not theirs, but mine. And a soul would be sold before I'd destroy the beliefs of my own sister. And perhaps a soul had been, there in the hallway of the place Dermot once called home.

CHAPTER

5

So small, that coffin in its Union Jack shroud.

Joe watched in the light rain as it creaked on the shoulders of the six Fusiliers, stepping carefully in their mirror-toecapped boots. Knife-edged trousers, stiff tunics, serious faces, young, innocent and old beyond their time.

He had never been a big man, David, just square and muscled with the compact, sinewy torso of a coal-miner, which is what he had been before becoming a soldier like his dad.

Thighs like a thickened sapling, all the power of a dynamo as he sprung from behind the pack, chin jutting, ball under his arm, powerhouse legs going.

The flash of a moment. A playing field, rain such as this falling, the echoes of isolated cheers and groans. And David running with the ball, bursting out of tackles, the slap and thud as muscle met muscle. All that energy, all that life, gone for ever, gone in a series of muzzle flashes and confusion as voices sang of peace on earth.

Twenty-two years old, now cold and white in the box, uniform-dressed like a waxwork, eyes closed for the endless journey into oblivion.

The rifles slanted up towards the grey, weeping skies, a series of sharp retorts, rifles lowered, then David's turn, deep into the wet earth.

Ashes to ashes. Litany for the lost. Then the young pallbearers turning, cropped heads soaked and glistening, joining the rifle party, sad but embarrassed, anxious to be away for a smoke and a pint.

The CO, grey-templed, face lined, and eyes that showed this was not the first time he had stood in such an English churchyard, his face solemn.

It was a picture of England and a landscape all its own. A momentary slice of what it meant to live in this damp island.

Boys coming back from foreign wars in coffins. The weeping faces of mothers and fathers, brothers and cousins, of comrades and friends; bemused and perplexed. It was worn into the fabric of the nation like some sad but inevitable tapestry.

Joe watched like an invisible man, as he always had before on these occasions. But this was not a mess-mate, not some fellow squaddy with a nickname, a Chalky, a Dusty, a Jock or Taff.

This was blood of my blood, flesh of my flesh.

But still he stood, the sun-tan incongruous in that tableau of grey misery, stood and watched as a military life received its prescribed farewell.

They filed past him and he took the murmured words, the half-mumbled condolences, shook hands, absent-mindedly patted some shoulders.

And he felt nothing but numbness, as though the big bullets had struck him and not David, as though he lay, as David had lain, paralysed and barely conscious. And just for that stretched moment, there on the damp grass surrounded by death gone by, he wished that the numbness, the paralysis, could end for him as it ended for David.

With a breath, a sigh, and an end to pain, an end to struggle.

And then the moment passed, and he wished to survive as he had always wished. To go on, for that was all there was until, like David, the option was snatched from you.

He turned on his heel, feeling the rain fly from him like spray from a dog, and strode out from the graveyard, along the gravel path and into the road. A brown leather glove saluted him.

'I was most awfully sorry, Sergeant.'

Joe stood, arms to his side. 'Thank you, sir.'

'If there is anything I can do . . . anything the regiment can do . . .'

'I appreciate that, sir.'

'I know you ceased to be part of the family, but I think we look on you as the boy who went away and made good. If we can help you through this, of course we will.'

'Thank you, sir.'

'Goodbye, Joe. If it is any consolation, he was a fine soldier. A tribute to you, and to the regiment.'

'Thank you, sir.'

The CO got into the Vauxhall Cavalier, whispered something to the woman in black beside him, then to the young army driver, and the black staff car went off in a slither of wet tyres.

A small, bald man in a grey suit and black tie came over to where Joe was standing. The man's face was grey-scarred, where the coal dust had ingrained itself in the cuts.

'Want a lift with us, Joe?'

He shook his head.

'No ta, Billy, I'll walk.'

'We'll be in t'club tonight, come in for a pint.'

'Mebbe.'

'There's nowt worse, lad, nowt, I know. And there's nowt anyone can say or do. But drink helps, and don't let anyone tell you different.'

'Aye.'

'It weren't your fault, so don't go thinking it were.'

'No.'

'He would've joined, no matter what you said, and if it hadn't been our lot it would've been the Foreign Legion. He were a soldier, it were in his blood.'

In his blood. Blood. My blood became his blood, and so he became a soldier like me, and then the blood was spilled.

'Perhaps I'll see you at the club.'

'Take care of yourself.'

'Thanks, Billy.'

The cars passed him, one by one, the dark, sad faces staring out at him, drinking of his sadness. Then he turned and began to walk, first down the roughly tarmacked road, then off into the side-streets across the slithery-wet cobbles and the fractured pavements, the smell of coal smoke in his lungs, an echo of another time, another man.

On he walked, sodden and tired, as the phantom-cloaked sky closed its folds over the dejected town.

For every year of David's short life Joe had been a soldier. Borneo, Aden, Cyprus, then Ulster at the very beginning. The bad days of '71, internment, Bloody Sunday and the protracted gun-battles of '72. And had survived it all, gone to the funerals like this one, seen the youngsters come and go, some missing limbs, avoided the faces of the child-widows.

David's childhood had been a series of blurred snapshots, and crushed weeks in awkward friendship.

Always the army, and when she had suggested that perhaps it would be better if he were home, he seriously thought about it, went down to the Labour Exchange, or was it Job Centre by then, he could never remember.

And they asked him what could he do, and the answer was that he could do nothing except be a soldier. He had joined at fifteen and a half, he had no pieces of pseudo-parchment to attest to his worth. He could not rewire a house, or fix a pipe; he could not file papers or add up columns of figures. He was a soldier.

He was a marksman, he could walk twenty miles with a pack on his back, and still stand at the end of it. He could set an ambush, kill with a knife, use a GPMG, and two varieties of mortar. He could do all the things a country needs but does not want outside that small group of people it detests, despises, but calls upon. Its professional army.

And more than that: he liked it. He had joined in the early sixties when few travelled, when the idea of a holiday was a coach-ride fifty miles to Blackpool and a week in a miserable boarding house watching the rain through misted windows.

The army had taken him to Asia, to Hong Kong and ultimately to Borneo for the 'confrontation'. He had nothing personal against the Indonesian commandos infiltrating across the jungle border, it was just a soldier's job and they were his country's enemies.

But he liked the jungle, its stillness, its menace, and its promises. He liked the self-containment of his life there. One man, a few trusted mates, carry what you need, live off the jungle and a few rations. For the first time that he could ever remember he felt free.

So when Margaret suggested that he leave he asked the simple rhetorical question, 'And do what?'

And she could not give an answer, for she knew there really wasn't one. The pit? Hours in the poisonous darkness, rheumatism at forty; or worse, coughing up your lungs into a mug as silicosis took its hold. A mind-numbing factory job if you could get it? Or the dole queue, that catch-all for those without marketable skills.

But worse for Margaret. Worse because she knew he did not want to come home each night to the small council house, to a crying baby, to drying nappies, to the blaring

TV and the boring recounting of a housewife's day.

So he stayed in the army, and David grew up without him, an only child, fate and absence proving an effective barrier to more children.

And then one day when David was eleven and at Scout camp and Joe was in Ireland, Margaret went to the pub with some friends. She was just lonely and this was a small break for freedom. She loved Joe and David, but everyone needs something, some warmth and colour. Kind words that are spoken not written.

He was a salesman, good-looking and witty, and she enjoyed talking to him, and that was that. But a week later, when the friends persuaded her to go back to the pub, she wanted him to be there, and he was. And again they talked. And the same the next week, and the next, until one day he asked could he take her out and she said it was impossible because she was married.

Just the pictures, and no hanky-panky, he actually used the words. So she went and he was as good as his word, and suddenly she realised that she wished he wasn't. That what had existed between her and Joe had died from absence, had withered away from thirst or starvation or whatever word can be applied to an unfulfilled longing for the physical presence of love.

David went to a weekend camp two months later and she went to the Lake District with Andrew, and it was rebirth. They made some decisions, there in the shadow of Mount Coniston. When she went home she wrote a letter, packed two suitcases, and the blue Cortina pulled up outside the council home and removed them both, a tearful, ecstatically happy Margaret, a bewildered David, to a new home fifteen miles away.

Joe got the letter in Londonderry after coming back off patrol, read it with the camouflage blacking still on his hands. He knew where his priorities lay when he found himself searching for the words . . . 'you can still see David'.

You cannot be angry or hurt when a stranger decides she will no longer take part in brief reunions.

In the ensuing years he had seen her just three times. Once at a school prize-giving where she had been polite and warm, recognising his pleasure in his son.

Once at David's passing-out parade, where she sat, without her new husband, severe of face and uneasy at whether to feel pride or fear.

She had been polite again, but not warm, and she gave him a strange parting look as though perhaps she blamed him for her son's choice of career, though Joe had done everything in his power to dissuade him. Had he not agreed to the lad taking an apprenticeship in the mines, anything but that he should become a soldier?

And the third time, just minutes before in that sodden churchyard. He had stood apart from her, a bent figure in black as she was, broken from weeping, her new husband so Joe thought of him still – tall and strong, his arm encircling her.

Joe had not spoken to her, nor she to him, there was nothing either could say to comfort the other. But he had caught her glance, impossible to decipher from beneath the black veil, but communicated by the strength of its venom.

You killed him, it said. You killed him because of who you were and who you are.

Joe pounded on, feet wet and hurting, on through the neon-lit town, past the cheap shoe-stores and food-stalls, past the miserable housewives and bowed husbands still shopping despite the rain and the failing hour. At last he reached the familiar brown door and inserted the Yale key.

She was sitting huddled by the sputtering fire, face red from weeping, her huge swollen legs like diseased tree-trunks, anchoring her to this tiny, circumscribed world. She looked up, and he observed the dirty tramlines the tears had cut down her cheeks.

'Is it done, Joe?'

'Aye, Mam.'

She turned from him to look into the fire, and he went through into the small kitchen, put water into a kettle, plonked it on the cooker, struck a match and watched the fierce blue gas jets burst into life.

'I'll make a brew.'

Tea. The elixir of English life. Have a cuppa, make a brew, drown those real sorrows in a mug of something warm and brown.

He wished he could cry, perhaps it would melt the awful grey iceberg that lodged in his heart and threatened to freeze him.

He tried to force it, screwing up his face like a constipated man, yet nothing came. But it will, he thought. And then nothing will stop it; time, place, company, control or reason. It will be like a flood and it will not stop until my heart is drained like a breached reservoir.

Over the tea they sat in silence, his eyes on the small, old clock on the mantelpiece. It had been there as long as he could remember, measuring out his time.

Next to it a small brass holder was stuffed with envelopes, bills, jumble-sale circulars and a parish magazine. Then he saw the tip of an envelope that had not been there that morning, buff-coloured and virgin, peeping from behind the rest.

'Something come for me, Mam?'

He got up, fiddled among the papers, took out the envelope. On Her Majesty's Service.

'Came this morning. Sorry, love, with . . . with everything, I forgot to tell you.'

He slit it open with his thumbnail, and read.

Then he crumpled the envelope and its contents and threw them on to the fire where they smoked, browned and finally exploded into a yellow flame that consumed them.

'They want you back?'

'Yes, Mam.'

'Back to the Middle East again?'

'No. Ireland, Lisburn.'

His mother started to weep.

'Don't, Mam. I've been there before, and it's not as bad as it was.'

Not as bad as it was. Not as bad as '72 when the coffins were coming back at the rate of two a week, but bad enough still now for David to come back in one.

'I couldn't take it again, Joe, not a son as well as a grandson.'

He knelt down, stroking the thin grey hair with his hand.

'I'm indestructible.'

'I loved him, Joe. I loved him like he were my own.' Her face was red from the days and nights of tears.

'I loved him too, Mam. He was *my* son, remember?' He said it angrily, defensively.

'Except you were never here, not for the birthdays or the Christmases, the times a boy needs his dad.'

The words were like punches, fierce and hard.

'Didn't have much choice, did I?'

'You'll go back?'

'Yes.'

She wiped a gnarled hand across the wet of her cheeks, and looked into his eyes imploringly.

'When will it end there, Joe? When?'

'Ireland?'

She nodded her assent, snuffling and searching for her already sodden handkerchief.

'Never.'

'And poor David, and all the other lads, ours and theirs alike. You're telling me there'll never be an end to that?'

Far sooner than he could ever have imagined, it was

starting to happen. Ice shifting, great blocks of it, cracking and splitting under the pressure of some awesome thaw. Crashing down, deep within him, crushed under his pain and his grief, sending up great sprays of tears that now reached his eyes and began to spill out down his cheeks.

'No. Because we won't give up, and neither will they, and neither of us can win, because it can't be won. There's no result and no prize.'

He was swallowing the tears, tasting the salt.

And his mother was looking at him, not old and stupid now, not crippled and damned-near senile, but frighteningly wise.

'Then you're all mad.'

He was seeing her through a curtain of tears.

'And David died for nothing.'

'Not if I can help it.'

'Oh aye, and what do you propose to do about it?' But he couldn't speak now, because he was drowning in his own tears.

CHAPTER
6

They waited until the pick-up. Two car-loads of them, SAS. Not an ordinary squaddie or an RUC man in sight. This was dirty, killing work, not an arrest. There was to be no Diplock court and no twenty-five long years in the Kesh.

Dermot was paid for, outside even the rough and grubby rules of Ulster. He was the Man, and he'd taken the big gun down to Cross and left five corpses.

Dermot was something to be disposed of.

Nothing was enshrined in paper to be brought out later and handed to a tame journalist, or sold to the highest bidder. No document to embarrass the army or the government of the day. It was done with the lack of words, the lack of orders, the absence of things said by men in deep leather armchairs in Whitehall and the lino-polished rooms at Lisburn.

They needed a body, a spectacular one, a Provo whose death notices would run to column after column in the Republican news-sheets. They needed the Man, this down-at-heel revolutionary who'd spread so much death in the name of his cause. And they had worked carefully, knowing that only intelligence would bring them to Dermot. They planted the word, and sowed the seeds, played on the guilt and the greed, on the fear and the need. This night the seed had pushed its way through the earth and flowered. A single telephone call, a code-word, and then the operation. Five men, two in one car, three in the other. Two drivers, three men to take out Dermot. Nondescript cars, plates put on that night and destroyed the next day.

Each man had a Heckler and Koch German-made automatic personal machine-gun, painted matt-black, a magazine in the breech, two more beneath the car seat. In addition a Smith and Wesson .357 handgun, each of its six chambers loaded with soft-nosed bullets, kept by each man, including the drivers, for close-work protection if things became difficult.

And for a *coup de grâce* if that too was necessary.

Beneath the dashboard of each car, a Winchester pump-action shotgun to take out the front and rear windscreen and side-windows.

The men were older than Dermot, two of them in their thirties, ordinary-looking men, wrinkled, suntans beneath the black camouflage cream, bodies hard and wiry. Their teeth were not in good shape, and at least one had an upper and lower set of dentures.

They had all killed before for their country.

And they had waited until the pick-up, hiding out of view on the edge of enemy territory by the bottom of the Falls.

These men would not have needed a reason, but if they had and if the tally at Cross was not sufficient, there was always the RUC inspector from Ballynahinch, the young Guards officer sniped on his birthday in Andersonstown, two RUC constables blown to pieces on the road to Newry. All down to the Man, or so the legends and intelligence said.

So they'd hit the car, riddle the occupants, return to base, re-spray their cars and fly back to Hereford while the planted rumours went out that a UVF killer squad had been going in for a bit of personal retribution.

And Dermot would be for the morgue and the men in green, with knives and plastic aprons. The butchers who would carve him like the dead meat he was; counting the bullet wounds, points of entry and exit, lung and cranial damage, listing it in their passionately neutral voices.

The men who would hand the remains of Dermot McGarvey to the morticians and embalmers who'd need all their skills, so they could leave the coffin lid open in that cramped council flat in the sky.

And the men who'd done it would watch the last slow ride to Milltown on the BBC or ITV news, sip their pints in the mess and never speak of it outside the regiment. But know that whatever they had done to Dermot he had done to others before him.

As the Cortina pulled away from the Divis, the two cars, lights off, smudges in the black night, pulled out and followed. Dermot was tired. He'd slept for only two hours, lying on the nylon sheet in his old room, fitful and cold. His mum and dad were sleeping when he left, Colm too, just a humped mass beneath the sheets.

He had lied, telling them he was leaving at first light, so that no goodbyes would be necessary.

Only Fionulla was awake, as though some sixth sense had told her he would sneak away with the marches of the night. When he peeped in she was sitting up in her single bed, the optimistic, defiant crucified Christ on the plastic cross above her.

'You'll be away then?'

He came in quietly on tiptoe.

'You should be asleep. School tomorrow.'

'Will we see you again?'

'Aye.'

He sat down on the bed, feeling the shape of her legs through the coverlet. He stroked them gently.

'It'll be over one day.'

'Will it?'

He noticed for the first time that she was crying softly, eyes haloed with tears.

'Sure as eggs.'

She hugged him viciously, crushing him to her, squeezing him until he winced in real pain.

'For God's sake, Nulla, will you be after breaking my ribs?'

She released him. 'I don't bloody care. About any of it, a united Ireland, the Cause, anything. I just care about you. My stupid bloody brother.'

He wiped her eyes with the back of his hand.

'You take care, Nulla.' He kissed her cheek.

'It was the truth, wasn't it, Dermot?'

CHAPTER SIX

'The truth?' He eased himself up from the bed, anxious to be away, the danger suddenly more real now that he was actually leaving.

'About Cross? About it not being you, who killed the mother and her bairns, I mean?'

'Gospel.'

''Cause if it was you, Dermot, on the Mother of God, I'd hope they shot you if you did such a thing.'

But he was gone, a figure in the half-darkness, closing the door behind him, closing it on the pop posters, on the fluffy toys, on a schoolgirl who loved him and hated what he was, or might become.

Late for the meet, twenty minutes, and the driver was angry and scared.

'For Christ's sake, Dermot . . .'

'I was held up. Shut it and drive . . .'

Up the Falls, slowly in the dark, because who knew what the hell you could crash into in this blackness; a hole in the road, the burned-out skeleton of a bus.

But Dermot wasn't looking, he was thinking. Thinking of the kid caught by the stray rounds in Crossmaglen, picked up by that invisible hand, wrenched away from the screaming mother. Both of them dashed down, bloodied and broken on to the wet cobblestones.

Peace on Earth. Goodwill to all men. Christmas Eve, and I wonder to God what toys were waiting. And what that house was like on the morning, the tree, the parcels, perhaps a bike, or a doll, and . . . snap out of it, Dermot !

Snap out of it! You lied to Nulla. And if you hadn't it would have been worse, because she'll never know, can never know. And if she did, if *you* confessed, then she'd hate you for the rest of her life.

God Almighty, we kill for the Cause, why can't we lie for it too, even if it is to the person we love most?

Not alert, damn yourself, Dermot. You took a sentimental risk, stayed too long, talked too much, even if it was your own family; what did it matter?

You are in the Movement and you have no friends, only people who pose a risk. The boy in the hallway, the widow on the stairs. Jesus, your mouth was working like a chainsaw. Blab, blab, the curse of our people; how many do you know who died by the blarney? Died because they couldn't keep their traps shut, had to sink too many pints then strut and talk, strut and talk. And one day the Peelers came for them, or the front door was kicked in and a couple of Prods put a chalk mark up for King Billy.

Keep it well buttoned in the future, Dermot my lad, keep it zipped tight. And keep out of Belfast, out of the Falls, out of the bloody Divis.

Feel like death. Pull down the vanity mirror on the sunshield to look at the face, and see them, behind, perhaps fifty yards, two things, dark but moving, detached from the rest of the blackness.

'For fuck's sake, we've got a tail.'

The driver swore, checked his mirror, started to

sweat, tremble a little. But foot on the accelerator, car picking up speed.

Dermot's eyes riveted on the mirror, scratched and fingermarked, pocked with rust, and now his saviour or the herald of his doom.

'Move it.'

'They wouldn't bloody dare, not here, not in the Falls.'

No weapon, *nothing*! Like a naked man. Dermot felt fear, real belly-aching, bowel-emptying fear. A cold sweat started to spread over his body.

They'd dare; the fuckers from Hereford would dare. Who Dares Wins. Isn't that what it said on their motto?

'You carrying, Dermot?'

'You bloody know I'm not. You?'

The driver shook his head.

'Take your first, left or right, and then fucking shift.'

And the burning thought like a red-hot poker through the arctic sweat. How did they know? Who had told them? WHO?!

Then it all happened.

A BOOM like thunder, BOOM-Crash! They were so close together, a blast of cold air, and a molten sting like a hail of gravel on his shoulder.

And his mind was still going. Shotgun, back window out, hit, pellets, not serious, no real pain, now it will come level, and . . .

Down, down as low as he could get, and fiddling for

the door catch, then bkbkbkbkbkbkbkbkbkbk . . . Like a low drill, the pop of steel punching through metal. Blood, the driver's, splashing on to him, a high cry of pain and fear like in the van at Cross, then another BOOM-Crash! and a waterfall of shattered glass cascading on to him.

Bkbkbkbkbkbkbkbkbkbkbkbk . . . The punch-whack of more rounds hitting the metal, a heavy fist in his thigh, like a knuckled punch, and hearing his own voice crying out loud at the pain.

The Cortina swerving, out of control, and the driver's body slumping on to him, hot, wet and warm with its blood, mouth gurgling, eyes closed, arms flung outwards, trying to bring Dermot into the coffin with him in some last horrific embrace.

Catch down, door open, dark blur of the road, tipping himself out, out into the road, then the gravity yanked him on to the hard ground and he squealed like a pig from the shock of it and the pain from his thigh. A great crunch and tear as metal hit brick and the Cortina halted, crumpled and crippled against the side of the house.

Dermot looked up from the pavement, a wave of misty coldness threatening to sweep him into unconsciousness. He beat it back with an effort of will.

Screeching brakes, the SAS cars coming to a halt, one behind, one in front. Trapped, hurt, a dying stag at bay in the stream, hounds closing in.

Fight it, Dermot, don't die. Fight.

Shielded by the Cortina, a barricade against the

killing guns. But yards away, then they'd be over him with the submachine-guns ready to riddle him.

Get up, off the floor. Sod the pain. Awful pain, burning into the flesh. Get up.

Half-crouched. One victory. Up. Do it, Dermot. *Do it*, because if not it's just a worm's-eye view of a pair of dirty plimsolls and ill-fitting jeans. Then upwards in the last-ever look. Up to the olive-green combat jacket, the balaclava, and the muzzle of the gun.

Stagger into brickwork, a window ledge, then a shabby door, which is opening, a frightened white face peeping out.

'This way, lad . . . run . . . run.'

That's a bloody joke, grandad, run, the Man can't even walk, let alone run. But look at me, old fellah, look at me go, and Christ the pain is something awful.

But in, through the portcullis, snapped shut after him, down the hall, eyes fixed on the threadbare carpet, feet snagging in the folds, no energy left to lift them high enough.

A tiny living room, sepia prints framed in wood, a holy picture, a bloody crucifix. Ducks, flying across a wall; picture of a kid with crying eyes. Weep for me, lad, I'm too hurt for weeping.

Conscious now of the old man in front of him, striped pyjama bottoms held up by a knotted tie; vest, a bony white arm beckoning. Dermot laughed against the pain, antagonising it, making it bite harder until tears sprung in his eyes and he bit his lip for comfort, tasting the blood.

It's a dream, lad, you'll wake up in a minute. One of the dreams where the bear chases you from room to room and your feet are like lead. Sound of a splintering door. Come on, Dermot. 'This way . . . Jesus sakes, be quick.'

Not on the Falls. Not here. They couldn't come in here and shoot me.

A liquid red volcano pouring out of his thigh, spilling down his leg, frying his clothes, burning him alive.

But run. Run for your life.

Through a scullery, door half ajar, out through a back door, into the damp night air, leg leaking like a punctured can, the reservoir of his life pumping out.

We never thought they'd dare. Jesus, we're going bloody soft. Pain, but elation too, elation at what . . . running for your life, surviving, loss of blood?

Into an alley, and the face of a kid.

'This way . . . run.'

Always run, what is this, the cripples' Olympics, the one hundred metres for nearly murdered boyos? But still running, obeying, lungs heavy, air frosting his throat like a winter wine.

At least no kids left to mourn. Just Nulla.

Stumbling into a rough brick wall, a jagged razor scraped raw across his face. Eyes closing. Don't! Not yet. Let the Brit killers do it when they've stuffed you down in the box and folded your bloody arms over your chest.

'In there.'

Pushed in the small of the back, legs collapsing under

him like a foldaway table. Then jagged mountain peaks, penetrating the heart of the volcano.

Christ, but the bloody planet is shifting, it's the end of the world. There was a strange sound like a dog crying, coming from somewhere down inside him.

'Lie down, and SHUT UP! They'll hear you. You're in the coal bunker, lie down, be still . . . and don't make a sound.'

But how can you lie still when the very earth beneath you is shifting with this slow earthquake? Lie still and feel the unseen hands around you, picking and shifting, lowering the pieces on to you, weighing you down with the black gold, pressing you into your tomb.

Buried alive. Rest In Peace.

Then the last glimpse of a frightened white face, and his own covered like the last piece in a nightmare jigsaw.

Buried me alive; my own people. I beat the SAS killers only to be buried alive behind the Falls Road.

Something in him wanted to laugh at the absurdity and irony of it, but there was no sound, even the whining dog in him had died. Now there was only blood and tears and a yawning silence where the laughter should have been.

And the thought, persistent and nagging as pain, who? Who? Who knew? And who had told them?

They pulled him from the coal bunker when the riot was in full swing.

The SAS men had gone immediately, their fruitless

and dangerous chase abandoned. The job was botched, and the men knew it. It was one thing to gun down a Provo in the early hours, car to car; it was another to kill him in a back alley with witnesses, surrounded by hostiles who might turn on them in mob fury.

Got one of the fuckers though, half his neck and head spread over the Cortina's speedometer, blood, brains and sinew on the cheap glass and plastic.

But not the one they'd come for. They'd followed the blood trail as far as they'd dared, down the crude hall, through the foul-smelling living room, along the damp backyard . . . then it was too late, the windows were opening, the clamour growing.

It had to look like a sectarian killing, UVF or UDA, Protestant paramilitaries wreaking their own brand of revenge.

So they got out, fast, then a coded call to the RUC. Wanted man, Dermot McGarvey, wounded. A location. Get him!

But when the first PIGs and grey RUC Land-Rovers roared up the Falls it was already too late. The war-cry was up, dustbin lids rattling out the tempo of riot.

Brit killer squads gunned down two of the lads. The word spread like a rip-fire, guttering down the dark but waking back alleys. And the crowds gathered, feeling for missiles in the growing dawn, kitchens alive with housewives filling empty milk bottles with petrol, gnarled men twisting rags for tapers.

The young fresh-faced squaddies came out, alert and

scared, SLRs and Stirlings cocked and ready, eyes eager and searching behind the visors.

Then the first hail of bricks and bottles came over like a shower of arrows. And the first fiery arcs, yellow and vivid against the grey dawn sky.

Transparent riot shields up, baton rounds loaded, warning screams, clicks, bangs and whooshes and the projectiles skidding into the rioting crowd. Soon some rifle would open up, sending the soldiers scurrying for cover. A token really, not a serious attempt to snipe, but enough to indicate this was a deadly business.

And the word going out to the local commanders: the Man is down. Telephone calls, doctors alerted. No hospital for Dermot if he survived, not until – and unless – they could get him down to Dundalk.

Shouts and screams, orders and curses in the same language but accents a world apart. Two answering cracks from the SLRs, the deadly rounds searching in vain for the amateur sniper.

And Dermot unconscious through it all, dug from his premature burial place, lifted, covered, rushed through the narrow back alleys, his carriers cursing his weight and the growing light.

A waiting van, a bumpy ride to the Whiterock estate, mercifully no roadblocks, then an anonymous council house, clean sheets, a man with a doctor's bag. A grim-faced man, cheeks broken-veined with drink, but sober now. Dermot washed and laid carefully on his belly, the blood- and coalstained clothes cut from him with sharp scissors.

Wounds cleaned, examined, entry and exit hole disinfected. Blood-pressure check, low. An injection through the buttocks.

A young man in a T-shirt said, 'What's his chances?'

'Bullet didn't hit anything, another half an inch and his femoral would have emptied him in three minutes.'

'So he'll live?'

'Should do. He's in shock, and he needs some blood. BP's very low. Get him out as soon as you can.'

'Too bloody risky.'

The doctor shrugged and closed his bag. He'd seen too many of these early-morning call-outs. Young men, *too* young, hit by high-velocity bullets, whole nervous systems ravaged, and instead of intensive care and the latest surgery they got a hungover has-been and first aid.

And if the patrols got *him* he'd be for ten in the Kesh too.

He looked again at T-shirt, at the cruel mouth, the young face and ancient eyes.

'Then he'll probably die.'

He didn't, but afterwards more than once Dermot wished he had.

They got him to Dundalk that night, and then to a private clinic, and in three weeks he could walk with a stick and felt only itching from the wound and stiffness in his thigh.

He knew how lucky he'd been. The round could have shattered his thigh bone, destroyed his pelvic girdle, and mashed his testicles and penis in the process. Then he would have been an emasculated, hospitalised cripple. Or it could have severed his femoral artery, in which case he would be dead.

Instead he was limping slightly.

And as he did, leaning heavily on the cane, pushing himself around the gardens of the clinic, desperate to gain full mobility, only one thought exercised his mind.

Who?

And eventually there was only one answer. His family knew he was home and they would not tell. Then there was Rosie. She had mouthed him badly, hated him even, but when it came to it she would not tout.

Even if her honour allowed it – and he doubted that – her sense of survival wouldn't. The Brits could offer anything they wanted, tickets to Canada or Australia, a so-called new life if you squealed, but Rosie couldn't shake Belfast, her husband's death, nor the looks of her two kids when they grew up and learned the truth.

So that left Danny, the lad on the stairs. Danny the gluesniffer. God have mercy on him, because the lads wouldn't when he told them. He'd like to see him before the end; tell him about Gerry's brains spattered over him, about what it meant to fight for Ireland.

Had Danny seen the news bulletins, or read the papers? Had he seen the tortured, drawn face of Moiread at the graveside and those dotted, uncomprehending eyes of young Ruraigh and Kevin?

Five weeks to the day that he'd been wounded, they smuggled Dermot back into the North in a meat lorry.

The red swinging carcasses seemed appropriate.

The local Provo commander met him in the front room of a house close to the empty garage where the job would be done.

The man stood and warmed his backside against the gas fire, behind him on the mantelpiece a football trophy and a plastic model of Christ the Saviour.

'We have the tout, Dermot.'

'Danny?'

'You'll see.'

The commander looked nervous. He'd never met Dermot before, probably never would again, that was the way of things in the Movement. But he wished he was not meeting him now, not like this, not under these circumstances.

'Why the mystery? It was Danny, you lifted him, you told me.'

'The Branch offered him five thousand and a ticket to Canada. He decided to take it.'

'And it *was* Danny?'

'Like I said, you'll see.'

'Where is he?'

'In the garage.'

'Who's doing it?'

'Our friend from Derry.'

The publican. Dermot shivered. What was it about

publicans? The English had always recruited their hangmen from the licensed trade.

'Unless you'd care to do it yourself.'

'I'm a fighter, not an executioner.'

'But you'll be there.'

'Yes.'

Once before, when Dermot had first joined the Movement, they'd brought him up here, a test of loyalty or guts perhaps.

Some anonymous tout, bent from fear, the stench of his voided bowels awful. Pistol pressed behind the ear, through the hood, an awful gagged last whisper of fear, the bang, head jerking, the fearsome slap as the body hit the concrete floor.

'Yes, I'll be there.'

The penalty for touting was death, it was the only way. Any other, and out would come the money, and the Movement would be riddled with informers. Only the fear of this shabby, terrifying end kept the waverers in line.

He followed out through the back door. The man's wife was frying chips; the crisp odour made Dermot's stomach contract with hunger, and he salivated despite himself.

Gardens, shabby and untended, a concrete path, weeds poking through, confident that they would reclaim it eventually.

Then the garage door swung high. Three men inside. Two standing, automatic pistols held low, and outward. The third seated on a small chair, an eyeless hood over his head, shoulders slumped in defeat, just as Dermot had remembered it.

And the stench again, urine and fresh faeces, the last indignity before death.

The commander said, 'Take the hood off the fucker.'

One man stepped forward and yanked at the hood, and Dermot said, 'Jesus, Danny, I warned you –'

Then the hood was off and the tear-stained face was looking up at him in fear and surprise.

It was his brother, Colm.

'Colm?'

Thin face, cheeks hollow and stark over the raised cheekbones and the livid bruising. Wet with tears.

Dermot whipped round. 'OK, what's the fucking game?'

One of the men with pistols said, 'Your brother. A tout. And no game, Dermot, no fucking game.'

'You're lying.'

'No. He confessed. Ask him.'

Dermot could feel the heat leaving him, like water from a sick man's bowels, with pain.

'Facts. Bloody facts, and they'd better be good.'

Colm, a tout, an informer? It wasn't possible. His own brother prepared to sell his brother's life for money and an airline ticket?

'Talk!'

'They lifted him and your dad at Christmas.'

'I *know* that, they *both* told me.'

'Hear me out, Dermot. Two days in Castlereagh and he needed clean underpants.'

They watched Dermot's waxen face, saw the white-clenching of the knuckles.

'After that we kept an eye on them both, your dad and him. That's the way it is, the Branch have been turning too many.'

'And?' Chest tight, breathing constricted.

'Your dad was fine, usual stuff, stays in most of the time.'

'And Colm?'

'He took a ride, didn't you, Colm boy?'

The red face began to sob, and it was like an ugly sore, the scab breaking off, all the badness seeping out.

'Into the city centre, a wee drink in the Europa. Then a chap comes in with an *Irish Times* under his arm. Like some fuckin' spy novel. Then off they go like long-lost pals.'

'Who was he, the man he met?'

'McClelland, Special Branch.'

'In broad fucking daylight at the Europa, don't make me laugh. You lifted Colm on that?'

One of the men made great show of putting his automatic in a shoulder holster. Dermot noted with clinical detachment that it was new, Colt .45 Gold Cup. Good stuff for a sidearm.

'We left him, Dermot, left him to see what he was up to. Of course, no one told us his little brother was coming back, did they?'

'You didn't need to know.'

'You broke the rules, Dermot, it was our territory, we should have been told. That way we could've warned you that Colm was under suspicion.'

'Evidence!'

'After we fished you out of the bunker we lifted Colm. Just in time. He had a bag packed. In an hour he would have been at Lisburn. Then a chopper to Aldergrove, a military aircraft to England, and his new life in Toronto. Am I right so far, Colm?'

The jagged face shook silently.

'Did he have this money on him, a bloody airline ticket? What?'

'Don't be stupid, Dermot . . .' This was danger, Dermot recognised it. There should have been fear, at the least respect, and there was none. These men thought his brother was a tout and, true or not, it was threatening to drag him under. '. . . they wouldn't be so daft as to give him that.'

'Then you don't bloody *know*!'

'We know all right. Because we found this under his mattress.' The man handed Dermot a scrap of paper with a Lisburn telephone number scribbled on it in ballpoint.

'It's the phone number of his contact. And yes, Dermot, we rang it. McClelland. It'll be changed by now. It was enough, and Colm told us the rest himself. The bank-account number in Toronto, the flight number, even the number of hairs in McClelland's nostrils.'

'You beat him up so he told you anything.'

'Jesus and Mary, Dermot, will you believe me there was a scuffle when we lifted him, nothing more. Ask him yerself for God's sake. He told us everything and been crying like a baby ever since.'

'Colm? Are they speaking the truth?'

The piteous, hopeless face lifted and gave its reply.

'Why, Colm, why?'

'One instruction only. When you came home or telephoned with your whereabouts he was to telephone McClelland. Then he was to disappear.'

'Colm?'

His face behind the *Sporting Life*, then suddenly deciding to go for a pint. Careless talk costs lives. *And I even said the time I was leaving!*

'Tell me he's lying, Colm, *please*.'

'If it was up to him you'd be in a plot in the Milltown by now, and he'd be screwing Canadian broads on his bloody money, fucking tout.'

The man spat on to the cold stone floor.

Dermot put his arm out, encircling Colm's head, bringing it to him, wet and raw from weeping, into his wounded thigh.

'Oh, Colm.'

Thin Colm, knobbly knees in the small of his back in the double bed they had shared, cold feet against his own.

Colm and his collection of rubber bullets from the early days, Colm and his catapult and cowboy neckerchief, like a ragged-trousered bandit firing stones at the soldiers.

'Yer big brother was emigrating over your dead body.'

Dermot took Colm's head in both hands, willing the eyes to open with a different message. And open they did, slowly, reluctantly like a locked gate, opened to reveal only confirmation of the awesome truth. Now he knew.

'He slipped out, made the call, and they were ready. No Diplock for you, just the cemetery.'

Dermot stroked the fear-sodden hair tenderly, then drew his fingers through its thick strands like the teeth of a giant comb through fur.

'Why?'

The head shook again in his hands, side to side, side to side.

Dermot grabbed it in both hands, forcing the face upwards.

'Why, Colm? I'm your bloody brother.'

'They told me you were a mad dog . . . said you'd killed a bairn down at Cross. Then they held me out the window by the ankles, I swear, Dermot, on my life. I thought they were going to . . .' His body shuddered as though racked by a fever spasm.

'Go on.'

'Said they'd do for me . . . they put a pistol in my mouth . . . pulled the trigger . . . I was scared, Dermot, never been so scared. I thought if I just agreed to meet, once or twice, go along with it . . . pretend like . . .'

'Canada?'

'They showed me a picture . . . of the bairn . . . and, then, this money, lots of it, more than I've ever seen . . . said they'd get you anyway, it was a matter of time. If I'd just phone, but they never said nothing about murder, Dermot, on my mother's life . . .'

'*Our* mother's life . . . And you were going to leave it all, Ma and Dad, Nulla . . . me . . . everything . . . with *their* money?'

'Why not? What's here for me, *anyone*? Nothing, it's a wasteland.'

'What about the struggle?'

'Not for me, Dermot, I haven't got the guts. It's all right for you, but I'm *afraid*, I've always been afraid.'

'Dermot . . .' A man's hand touched his sleeve and he brushed it angrily away.

'And you couldn't have backed out if you'd wanted to?'

'They said they'd taped me, taken a picture, if I didn't go along they'd send everything to the boys and then . . .'

'I know. So you thought . . . Canada.'

A fearful parody of a laugh burst nervously through Colm's tears. Dermot was here now. *He'd* understand. Just a kneecapping, dear God . . . two knees, but not . . .

They'd looked at pictures of the forests of Canada together in school when they were young enough to believe in dreams, and they'd vowed that one day they would take a boat to Montreal and live as lumberjacks.

'Remember the books, Colm?'

'Lumberjacks.'

'Aye, lumberjacks.'

The man with the holstered automatic spoke. 'Time's pressing, Dermot.'

'I never thought they'd try to kill yer, on the word of God. I never would've if I'd known, never.'

Dermot broke their embrace. 'I know that for sure. Now wipe your eyes.'

Colm did it with the edge of his sleeve, and Dermot saw the snot peeping guiltily from the end of his brother's nostril. He took out his own handkerchief.

'Give it a good blow.'

Colm took the handkerchief and blew noisily.

'Keep it.'

'Ta. Dermot, I'm sorry. I'll do anything. You wouldn't let them . . . would you?'

'Shush...' Dermot soothed him like a frightened child. 'I'll be back in a while.'

A kitchen table, empty chip plates, the smell now vile to him, half-empty bottles of Guinness on the stained cloth.

A star chamber, he one side, two officers of the Belfast Brigade the other.

'He's a tout, Dermot, only one fucking penalty.'

'He's also my fucking brother.'

'And if it was up to him you'd be an epitaph.'

'He was duped, for Christ's sake.'

'Rules. You know them, he knows them. If he gets away with it the whole thing comes apart. You know that better than anyone. If it was Danny?'

They were right, *right*. But Colm!

He took a deep breath. 'Knee-capping; both legs. He'll be on crutches for years. My own brother.'

The man in the centre took off his bottle-green spectacles.

'Not possible.'

He nearly said please. Nearly said the fateful word that would have exposed him, but he swallowed it. Dangerous this. Not my brigade, though I'm local. The Man. They know my reputation, but still at risk. My brother a tout. Who could tell how deep the paranoia might go? Mam, Dad . . . Nulla . . . himself?

And then he knew and he accepted it with a mute feeling of horror. They would do it whatever he said.

Tongue cardboard, he said, 'The man from Derry's here?'

'Ready and waiting.'

'Hood, till the last?'

'Yes.'

'You pronounce on him and he hears the gun cocked before it happens?'

'The works, Dermot . . .' Lips parted over yellow dentures and arms spread wide . . . 'That's the purpose, they have to know why, and they have to be frightened.'

Even unto death, thought Dermot.

'Let me do it.' *My own brother*.

'Highly irregular.'

'The result is the same.'

'Give us two minutes.'

Dermot left the kitchen, went into the living room. A small, bald, pot-bellied man sat there drinking tea and watching the television. The publican. He did not even acknowledge Dermot's presence.

They called him back, and he sat down.

'Like I said, highly irregular, but then so is the circumstance . . .'

They pushed a cardboard box the size of a hardback book across the table.

Dermot opened it. A Spanish-made .38 Star automatic. There was a magazine in the box too, and he checked that it was loaded to capacity.

'You wouldn't think of . . . well, you know, him being your brother and all?'

Dermot shrugged and shook his head. He took the magazine, inserted it in the empty butt of the Star, made sure it was secure, then worked the slide, cocking the pistol.

The man in spectacles cleared his throat.

'Do it. You've got five minutes.'

Dermot smiled, lifted the pistol and pointed it directly between the green false eyes of the man sitting opposite him.

'Or maybe you.'

The man went white, and the other froze like a statue. The only sound was their frightened breathing.

'And then after you, this fuckin' rabbit . . . Then the publican. A bullet for each of you . . .'

The sound of the TV rose and fell.

'Then me and Colm are away to Lisburn, Aldergrove and a new life among the fir trees. Eh, lads?'

Dermot's finger curled around the trigger. Five long seconds, pistol pointing, two men not knowing if they really were waiting for death. He was the Man. If he wanted to do it he could. This was his *brother*!

Then he lowered the gun, released the slide so the gun was safe, and ejected the magazine.

'Dangerous tricks, Dermot,' the man in glasses said.

'I'm a dangerous man.'

And they knew it, and he saw that they did, and they both smiled, more from relief than from anything else.

Except that they did not realise how close he had come to pulling the trigger on them, and not on Colm.

His brother's eyes brightened as the garage door opened.

'Dermot?' The lad's eyes were full of hope, and desperation.

'Wait outside,' Dermot told the man left to guard Colm.

'My orders are to stay here.'

'Paddy says to fuckin' wait outside. You want to argue with him, or me?'

Reluctantly the man holstered his pistol and left.

The Star was in Dermot's inside jacket pocket, tugging at his heart. Something was moving in him like a great, shifting cancer, some agony that could never be explained.

No alternative. I believe in it. Believe in the struggle, and if I believe in the struggle then this thing has to be done, and if I didn't do it, they would, and it would be a nightmare torture.

'How'ya feelin'?'

'I'm OK. Dermot, did you fix it?'

'Easy. Dublin in the mornin'.'

'Jesus God, Dermot, I'll never be able to thank you . . .'

And Dermot winked. A terrible, God-awful thing to do. His Judas kiss.

'Why are you doing this for me, Dermot? After what I've done?'

Dermot looked deep into his brother's eyes. Could Colm see the deep, deepest treachery in his?

'I'm doing it because I love you, Colm.'

Dermot knew it was true. And that no one would ever understand, because it could not be explained. Colm was to die, and there was no way out from that. Dermot could not prevent it. But he could make it easier. He could rob it of its parody of ritual, so that the last voice Colm would hear would be a voice of love.

So he would not have those last, long seconds of unspeakable terror.

'Because I love you, Colm.'

'God, but you've been a brother, Dermot.'

'Now will you turn around while I untie these bloody ropes.'

And Colm turned, and the automatic came out, and his eyes were staring at the garage wall. And if Dermot could have seen them at that moment he would have seen them wide with hope and reprieve.

But Dermot was looking at the back of his brother's

head, at a point near the base of the neck, for he wished the minimum of suffering.

Because I love you, Colm.

And with his left hand on the ropes in a pantomime of untying, his right pointed the pistol at the spot, and fired.

The blow jerked Colm forward off the chair, face forward on to the concrete with a cold, abattoir slap of flesh.

And Dermot thought, I should have untied his hands first, he shouldn't have died with his hands tied.

The garage door opened and the guard peered in.

'Let's get it out. We have to be away.'

Dermot stood up, ejected the magazine from the pistol and handed it, butt first, to the man.

He said in a low voice, deadly with purpose, 'Tell them. He'll not be named as a tout. Do not wire or booby-trap his body. He was a victim of a sectarian killing. He'll get a proper funeral, with priests and a mass, a coffin and a fucking grave as befits the Man's brother. D'ya hear?'

The man nodded, his face neutral. 'I'll tell them.'

'You do. And tell them if my brother is named for a tout and dumped I'll come back, for them, for you, for the lot of you. And I mean it.'

The guard could see the dark, hooded eyes, burning with the guilt and the desire for revenge. He knew he meant it.

He said again, 'I'll tell them, there'll be no problems. It was a bad business, Dermot, no one wanted it this way, it's just . . .' He shrugged.

On the way back south Dermot could not keep his mind off Canada. Forests and lumberjacks, black and white encyclopaedia photographs of a man balancing on floating logs. Of a pair of cold feet on his in a bed.

And of the Biblical story the priest had once told them, about the man who killed his brother, and carried the mark of shame with him for ever.

CHAPTER

7

Older man, younger woman.

They sat at the table like a cliché, hands entwined, and the eyes of the fellow diners occasionally flickered in their direction. Knowing, disapproving, sometimes hostile. They looked at each other as lovers will, shutting everything else out.

The man said, 'Why?' and squeezed the girl's fingers even harder.

'I've told you a thousand times.'

'One thousand and one, please.'

'Because if I don't I will always wish I had. That simple.'

'And me?'

'You'll survive, I'll write, and next Christmas I'll be back.' He tried a smile. 'I'll miss you. More than you'll ever know.' She felt a tear start. 'I you – and you *do* have Margot.'

'Touché.'

The waiter brought their cognac, and when he left she leaned back and took in the glances, the curiosity and the disapproval. If only they knew. She enjoyed minor games like this, and he did too.

She smiled across at the tall, strong man whose heavy hands touched hers. She looked into the cool, deep grey eyes. How much would he miss her?

At last he said, 'When will you leave?'

'Monday.'

'And shall I see you before that?'

She shook her head. 'I don't see the point – do you? This was supposed to be our goodbye dinner.'

He pulled a face. 'A year's a long time.'

'And Europe is just a plane-ride away – if you can slip Margot's leash.'

He sucked air, making a wet noise of regret. 'That could be difficult.'

'I just thought it might.'

'Dammit all, she is my wife.' His voice was raised and heads turned.

'I've never forgotten that.'

She raised the brandy glass. 'To study and the broadening of knowledge. *Santé.*'

He raised his. 'To Christmas.'

Outside, the wind was up and they could feel the sting of sand, and see the phosphorescence of the breaking waves. They stood and listened to the slap and hiss of the Atlantic as it pounded the shore.

'Be careful over there.'

'Because of you – who you are, I mean?'

'Well, that – but it's a dangerous place anyway. To you it's just a trip. To them it's their life. It's tribal and you're a stranger.'

She laughed, high, and the wind caught it, lifting it like a bird cry. 'Not after *your* speeches.'

'Here I'm a senator, *there* . . . well, a busybody

maybe. I don't think I know any more.'

She loved him more than ever. And because of that she had to leave him. For if she didn't she would always shelter under that umbrella of love. And she knew that at the end of the day – literally – there would always be Margot.

She leaned forward and kissed him on the cheek. He turned and held her, fiercely, protectively, as he had done through the years.

The desire to stay was overwhelming then. Instead she broke free.

'I love you, Dad – more than you'll know – but I have to go.'

'I know. You're all I've got, and I promised Mom I'd take good care of you.'

'And you have.'

'Write – all the time.'

'I will.'

'If I can persuade your wicked step-mum to come to Europe with me, will she be welcome?'

'With open arms.'

Then the wind got colder and they walked back across the car park, through the eddying whirls of driven sand, back to their cars and a silent parting.

And across the Atlantic, in the old world, the islands waited. Old, wise and infinitely dangerous.

By the insane logic of Irish history, politics and passion, of its fear and its paranoia, the decision made evil sense.

Dermot had gone wrong. Dermot was a rogue bull.

Dermot was the man who had botched the big job and brought calumny down on the Movement. He had been betrayed by his own brother – and had executed him for that crime. Dermot was clearly cold-blooded and dangerous.

For had he not also levelled his gun at two top men of the Belfast Brigade and threatened their lives?

The Man was a mad dog, unreliable. He was an individualist, who sought the cult of personality, encouraged it, fostered it, feeding it like his pet animal with tales of his own daring.

But when they'd given Dermot McGarvey the Big Gun, and sent him to Cross for the Christmas Eve spectacular, he'd botched it.

It should have been British soldiers; five, six, maybe ten of them at one sweep. That for the Christmas Day news in England, that for the BBC to report on, for the British Army to explain away. And instead there was an Irish mother and child, good Catholics up from the Republic on a last-minute shopping trip.

So instead of rejoicing, outrage. Items on the American big three, CBS, NBC and ABC, a statement from the Taoiseach, a mob threatening the Dublin Sinn Fein office, Irish Special Branch raids on the lads in Dundalk.

And the Brits were crowing.

Christmas Eve, too, the TV-programme pundits and the politicians said; was nothing sacred? The faces were never off the damn TV screens, and even Radio Telefis

Eireann ran a special on Boxing Day: 'Dying for Christmas', and word was CBS wanted it.

Phone calls from New York and Boston. NORAID were angry. How the hell could they get people to dip into their pockets and fill the collecting boxes when it was *Irish* women and kids getting wiped out by the people who were pledged to protect them from the murdering Brits?

Takings were down all over the eastern seaboard. In Queens, where the murdered girl's relatives now lived, one collector even got roughed up. Fewer folded dollar bills in turn meant fewer Armalites, RPGs, plastic, timers, fuses; less money to pay the crooked trawlermen meeting ships stopped dead in the night in the heavy seas off the deserted beaches and cliffs of the West of Ireland.

And ultimately, like a balance sheet of profit and loss, that meant one less snipe at an army patrol in the Andersonstown, one less culvert bomb in Tyrone or Armagh to catch an unwary RUC patrol, one less incident to keep the Brits and the Peelers nervy and unsure. The acceptable level of violence, the British government callously called it, and it would be even more acceptable if the guns and money dried up.

And perhaps because of the Man, that would happen. So if they had needed reasons, there were reasons aplenty, and many a man had been knee-capped for botching an important job.

But beneath the skin of logic, running like a throbbing nerve, was the moment Dermot had pointed the black muzzle of the Star automatic at the green sunglasses.

From that moment Dermot had put himself in deadly danger. It had been the joke of the execution shed, of course, and Dermot had turned the barrel away, walked from the room and put to death his own brother.

The man who had fallen under the shadow of Dermot's pistol was a one-time barman, merchant seaman – even a former soldier in Her Majesty's Royal Irish Rangers. He rolled his own cigarettes and had armsful of tattoos proclaiming love to his mother and a long-gone girl called Alice.

He had also read Marx, Clausewitz, Machiavelli, de Tocqueville, Napoleon, Lenin and Giap. He had personally killed four British soldiers with a rifle between 1974 and 1978 and singlehandedly planned a mainland Britain bombing campaign that had cost the British eight lives. His own son was in the Maze prison serving fourteen years on arms charges.

After Dermot had killed Colm the man had gone home and re-read his Machiavelli. If you strike at the Prince, the master had written, do not fail. If you fail, you are doomed and not he. And, of course, reasoned the reader, it follows logically that the Prince must then strike down the usurper who has failed to depose him.

The man with the green sunglasses was the Prince, and Dermot had struck at him. He smiled as he flicked the pages.

The Man should have realised the seriousness of his position. He should have pulled the trigger, killed them all, including the executioner from Derry and the man guarding his brother. He then should have fled with his brother to the dubious safety of the British. That, the man concluded, is what I, myself, would have done once I pointed the pistol across the table.

The lover of Machiavellian works talked to the Belfast Brigade, and talked persuasively. One had sat next to him and seen that look in Dermot's eyes, a man an inch from murder and betrayal. And when they took their findings and their recommendations to the Provisional Army Council, the council listened too.

It had suffered badly from the debacle at Crossmaglen, had spent an awkward Christmas watching the bulletins, had damned near had its HQ burned about its ears.

Now to learn that this McGarvey, who the tame Republican journalists called the Man, had pulled a gun on a Brigade commander, threatening to free his tout brother, and murder his comrades? Well, now, the man was clearly unstable. And the Catholic in them said, but did not speak it, And a man who will kill his own brother . . . ?

And some good would eventually come of it when NORAID learned that baby-killers got summary justice from the Provos. Like the revolutionary he was, Dermot would surely understand Robespierre's maxim that the revolution first devoured its own children.

So the decision was made.

Dermot McGarvey, alias the Man, was to be devoured.

CHAPTER

8

Joe looked around him at England.

Inside the railway carriage he sat among it, outside it sped past him in a green and brown blur. Which was the real England, and which the myth?

Joe considered. Outside, the winding lanes, the rolling fields, the lone cottages from which smoke curled lazily. Glimpses of churchyards, small steeples, weathervanes and slumbering graveyards. Out there the village clock stood, even yet, at ten to three, and there was honey still for tea.

But it had never been an England he had known or could understand, excluded from it as he and so many others had been. It was an image, and a belief held in hearts. But it had no substance for Joe Biddle.

The real England, the England a decade away from the twenty-first century, sat around him in the smoky second-class railway carriage. Or – what was it they called it now in a euphemism that fooled no one? – ah, standard class.

This was England, the human shape and sound, smell and feel of the nation he loved but could not understand why. And it had no more substance for him than that toytown village England speeding past the window.

It had once, he remembered that much. It had been

faces of friends, uncles, aunts, kindly shopkeepers wrapping the two ounces of sweets in a twist of white paper. It had been open back doors, women in aprons, the pungent smell of fish and chips sprinkled with vinegar on a Friday night.

But that had been his youth, and his youth and England's youth had gone for ever.

He had been away too long, fought in too many foreign wars, small wars and vicious wars for his country. And all the while his country had been changing, week by week, month by month, stealthily, like a child long unseen, until at last he could no longer recognise it.

Was it the listless youth wearing earphones from which a tinny noise escaped? The face pitted with acne, the jaws working bovine-like on some meat concoction sandwiched in a bun. Joe looked into the youth's eyes and saw nothing, just apathy, again that cattle-quality of acceptance. England?

Across from his seat a woman – fifties? – it was hard to tell with her cheap clothes, ravished powdered skin and sunken, puckered mouth, read a magazine. Its subject was the royal family, and the woman swallowed it with more eagerness than the youth his bun. Royalty, patriotism, welfare-socialism, a TV and refrigerator in every home, cars, two weeks in Spain, the National Front, pickets who murdered, patriots who killed.

God help England. Two Englands, inside and outside? More like a dozen, twenty, one hundred Englands, pulling, and tearing. He was in a land he didn't know, among a people he could no longer understand, living like a man whose life was beginning to spin out of control.

Perhaps it was David's death, perhaps it was the age he had reached, too much violence and death at last leaving their mark like alcohol on the face? But the sheet anchor of his nation had gone, ripped away by some psychic storm while his mind slept. He seemed to float now, as he had in his dreams as a child, inflated and weightless, high above the surface of his country.

I fought, have fought, fight, will fight, and for what, for whom? For the field outside, that church with the unkempt grave, for the youth with the dead-pig eyes, the woman in her fantasy royal palace?

Was it for these he fought? Was it for the faces he had once seen through the smoked glass of a London restaurant window? Well-fed faces smug and secure. Cosy faces in a restaurant where a meal cost more than his mother had to feed her family for a week.

Was it for the railway-ticket collector, union badge proud in his lapel, his face unshaven and dirty, loudly berating some unfortunate pensioner who had travelled when her reduced-rate pass was invalid?

For the yobs kicking each other on the football terraces or the city whizz kids with their £100,000 a year salaries and trendy homes?

For the Rolls-Royces or the filthy estates strewn with rubbish? For the vandalised high-rises or the private schools, for the white skinheads who fire-bombed the homes of helpless Asians, or the West Indian Rastas who terrorised the South London tubes?

He closed his eyes and sank down in his seat. For these? And if not, for what? And if for nothing, then why go on?

He remembered his grandfather, old by the fire, white muffler covering the dark scar on the chicken-like scrawny throat. Talking of Gallipoli, of being waist deep in the limpid water. Barbed wire pulling at him and the bullets ploughing into the men around him. Then months on the parched slopes, and thirst so bad Joe felt dry himself when the old man described it.

The withered, trembling hand still capable of feeling the terror over the years as he described the awful sound of the Turks charging: 'Allah, Allah, din-din.'

Joe had been fifteen and anti-war, and he'd asked innocently, 'Why'd you go, Grandad?'

And the old man had laughed that bubbling, pneumoconic laugh that always sounded like the beginning of weeping – and perhaps it even was. 'No choice, lad, no bloody choice.'

'But you volunteered, Grandad.'

'Aye, and bloody fool I was. Thought as how it'd all be over by Christmas.'

And again the weeping cough-laugh, and the bitterness. His grandfather suddenly strange to him, not cosy Grandad, mild, loving, but hard and far, far away.

'We didn't do it for King and country, Joe, lessen I

didn't. I didn't hate the Germans, or the Turks. I did it for yer gran and yer dad, and all of them, and now I wish . . . I wish . . .'

But he'd not been able to go on, and there was just the hiss and bubble of the coal fire. Joe found that he was holding his breath, willing his grandfather to go on.

At last the old man said, 'And we thought, we really thought it would be different when we came back. That if we went, it would prove we were men, just like them, and that when we came back they'd treat us *like* men, not like bloody animals.'

'Who's "them", Grandad?'

The old man ignored him. 'A land fit for heroes, that's what we were supposed to be getting when we came back – those of us who did.' Then he'd unwound the spotless white muffler, and dabbed his eyes without a trace of shame.

'Grandad...' Joe was upset, near to crying himself. He reached out and touched the old man's arm.

'. . . Well, I got back, and I made a promise. If they ever asked me to pick up a rifle again I would. But it wouldn't be pointing at no Turk or German, I'd be pointing it at them who'd sent me in t'first place.'

And the eyes were wet with tears, and Joe had fled because he couldn't take the pain in those eyes. A promise, if they ever asked me . . .

They hadn't. But they'd asked Joe's father, and he'd gone, and come back. And then Joe'd gone too, and so far he'd always come back. But when young David had gone, there was only that awful coffin and the Union Flag.

The train jerked, braking; jolting Joe back into the present.

The old man had been war veteran, socialist, anti-monarchist, trade-union organiser, and when Joe had his passing-out parade, his grandfather had climbed from his sick bed, pinned on his medals and stood with the rest of them, ramrod-stiff as his grandson went by.

He'd hugged him, putting tears on the new uniform, and six weeks later he was dead, lungs removed post-mortem and sent off to the Pneumoconiosis Board to see if they were of a percentage enough diseased from coal dust to grant his widow a pension.

The third-generation soldier of the Queen rubbed his eyes, feeling the effects of cigarette smoke and tiredness. Bloody mad, all of us English.

He would carry on being a soldier, carry on doing what they asked him – ordered him – to do, because he had come too far to go back now. Whatever path had led him here was too tortuous to retrace. He would only lose the trail, get lost and stumble into some abyss.

At least here he was familiar with the ground, even if he did not sometimes care for the view. He had signposts, markers and familiar objects to cling to, like uniform and tradition.

His own son had died for that uniform and that tradition. Had died because he was British, had died for his country, had died because of that strange thing called nation.

Now Joe could no longer define that, or remember quite what it was or what it meant. Perhaps it was something that reposed in the unconscious, or the soul, or the instinct.

Whatever it was still existed for Joe, somehow and somewhere. And if it ceased to exist then there would be nothing left, only a desire for extinction and nothingness.

For ever.

'Welcome to Lisburn.'

'Thank you, sir.'

'Sit down, would you, Sergeant?'

The sergeant did as he was bid.

'You've been overseas, I notice.' The intelligence officer was studying Joe's file.

'Oman, sir, then Bahrain.'

The officer smiled. 'Need to know, etc., eh? Did a bit of time there meself, in the seventies. With the Trucial Oman Scouts.'

'Really, sir.'

'Best time of my life.' The officer rolled up his sleeve and showed Joe a small scar. 'Tough buggers. Got that in a scrap.'

'Sir.'

'Back to business. You've been here before?'

'Three tours, sir. Derry, early seventies. Belfast, mid-seventies, then a spell with Intel here, sir.'

'Good man. Ever work undercover? You know, mixing with the locals, that sort of stuff?'

He looked carefully at Joe, and Joe looked back carefully and neutrally and said, 'No, sir.'

Joe knew the notion was laughable, or would have been laughable if the results had not been so tragic. Undercover in Belfast, or the rest of Ulster for that matter, was a way of getting keen young men killed.

Some con-tricks could work. Surveillance teams with vans and peepholes, laundry scams with false shops and pick-ups, collecting suspected Provo laundry and checking it for traces of weapons or explosives. That had worked for a few months until the Provos got wise and at least one innocent Catholic laundryman got shot by mistake.

But undercover, literally, putting an agent into the field: forget it. He'd done it in Aden when he was barely out of his teens, after a three-week crash course in Arabic, and he knew of others who'd done it in Cyprus and Borneo.

Belfast? Forget it. You could learn Arabic and stain your skin and the locals might fall for it if they gave a damn in the first place. There was a score of different Arabic dialects and accents and people wandered into Aden from all over the place. The souk Arabs couldn't have cared less.

But Catholic, Nationalist Belfast was tighter and more closely knit than any community he had ever known. Putting a man in there pretending to be a local, then trying to insinuate him into the Provos, was suicide for the agent concerned. And that wasn't just Joe's opinion, that was fatally proven fact.

The army had tried it, so had RUC Special Branch, and the corpses had turned up in back alleys or on border roads, wired to explosives, covered in cigarette burns, colandered with electric drill bits, beaten hideously, and – mercifully – dead from gunshot wounds.

For where did you stay? Who did you pretend to be? In the Catholic areas everyone knew everyone else, and strangers were treated with great suspicion unless someone could be found to vouch for them. And Joe defied the best mimic to impersonate a Northern Irish Catholic accent, day in day out, taken by surprise, intoxicated, beaten – tortured, perhaps.

They'd used locals, too, men who'd joined the British Army and who felt passionately against the Provos, but such men had a history, a past, relatives and old friends. They had died like the rest.

Brits? The Provos could smell them. They had a saying in Ulster about being a Catholic or a Protestant: 'You can tell by the look of him'. Years of in-breeding, habit, accent and custom had seen to that. So how much more they could detect an Englishman.

Urban Belfast and Londonderry were one thing, perhaps the rural and border areas were another. So they'd put men in, with carefully rehearsed aliases and histories, in unmarked cars, passing through, hands deliberately calloused to show they were men of labour.

At first it had seemed to work, the brave agents passing tidbits of information over their carefully concealed radios. The Provos let them have their tiny triumphs, then took them, cars, radios and all.

More corpses, huddled and stiff in green fields both sides of the border, then posthumous medals, and grieving, noble famlhes. And quietly, without fuss, several middle-ranking intelligence officers found themselves moved to England, their careers on hold.

The officer said, 'Why not?' and Joe told him.

'Really? Ever tried it yourself?'

There was contempt in it, Joe knew that. The officer before him was a brave man, he had the medals to prove it, he thought Joe was some Johnny-come-lately intelligence man without the bottle to actually take risks himself.

'Yes, sir. Once, in a manner of speaking.'

'Really?' The man's eyebrows raised in question.

Joe had gone up the Falls, 1972, at the height of the troubles, strictly without authorisation, buzzing with the danger and dare. He chose the dirtiest anorak he could find, tucked his Browning service pistol in its pocket, hunched himself up, ice-cold with the risk of it, and went.

He was not even quite sure what he was looking for. A patrol had been sniped; perhaps it was a regular snipe position he was looking for, perhaps just random information. Perhaps he was just proving to himself that these people were not unbeatable, that this territory could be breached, that he – Joe Biddle, twenty-seven – had the guts to do it.

He walked a mile without being challenged, then

someone simply passed him the time of day, and he could only grunt a reply, fearful of his accent being detected.

The look he received in reply knocked the plug out of the barrel of his courage. Joe turned a corner, eyes flickering, looking for something to justify this insane excursion. He was in a narrow street of typical Belfast back-to-back terraced homes, and suddenly out of one front door came a woman, randomly flinging a pail of water into the gutter. She looked up at Joe with a half-smile, and made some remark with a query in her voice, but the accent was so strong Joe could not understand her.

He cupped a hand to his ear, feeling rising panic, and when she repeated it he still could not make out the sense of it, something to do with the weather, or water? The blood was coursing to his cheeks, he saw the woman's face change from good-natured cheer to half-suspicion, so he blundered on, hurrying, suddenly terrified of discovery, terrified of the particular purgatory he knew could dwell for the wrong person in these innocent-looking streets.

Joe turned left at the end of the street, then left again at the next street, cutting back the way he had come, trying to quell the panic that threatened like nausea. He was no longer concerned with intelligence, with sniping positions and the miscellany of the Regular Army mind. He was concerned only with the urgent desire to be away from this hostile land.

Eight minutes later he reached the main road, a stroll

from safety now. And saw the barricade, the six men, and the growing crowd of bystanders. There was a hi-jacked bus, a milk float, some black taxis, and he knew with awful certainty that it was all for him.

He pushed a trembling hand through the holed pocket of his anorak, on to the firm butt of the Browning, trying to walk with purpose and without fear. Perhaps they would let him through.

One of the men shouted in a voice that was almost friendly, and in words he could clearly understand, 'Are yer all right there?'

Joe kept his silence, suddenly alert now, the fear metamorphosing into some determination not to be taken. Bluff was useless, surrender meant death, only action could save him.

Perhaps they were not armed. It had only been minutes, he *knew* that. They could rustle up two taxis and a milk float, hijack a bus, perhaps that was planned *anyway*.

But surely they'd keep the weapons hidden, deeply hidden.

They couldn't expect a British soldier in civvies to walk up the Falls.

The man said again, 'Are yer all right?'

Joe laughed without mirth, and the fear in it seemed to explode into the air like startled pigeons.

'Fine.'

'Shouldn't be here, lad. Wrong side for you.'

'Really? Thought I was in the United Kingdom.'

Steady Joe, the inner, still-calm voice said. Don't fall

victim to the false euphoria of danger. This is the worst possible position, don't forget it.

One way, that's all, one way, past them, round the barricade and out of the Falls with your life. Calm, Joe, and *think*.

'British Army? Or is it a Prod you are?'

'British Army.' No point in denying it, and if they thought he was a local, UDA or UVF, then they might just rush him in anger.

'Liverpool?' the man asked.

'Close.' Keep alert Joe, hand on the gun, eyes moving. There's space behind you, gamble they haven't got weapons yet. But when to make the move? When?

'We're not your enemies. You'll just be a working-class lad like us. We should be fighting together.'

Good try, thought Joe. It's worked with others. All cloth-capped lads together, let's fight the top hats. Well what class were the three Scottish lads you blew away while they were taking a piss that New Year's Eve in Omagh, fucking aristocrats?

Three acned eighteen-year-olds from a Kilmarnock council estate, who'd joined up because there was bugger-all else. Befriended, betrayed and murdered.

'Sure.'

'Come on, soldier boy, you know you can't get out of here. Come and have a chat with us, a cup of tea maybe. We get your pistol – you *are* carrying, I presume – a bit of information, that's all.'

'Then ?'

The lying, agreeable smile. 'You go back to barracks. You'll get a bit of a bollocking, that's all. They might even send you back to England, away from us mad Irish.'

For an insane deadly second Joe considered it. Perhaps they *would* let him go, it had happened before. Those two officers who got lost in Derry and wandered into the Bogside no-go area, wearing civvies. The IRA had captured them, taken pictures of the hapless officers, flanked by masked gunmen, then released them. The propaganda coup had been worth ten corpses.

So perhaps?

But those were the early days, the days of relative innocence. Now? No chance. Joe remembered the young soldier who went adrift from his patrol in the Whiterock, scared shitless, cornered up an alley with his SLR and a dozen rounds.

He should've waited, should've hung on, fired a shot every now and then to keep the crowd at bay until the lads realised what was going on and the PIGS and Saracens screamed in mob-handed and pulled him out. But the local Provo had been a smooth-talker, the lad had listened, come out, handed over his rifle, then the crowd had set on him and cracked his skull like an egg.

Only one way out, Joe, down the Falls with blood in your veins, or to the morgue with a bullet hole in your neck.

The man was talking again, words Joe couldn't follow, just syrupy, comforting words, seductive and warm, like the lure of peace and comfort in the Arctic night . . . Lie down, go to sleep, surrender.

Joe moved, pulling the Browning up through the jagged hole of his anorak pocket, hearing the material tear like calico.

The crowd was scattering, stumbling over one another, the speaker's mouth was open in fear.

Browning up, Joe cocking the slide, two hands, into a crouch, foresight on the man's silent round scream.

And the small voice said, No, Joe, No, No.

Last second, jerking the barrel up, two deafening reports, and the man quivering in fear, and the rounds whacking into the metal of the hi-jacked bus, and whining off, fragmented.

'Keep back.' Voice a scream, and hoarse with his own terror, running then; running straight at the scattering mob who parted like sheep for him, through the barricade, tearing skin from his arm, feeling the warm burn of pain, and out, down into the Lower Falls.

Pistol held out and to one side, finger still in the trigger guard, heart pumping, feet slogging red hot on the pitted road.

Stopping only when he saw the patrol at the bottom of the Falls, hard by the Divis flats, saw them turn and scatter, seeking cover, going into firing positions at the sight of this armed, running man coming from IRA territory.

He flung himself into the road, feeling the kiss of the stone and the jar that knocked breath from his body. The pistol flying from his fingers in a wide arc, and Joe summoning everything from his starved and tortured lungs, screaming, 'Friendly, friendly . . . British Army, Corporal Biddle . . . not hostile, not hostile.'

And he lay there, cringing into the hard embrace, dreading the awful sound of the SLRs opening up and the fiendish imagined hurt of the rounds hitting him.

He lay there, and to his everlasting shame felt the urine warm and wet in his pants. As the patrol loped warily towards him, rifles tight into shoulders, Joe was aware that the awful lavatory smell that made the men curl their mouths in disgust was coming from him.

'Not successful, I take it?' the officer said.

'No, sir.'

To say the least. Close arrest, confined to barracks, CO's hearing, bloody near court-martialled and kicked out. Loss of two stripes . . . fined a month's pay. Damn good job he hadn't injured anyone when he'd used the firearm, the CO had said. And Joe shivered as he thought of the moment he'd had the Provo – for what else could he have been – in his sights. That split second when he had to decide whether a man should live or die.

Thank God he'd pulled the shot. As it was the newspapers were full of wild talk about British killer squads operating in plain clothes in Catholic areas.

Joe felt he'd been lucky to stay in the army.

'So I see.' The officer seemed to draw some wry amusement from the file which outlined Joe's earlier predicament. 'Well, I think you'll find there's nothing quite so dramatic these days. We've got most of the lads on computer tabs, know where they live, who they drink with, etc. When they move we jump on them.'

But they can still send a team down to Crossmaglen, park their van on the market square and take out – take out . . . Joe felt a lump in his throat, *kill* my son.

'Mostly routine, lot of filing, bit of interrogation. We're on the ball now, got them on the run. Let's keep it that way.'

'Of course, sir.'

'Sarnt Biddle, everyone here is . . . aware . . .' the officer coughed behind his hand . . . 'of the events of Christmas.'

'Yes sir.'

'If one can be of help.'

'Thank you, sir.'

'You come to us with a fine record. I gather you managed to apprehend an Iranian commando unit while you were in Bahrain.'

He pronounced it Bach-rain, like an expert, and Joe knew he was making a point. That he was on top of the game and Joe was a sergeant and had better not try to get too big for his boots.

'Sir. A team effort, sir.'

'Of course, best way, work as a team.'

The officer shuffled some papers and Joe said, 'Will that be all, sir?'

'Yes. We'll meet on a regular basis for briefings and so on . . . so . . .' the officer thrust out his hand, and Joe took it . . . 'welcome to the team.'

'Thank you, sir.'

'And Sergeant –' there was a small gleam in the officer's eye – 'do us all a favour. Don't go walking down the Falls with a pistol in your pocket all on your ownsome.'

'I shan't, sir.'

'See that you don't. It's maybe more than a couple of stripes you lose next time.'

CHAPTER
9

Three men in a room. Three hole-in-the-sock revolutionaries. Terrorists in cheap chain-store shoes, worn down at the heels.

The kind of men you'd pass in the street without a second glance as they merged into the damp pavements like drab chameleons. Each wore a faded, dirty anorak, that working uniform of the rag-bag army who bombed and killed for a thirty-two counties united Ireland.

Their faces were rough and red, broken-veined from drink and fear, from late nights and poor diet. If you'd seen them in a pub they'd elicit only pity or perhaps contempt, certainly not fear.

They looked losers, men who'd fallen off the fast train of prosperity and purpose, to aimlessly shunt around in life's sidings. And never would appearances have been so deceptive. They *were* dangerous men, killers all. They looked up as the door opened.

'Y'all right, Dermot?' Each man nodded in turn to him and he returned their muted greetings.

Dermot pulled up the only other seat in the room, a hard wooden chair, and the men told him what they wished him to do, and how.

When they'd finished, one said, 'Can you handle it, Dermot?'

'No problem.'

Two of the men exchanged subliminal glances, a momentary flicker of the eyelids, no more.

'It'll take a few days, you understand. We've got sketch maps and the like. Don't want to go nosing around. Isolated house, but word travels fast, what with what's gone on, and all.'

The Provos had killed twelve men in as many months in forty square miles close to the border.

'Right.'

'We'll lay the weapon on. House to pick it up on the other side, and a car. Drive over, lay up for a couple of hours, hit him, and then out before the fuss.'

Dermot was studying the men. Too much blinking for his liking. Why so nervous, just another hit?

He said, 'You sure he travels alone? No wife, or bairns?'

'We're sure.'

One of the blinkers said maliciously, 'You'd be sensitive about that, Dermot? After Cross, and all.'

Somehow the malice and aggression dampened his earlier sense of suspicion.

'Just being careful, Donny.'

'Well, you needn't worry. Just our RUC friend, all alone.'

'Personal weapon?'

'Of course, never travels without it. May have a Stirling in the boot, but it won't matter because you'll have him before he has a chance to go for either.'

The man Donny leaned forward and traced his finger across the sketch map. He drew a dirty line down a drawn road.

'Comes out of the house, into the locked garage through a side door. Checks his car for explosives, then comes out at speed, left on to the main road.' The dirty finger continued its journey. 'Here! A tight bend, left, couldn't go round it at more than twenty. That's where you hit him. Wall on the left, lay up there, take him as he brakes for the bend.'

Dermot grunted approval. 'When?'

'Monday's a good day. Off his guard then, Sunday with the family, church, too much roast beef and red wine.'

'Monday then.'

'Monday.'

The glasses were half-empty, and the younger man said, 'It's dangerous. Suppose the Brits take Dermot, instead of killing him?'

'It won't go wrong. One man? Even the Brits are not that bloody stupid, and they'll gun him down, it's their way.'

The pint was lifted, beer downed, a sleeve wiped across a mouth.

'One man? *The* Man.'

Gurgling, beer-filled laughter. 'Don't fall for the personality stuff. Dermot's just another boyo who went too far. He's to be finished and that's the way it is.'

'Then why not the usual way, why not at least a hearing?'

'Because Mr McGarvey can help us. Republican hero gunned down by SAS killer squads. We'll give him a funeral Belfast'll never forget.'

The men finished their beer and tossed down the whiskey chasers, grimacing.

'It's a fuck-awful bad business, all the same,' the younger man said.

'Bloody mad dog, got to be put down. Better if he helps the Movement on his way out.'

The other man signalled to the barman for refills and said with a sudden burst of bravery he did not feel, 'I'll not make the call. I'll not be the bloody Judas.'

'My job.' The older man stood up and went into the payphone alcove, careful that he could not be heard, his hand over his mouth so that his lips could not even be read.

He dialled the special number, laughed at the suggestion that he reveal his name, then gave a time, a location, a description, the type of weapon, modus operandi, name of victim – everything.

They asked for a meeting, he laughed again and replaced the receiver.

Back at the table the drinks waited, heavy and full of promise.

'Done?'

'No problem. They've got five days so I doubt if even the Brits could fuck this one up.'

The younger man glanced at his mentor, searching for anything in his eyes, anger perhaps, regret, compassion, that thirst for revenge?

But there was nothing there, just, as always, the opaque screen of the dark-green sunglasses.

The plane banked sharply, the clouds parted and the girl glimpsed a glimmering sheet of water as Belfast Lough appeared below, then just as rapidly disappeared as the cloud closed in.

Kathleen felt a lump, a real lump rise up in her throat. Ireland, Ireland at last. The land of her forefathers, a cliché but oh so true.

Everything that pumped through her, every gene, every inherited instinct led her back to this green chunk of land, its history and its troubles. Now at last she had come to see for herself. To travel, to talk, to meet and to write. To soak up Ireland and her father's past, *her* past, like blotting paper.

She wanted to be changed, and she wanted Ireland to change her. She was an American, but an American of Ireland, and she wanted to feel that now, so that in the life that was to come she would never regret that she had not reached out and embraced the country that had made her existence possible.

It had been necessary to stay in London for a while. She had to look up friends of hers and her father's, meet Senate contacts, have lunch with the Ambassador.

She was not just anyone, she was the Senator's

daughter, and she had to act as such, but soon the tide of minutiae and small talk began to engulf her and she longed for the date she had set to leave for Ireland.

London was stultifying, its climate soporific, sometimes cold and grey, then humid and grey, but always, it seemed, grey. The city was dirty, the people rude, and the dull government officials and members of Parliament she met were on the defensive because of her father's outspoken views on Ireland, and the British presence in the North.

It was clear Senator Joseph Minihan was hated, and she winced at the cruel cartoon caricatures she had seen in some of the tabloid newspapers and satirical magazines.

But it was also clear he had both power *and* influence. Any speech he made on Northern Ireland was eagerly reported on television and in those very same newspapers that mocked him.

She had lunched in the House of Commons dining room, watched a debate, met the editor of *The Times*. And never, for one moment, did she feel she understood what England was, what Ireland meant to it, or what that bit of Ireland they called 'Ulster' or 'Northern Ireland', meant either.

Then one day she was drinking alone, in a pub, up against the bar, listening to the chatter around her. A large colour TV sat at one end of the bar, and some of the drinkers were watching a lunchtime news bulletin.

She could not hear the words, but saw some film footage of a wrecked army vehicle, then troops with rifles at the ready moving into Irish-green fields.

The man next to her, middle-aged, a checked flat cap on his head, turned away from the TV and said to her, without preamble, 'Murdering Irish bastards. That could have been my lad.'

She felt the hairs rise on the back of her neck, a surge of anger in her throat like bile against the taste of her warm beer.

'Maybe your "lad" shouldn't be in Ireland.'

The man eyed her first with surprise, then contempt.

'American, are you?'

She nodded.

'Think we want to be there, stuck in the middle of two bunches of murdering Paddies?'

'Oh, I hadn't realised it was that simple.'

He ignored her. 'We don't want to be there, none of us, my lads don't, I know that. Being spat at, shot at.'

She took a sip of beer to calm herself. 'Then I would have thought the simplest thing would be for you to leave, and bring your troops back to *England*.'

'Then you'd see a bloodbath, my love, then you'd see 'em go for each other's throats like dogs.'

'I'm sure Irishmen could settle their own differences.'

The man turned to the TV, but the images had faded now, and it was footage of the floor of the Stock Exchange. He turned back.

'You make me puke, you lot. What the hell do you people over there know about Ireland, or sodding anything, eh?'

She winced from the venom of the man.

He continued, 'You were pretty damn quick to sort out Vietnam, weren't you? With bloody napalm and bombers too. Well, this is our own bloody doorstep. Wait until they start car-bombing you, or trying to blow up your President, see how you'll feel then. In the meantime *piss off* and don't meddle in things you don't understand.'

She slammed her glass hard on to the wet counter of the bar, and the beer whipped up like a small wave.

'My whole family comes from Ireland, if you must know, so don't patronise me about the political situation.'

Heads turned, eyebrows raised, it was a middle-class pub, full of men in checked jackets and hats like her tormentor's.

The man instinctively lowered his voice; he might feel hate, he might feel anger, but he would not make a scene.

He said quietly, 'But they got out, didn't they? They got out of Ireland because anyone with any sense has. And if we'd had any sense maybe we'd do what you suggest, get out and leave them to it.'

'And do all the English feel this way, may I enquire?' she asked with a restraint she did not feel.

'British, actually, young lady. *British*, that's what we are, a bloody nation, not a concoction of mongrels like Americans, and yes, if you ask my opinion, if you took a poll tomorrow ninety-nine per cent would say get out and leave 'em to it.'

She hated every inch of him. Calmly she buttoned

her coat and said, 'Well, I have a message from Irish-Americans everywhere.'

'Which is?' Something strange in the man's eyes, and she felt pity and fear at the same time.

'Fuck you.'

She pushed her way through the drinkers, and fell into the fresh air of the street, face red, anger coursing through her.

There was a touch on her arm, and she whirled round, ready to strike the man. But it was not the person with whom she had argued. It was a younger man, a man who had been standing next to the flat-capped loudmouth.

'Don't touch me!'

'I'm sorry. Look . . .' The man was red, embarrassed, struggling to find the right words. 'You just had an argument with Freddie in there, yeh? Well, look, I'm sorry if he was rude to you, he'd got no right, you're a visitor, and well . . .'

She was agitated, anxious to be away. Maybe this was some kind of English . . . sorry *British* . . . attempt at a pick-up.

'I have to be somewhere, it has been pleasant meeting you, thank you for the apology, now if you don't mind I–'

'His lad lost a leg in Belfast.'

'Pardon me?'

'Freddie. He has three sons in the army, same regiment. About a year ago the middle lad was on patrol when he copped a booby-trap. They had to take his leg off, above the knee.'

She felt very cold.

'I'm sorry – if I'd known . . .'

'Forget it, how could you have? It's just that old Freddie, well, he took it very badly and he has a bit of a bee in his bonnet over it now.'

'It must have been awful.'

'Fortunes of war. Anyway, don't take it to heart, what Freddie said, I mean. We quite like Americans really.'

He went back inside the pub and Kathleen stood on the pavement feeling dizzy and unsure of herself. She began to walk, hardly registering the passers-by who pushed into her, jostling, city-indifferent, anxious to reach their destinations.

She found herself by the Thames at Blackfriars Bridge. The river was at the turn, grey and sluggish, and filled with polystyrene cups. She gazed into it as it dully reflected her feelings. God send me soon to Ireland, she had prayed.

And now she was here. Occupied Ireland stretched out below her. She would visit her father's birthplace, walk in the cemetery where her great-grandfather was buried, then travel Ireland without design or conscious plan. Perhaps if she had time she would even try to look up her father's cousin Michael, though she had little stomach for his political stance on the North.

The cloud parted again and she saw green fields beneath her. What would she find here? The change she sought, the answer she felt might be there to a question that had not yet even been asked?

A sense of belonging?

Disillusionment? Danger?

The possibilities lay beneath her on the green carpet of Ireland on which so many hopes had foundered, so many ideals had been wrecked, so many lives cruelly shattered.

It was to be a simple army operation of the type that had worked so well in the past. The British liked them, were good at them, and enjoyed their cruel sense of irony.

The biter bit, the hens waylaying the fox. All you needed was information, the telephone call or the anonymous letter, and you could go, as long as you thought it was reliable.

There was always the double-double bluff, and no one wanted to send an ambush team *into* an ambush.

But there were satisfactions in it not gained elsewhere. Like when they got the two-man Provo motorbike team, who had three kills to their credit.

The Provos had planned to hit a UDR man, a foundry worker as he came off shift. But someone was jealous, or angry, or wanted revenge or money or perhaps both, and the call was made. So when the would-be killers roared up on their 650 Yamaha, one rider, one assassin with a Magnum, the army hit them.

They shot the back-seat cowboy first, three SLR rounds punching him off the pillion and into a wire fence, spreadeagled, contorted, a look of violent, hurt surprise on his newly dead face.

The rider panicked, tried to brake, to slew the bike round in a long circle, lost control just as the first round hit him in the back and dragged him, bike and all, into a long, bloody, braking skid.

They'd been kids, really, nineteen if you believed the Republican news-sheets, but there'd been laughter and pints in the mess that night, and much talk of the dangers of riding without a crash helmet.

This one was country, not town, so surveillance and concealment was more difficult. You couldn't use buildings or closed vans, it was like in Germany on exercise with the Americans and the Bundeswehr.

Proper soldiering, not dirty back-street stuff. Go out early, drop men off secretly, leave them to build hideouts, and then wait. Then on the morning, move men into stop positions, wait for your man and take him out.

It had all gone back to Whitehall, and the word was that Dermot McGarvey was to be shot without question. He was a dangerous killer who had murdered British soldiers, children, and policemen. He was not to go to the Maze prison.

He was being caught red-handed in an ambush, and the government knew there would be no sympathy for him. Sure, they'd sing their laments in the bars of Dundalk, Derry . . . perhaps even Boston . . . but the world would soon forget Dermot McGarvey.

The RUC inspector had been warned, and had volunteered to act as decoy. His wife and kids were moved out under cover of darkness. He would wear body armour and his police Ford Escort would be stripped and armour-plated, toughened glass fitted in case the worst happened, and the Provo hit-man got off a shot.

The inspector would leave home at his usual time; the assassin would make ready to strike, and the moment he lifted his weapon he would be shot by a concealed army sniper.

The corpse would go to the slab, and the publicity machine would spring to life. The security forces were desperately trying to put a stop to Provo assassinations in the border areas, and perhaps a stiff, cold Dermot McGarvey – the Man – would make them think twice about hunting glory down there.

Everybody but the Republicans would rejoice, and then – who knew, for the British were devious in these matters – perhaps it would just be let slip to a favourite newspaper correspondent (the *Guardian* was respected in Republican circles) that the Man had been betrayed.

Cats among pigeons, fear, distrust and paranoia – maybe even a few 'own goal' corpses.

All in all it would be a perfect day for everyone, with the exception of Dermot McGarvey. At last his time had come.

He awoke at eleven to the clatter of the old alarm clock, and he quickly checked the luminous dial of his wristwatch.

Thirty minutes to dress, take his gun and equipment and leave. He lay there in the darkness, a strange feeling

touching him, leaving a sense of soreness and fever-
ishness as a man will feel when influenza threatens.

Putting the back of his hand to his forehead, he felt
heat and wetness. Perhaps it was the farmhouse, which
was damp and inadequately heated; perhaps he *was*
getting a mild dose of flu.

Or perhaps it was the fitful few hours of sleep in
which he had fretted restlessly on the bare mattress. He
had not meant to sleep, but had set the alarm as a
precaution.

For sleep was like an ocean. You entered it in one
state, and then it submerged you and deposited you on
the shore of wakefulness in another.

He had fallen asleep relaxed and confident; just
another job. Since Colm it seemed even more vital to
continue the struggle, to lash out and destroy the enemies
of Ireland. For if the struggle ceased, then Colm's death
was in vain and he, Dermot, was guilty of a crime and
a sin.

But when the sleep took him it took him like the
waves, tossing him this way and that, controlling him.
The flotsam and jetsam of fragmented dreams came back
to him now, washed up in separated slivers on his beach
of consciousness.

Togas; there had been togas, and daggers, and
Fionulla in school uniform, and Colm of course – but
there was always Colm in his dreams – and cars and
waterfalls.

The teacher, old Mr Walsh, poking him viciously in

the skin of his side, below the ribs, poking him so hard Dermot cried out in his sleep and the finger jabbed like a knife-thrust.

Dermot checked his watch.

He switched on the bedside lamp, recoiling from the molten glare of the naked bulb. The battered cardboard suitcase lay in the corner of the room, and Dermot considered it as a man will a favourite painting.

Fully clothed, he rolled off the bed and walked over to the case, flipped the rust-pocked locks and put his hands inside. He caressed the reassuring steel beneath its hessian cover and reclosed the lid.

Then he stripped to the waist, sluiced his face and upper torso with cold water from the chipped enamel basin, dried himself on a piece of rough towelling, and pulled his roll-necked sweater back over his head. He re-tied the laces of his down-at-heel scuffed Adidas trainers and pulled on the battered anorak.

He took the suitcase, went downstairs and put his load in the back of the Hillman Avenger, then drove off, headlights on, down the blackened lanes, heading for the border.

In position by three, first light by five, target on time, God willing by six, job done three minutes later, back across the border by six-thirty, farmhouse by seven.

He saw a fox dart past in his headlights and slowed, but the fox was away, an almost subliminal glimpse of red and silver in the yellow headlights.

Just after the unmarked border a rabbit was caught

petrified in the glare of the twin converging beams. Again he slowed, but this time doused his lights. When he switched them back on again, the road was empty, the rabbit vanished, freed from their spell.

Five minutes later he saw a signpost, stopped, checked his map by the light of a pencil torch, then branched left. About three miles further on he pulled on to the grass verge, did a three-point turn, and switched off the engine.

He sat there in the pitch dark and the silence that was broken only by the intermittent ticking of the cooling engine. Then he gently unclicked the door, just as gently closed it, and went to the boot of the car.

He unlocked it, left it open and returned the keys to the ignition. If he did need to rush away, then he did not want to waste vital seconds fumbling for the key. If anyone knew of his plan, or his getaway, then they would disable the car whether he left the ignition key in or not.

Opening the suitcase he deftly assembled the Armalite in the dim light afforded by the meagre bulb in the boot. He put a full magazine into the rifle, and a spare in the pouch pocket of his anorak.

He shivered slightly in the dark night chill, and again felt that touch of damp heat, this time in his crutch and his armpits. The danger fever, Dermot, nothing more, just the danger fever.

He looked down at the suitcase and this time it seemed to mock him. And what would the extra contents stop, Dermot my lad, a peashooter, an air rifle perhaps, a .22 if you were very lucky?

But togas; togas and sandals and Mr Walsh poking him in the side viciously like a knife blow. Colm and Fionulla, and cars and waterfalls, and daggers . . . daggers? Searing pain below the ribs.

Et tu, Brutus? Where had he learned that, school probably. You too, Brutus? Beware the Ides of March.

He opened the suitcase again, and looked long and hard at the object within. Is it pride that's stopping you, or just obstinacy?

Take it, lad. Take it. Dermot turned and faced out into the blackness, then back again, reached down, taking out the flak jacket. Slipping off his anorak he buckled the cumbersome armoured vest about himself, then awkwardly replaced the anorak, zipping it tightly, stretching its fabric to the limit.

Now it was time to think only of the job ahead, not of togas and daggers, of Colm and Fionulla, and above all not of Mr Walsh.

The hunters and the unknowing hunted waited for the dawn and the killing that would come with the grey light.

Dermot did not sleep, and neither did his watchers. He checked the land for human activity, for possible ambush, and saw nothing. Could not, for the darkness cloaked it all, and the soldiers were well hidden and camouflaged, and above all disciplined-silent.

In the silence and the blackness they waited.

At last grey dawn began to reach out, touching imperceptibly with its probing fingertips, and Dermot checked the road through the firing loophole he had prised out of the stone wall: up the road, and then back the way he had come.

There was mist on the hills, masking sound and movement had there been any, but there was just the serenity and stillness of the tomb.

Dermot shivered and steadied himself. It will work. It will work as it always has done, and tonight you shall drink to the death of your enemy.

He heard the engine noise first, travelling easily on the early-morning country air, like an old woman's cackle or a tinny death rattle, as the Ford Escort's starter motor shook the engine awake.

Dermot took the small Zeiss binoculars from his anorak pocket and peered through the aperture in the stone wall, then waited, his breath rising in the cold air.

He saw a squashed-up road, like something from a child's pop-up book, everything distorted and compressed by the magnification. Everything grey, grey road, grey grass, grey walls, life and colour drained from it . . . and then a splash of kingfisher blue.

The car!

Dermot's heart skipped and he felt that familiar pounding in his chest, skin tightening, goose pimples sprouting on his skin, a surge of heat in his cheeks.

Behind the windscreen one man . . . *check it, Dermot* . . . one man, no wife, no kids, no bodyguard, no trap.

Registration plates, letters and numbers. It tallies, right car, right man. Dermot lowered the binoculars, reached out for the Armalite, checked himself and quickly snatched up the binoculars.

Something about the car. Right car, right plates, and yet . . . what? What? They'd told him it wasn't a new car, yet it was so bright, as though it had been re-sprayed.

So . . . ? So . . . ? Seconds now, Dermot, seconds. But low in the road, this car, *heavier*, as though weighed down. With what? One man . . . just . . .

Dermot was sweating, globules of it sliding down his face, misting the lenses. He wiped them furiously, pushed his sleeve across his face, clearing it.

One man, bare head, face set and white . . . maybe that was the early hour. Was he tense? And the car. Why so heavy and new-looking? Hammer-blows in his chest, blood pumping furiously.

Low on the axles like an . . . Christ, it was ARMOURED! The fucking thing had been armour-plated.

HE KNEW!

Dermot leapt like a man convulsed by electricity, going for the Armalite and the ditch.

They saw the Provo move, going for the ditch. Something badly wrong, now or never.

'Fire!'

Target moving, but in view, just a fraction of aim shift required. The sniper squeezed the trigger, felt the satisfying recoil, saw the round impact with a flurry of dust and what probably was blood and tissue.

Then the Provo slumped, still clutching his rifle, and slid out of sight into the bed of the stream.

A bedlam of shouts, orders and running feet. But the sniper stayed, feeling the gentle pain in his shoulder, content. He was twenty and he'd just killed a Provisional IRA man.

The blow hit Dermot like a red-hot cannonball in his lower left back, smacking him into the dirt, sliding him down the tiny incline.

For long seconds he was dazed, hurting, then he heard the shouts of the running men and forced himself to sit up, wincing and crying out involuntarily from the pain, biting his lip to gag himself.

The flak jacket had saved him, taking some of the impact of the bullet, diverting it perhaps, for it had struck his flesh, he could feel it like a branding iron, and the pain was excruciating.

Togas and daggers and betrayal, and the bullet like Mr Walsh's finger, dagger sharp in his side. Ides of March betrayal, and not Colm this time, just a man with bottle-green spectacles, Dermot knew.

Then through the mist of his pain Dermot saw a face like a white mask, snarled in terrible fear and hate. The policeman, his pistol pointed over the stone wall at Dermot.

Two sharp cracks, a brief one-two of flame, the pistol jerking upwards from the recoil, and Dermot flinching, closing his eyes, as the rounds zipped past him and hit the bank with a plopping, sucking sound.

One-handed, the Armalite up, the notched 'V' of the sight on the white, hate-frightened face. The pistol jammed, and now sheer terror on the mask as the RUC man struggled to clear his gun. The 'V' like a tattoo of death over the man's shrivelled, brave face.

Kill him! Brave man. Fool. But kill him!

And suddenly Dermot screaming in a voice not his own, a stranger's voice, 'Get away, it's done, get away.' And the white face gone like a dreamed-of phantom on waking, and Dermot up now and running, bent double, back scalded with pain.

Two sharp cracks, live rounds, and a rush of hot air and a whine as they ricocheted from the stone wall. Running, tugging at the armour that had saved his life, but now threatened to fling him into the mud and pin him like the French noblemen at Agincourt and Crécy, so that another generation of English yeomen could do their killing work.

Eyes only on the woods and the life-giving shelter, and suddenly he was there, cannoning off a tree, tearing his clothes, falling into a roll, gun held out and away, then sprawling face-first into a bush, feeling the absurdly welcoming claw of the branch talons.

The major in charge of the ambush called for helicopters and moved up his blocking positions. Then he swore and swore and swore.

This could have been handled by special forces, the SAS were itching to take out McGarvey. But the CO had been adamant that a good infantry regiment was perfectly capable of staging a standard rural ambush.

It had always worked in exercises, the major had *never* failed to get a hostile. But they hadn't banked on the little bastard using body armour, because he *must* have been, everyone saw the round impact.

Now there was a live, deadly armed Provo in those woods who should have been a *dead*, *un*armed Provo.

The major swore again.

CHAPTER
10

She saw a small white signpost, fresh-scrubbed by the rain, and thin letters announcing a half-mile to the village of Killibrea, her father's birthplace.

A tightening in the gut, heart beating faster, hands clammy on the wheel of the hire car as she drove down the slow, winding slope.

Then the village spread out for her; white-washed Irish cottages, some thatched, all with an individual spiral curl of smoke ascending from their chimneys.

A small bar, Killeen's, she had heard her father talk of it; of the two British soldiers who'd had the insensitivity to try to drink there in 1916, oblivious it seemed to the rage and dismay after the executions that followed the Easter Rising.

How they'd sat, sat and drank, ignored, as the other drinkers stood in silence, caps off.

'They managed a pint, damn near choked on that, and couldn't manage no more,' her grandfather had told her father.

And the two Black and Tans, shot as they left one winter's night, drunk and arrogant, their list of crimes against the local community known to all, their deaths marked out and decided upon by the local battalion of Volunteers.

Killeen's. And there it still was, a repository of history, with its signs for Guinness stout, its stickers indicating its approval by the Northern Ireland Tourist Board. But strip away the cars, the yellow parking-restriction lines, the modern street lamps and the late twentieth-century dress of the passers-by and it would be the Killeen's of the sepia picture-postcard her father still kept, framed, on the mantelshelf in the big house on the ocean.

The whole village, too, an anachronism in the world in which Kathleen had grown up.

She drove slowly down the main street, a sense of history and fulfilment enveloping her.

The car reached the stern, granite Catholic church – Our Lady of Lourdes – the church in which her grandfather had married, in which her father had been baptised and married her mother.

She drove on, slowing by Devlin's. In the window little green shamrocks, jaunty, almost tongue-in-cheek, an Irish in-joke at itself – dancing next to the name of its first proprietor.

Seamus Devlin had died in the Twenties, during the bitter civil war, executed by the Treaty men for standing out for full independence for Ireland, North as well as South. Perhaps it was a grandson who ran it now, or maybe it had been thought sacrilege to expunge the name of a brave man who had gone South and paid with his life for what he believed in.

Kathleen turned right at the crossroads, knowing the

village from a thousand nights of telling at her father's knee. At the end of a row of identical terraced cottages, a figure waited, leaning on a wooden gate.

The woman wore a shawl, and a headscarf over what would prove to be a shock of grey hair – and a shock in the other sense, too, for Kathleen had only seen pictures of her aunt with thick, black tresses.

Her father's sister, Aunt Kathy, the woman whose name she had been given, the woman she knew only from posted black and white pictures, from scrawled, almost indecipherable letters to her father. Or from random, scattered long-distance telephone calls, crackling 'Happy Birthdays' in an accent so thick and foreign the young American Kathleen could scarcely understand what was being said.

A woman with the mane of hair, the woman on horseback, the tall, strong woman with a half-filled big glass in her hand, surrounded by laughing Irish faces. Aunt Kathy, grown old now, slightly stooped but still with that etched memory of strength and power and physical force in her frame.

The woman turned as she heard the car, leaned forward as if peering, a hand over her eyes like a seafarer. Kathleen brought the car to a halt a few yards from the gate, got out and walked the last stretch of the journey 'home'.

'Aunt Kathy.'

'Well now, and aren't you a fine-looking young woman?'

'You're just like Dad said.'

And Kathleen saw her father's face there, the strength and the humour, and some of the bitterness too, sketched into the craggy, weather-beaten features that had fought the familiar losing battle against age.

Then they were in each other's arms and Kathleen could smell wood and smoke, and feel the strength of the grip in the old woman's embrace, and the moisture too, as their tears merged.

For over an hour it was a helter-skelter tumble of conversation; their words jostling each other, pushing ahead, tumbling over, catching up, joining and parting, sentences crossing like tracks on a speeded-up rail journey.

Then the snapshots came out, first young Kathleen's, fresh and American, early Polaroids, out of focus Instamatic shots, then the more practised, professional shots from the expensive 35mm. Then Aunt Kathy's, some very old and sepia either from design or light-age, some black and white, small, badly printed and out of focus.

Men in baggy flannels, and gangster-like trilbys; and they'd laughed and pointed, and Kathleen said, 'I don't believe it' a dozen times, as hitherto-unseen shots of her father emerged. The senator-to-be in ludicrous baggy short trousers, football shorts that reached to his knees, and massive boots; even naked as a baby on a rug in front of the fire.

Then the two women, old and young, aunt and niece, grew suddenly silent, watching each other with the slight wave of embarrassment that follows early intimacy.

The old woman at last got up, breaking the uneasy spell they had cast over each other, and went into the kitchen, whence Kathleen heard cooking noises and smelled associated aromas.

Eventually Aunt Kathy returned with a large, dark brown pot and began to serve stew with a ladle on to white china plates set on a table laid with a soft, cream-coloured Irish linen cloth.

Kathleen had felt an unreasonable pang of disappointment when she learned that dinner had not been cooked, as she had fondly imagined, over the peat fire in the hearth – as her father had described to her. It was clear the village had electricity now.

She had imagined, too, that they would drink beer in jugs brought from Devlin's or Killeen's, an image from her father's tales that hung in the gallery of her memory.

Instead her aunt produced a bottle of white wine from the kitchen, and uncorked it. Kathleen noticed it had been brought from the chain-store grocery called Mace she had seen in the high street. The wine itself was a Reisling – not a wine that Kathleen liked – imported from Communist Yugoslavia, and the assistant had left the price tag, a tiny, white sticky label, on the neck of the bottle.

She translated the British pounds sterling into dollars and realised that this inferior white wine had cost her aunt the equivalent of seven US dollars. There was another unreasoning twist of something inside her, which she could not possibly recognise.

They ate the stew – which was delicious – in almost total silence, and drank the warm white wine without enthusiasm, leaving over half the contents still in the bottle at meal's end.

Eventually her aunt went across to an ancient sideboard, bent down – with a little difficulty, Kathleen noted – and brought out a bottle of Jameson's Irish whiskey.

Over the Irish the talk turned to history, and to politics, to the US, to England, and inevitably to Ireland, North and South.

Kathleen ventured, 'Why do you still stay here, Aunt Kathy, why don't you move South?'

The old woman laughed, then half-covered her mouth as old people do in embarrassment at long-possessed, ill-fitting dentures.

'Don't be soft, girl, this is still Ireland, even if it still has its British landlords, no matter which army comes patrolling down the lanes.'

'And do they – the British I mean?'

'Well of course they do. Drive through in their Land-Rovers, rifles poking out to the sky as though the birds were enemies.'

'It'd make my blood boil.'

The old woman took a gulp of her whiskey, then sucked it noisily over the artificial incisors.

'We're twelve miles from the border. The boyos come over, kill someone, dash back – so . . .' She shrugged her shoulders, and it seemed to contain both hopelessness and rage.

The two women fell silent again. At length Kathleen spoke, like the first boxer to land a punch after a temporary lull in aggression. 'Of course, if they weren't here?'

Aunt Kathleen looked up, eyes suddenly shrewd now, and irritated too. 'If they weren't here? If who weren't here?' Those eyes gave lie to the apparent incomprehension.

'If the British left, Aunt Kathy. Ireland for the Irish. Peace. And Irish men and women solving their own problems . . .' Her voice tailed off, the sentence and its meaning seeming to evaporate like morning mist under the hot-sun gaze of her aunt's eyes.

'Well, *wouldn't* it?' she said, her voice almost pleading.

The old woman gave that hopeless shrug again, and it seemed to douse the fire of her eyes. She spoke slowly, without enthusiasm or conviction.

'Perhaps. But they won't go, they're too bloody stubborn, the Brits. How do you drive them out – tell me? The boys have been trying since I don't-know-when.'

'The armed struggle has to succeed,' said Kathleen. But the words that sounded so resonant and sincere in Boston now rang hollow and empty in this Irish sitting room.

Her aunt snorted. 'Pah. It's past that. The Germans couldn't make the British see sense, what chance have we got? What chance have a bunch of bloody Shamrock Boys got? Forget it. It's all to do with the politicians now. Perhaps cousin Michael, and the talkers in Dublin and Belfast all, can jaw us into a united Ireland.'

Kathleen was genuinely shocked. This was her father's sister, a legend, a totem, and she could speak like this.

'Shamrock Boys, Aunt Kathy?'

'Aye, Shamrock Boys, that's all they bloody are now. The old patriotism has gone. It's robbing post offices and driving Mercedes on the proceeds now. Lining their own pockets, and a bullet in the back of the leg for those that dare speak out against them . . . !'

'I don't understand.' She didn't, she didn't understand at all.

'It's me. I'm an old woman, don't pay me any attention.' She put a hand almost protectively around her whiskey glass, and Kathleen noticed for the first time the brown, mottling age-spots, and the inflamed arthritic knuckle joints.

'But you always believed. You taught Father and he taught me. You know what he's achieved for the Cause, for what we all believed in, a united, free Ireland. You helped.'

Aunt Kathy pulled the drink towards her, an increasing gesture of protection, wagons pulling into a circle against hostile attack.

I am her brother's daughter, Kathleen thought, and still she is suspicious of me, frightened of me?

'Yes, I helped. It was different then. We knew what we wanted, probably would've had it, too, if it hadn't been for the big War.'

'Then why have you changed?'

'*I* haven't. The world has, politics has, nothing's simple any more. And the Brits won't go, you don't understand them in America. You think of bowler hats and umbrellas, and those chinless upper-class wonders drinking tea. It's not like that, Kathy.'

'It's not? You think I don't know that? You think I haven't seen the film of their soldiers . . . I'm not totally naive, Aunt Kathy, I don't take my images from Hollywood.'

The hand closed on the glass, brought it up, the old woman drank and replaced it on the table like a chess piece.

Kathleen said, 'You were with the boys . . . you fought?'

'I fought, I fired a Thompson gun at a British armoured car not three miles from this hearth.'

'Then. . . ?'

'At soldiers . . . not at babies.'

'Don't change history, Aunt Kathy, in the Thirties the Movement took the war to England. Bombs in postboxes. Irish boys hanged from British gallows.'

'Yes, and I was against it. Always was, still am. We didn't kill babies for Ireland, that wasn't *my* movement.

Now they blow up the British when they mourn their dead at prayer. They blow up their horses and their bandsmen even as they play the tunes.'

Kathleen said viciously, 'You sound like the spokesman at the British Embassy in Washington.'

The gaze that met her was withering. 'Don't you ever say that to me, *ever*! I'm an Irishwoman, a Catholic, a speaker of Gaelic and the thing I like most about England is the ferry that leaves Liverpool for Dun Laoghaire.'

'I'm sorry . . .'

'And so you should be . . . never clapped eyes on me since the day you were born, daughter of your father – a man I scraped for with my own hands so that he could go to America and become something, something more than a ragamuffin boy with a gun and the desire to get killed . . .'

'Aunt Kathy!'

'. . . and you come back to tell *me* the solution to the problems of this accursed place.'

'You feel that way about Daddy?' Kathleen felt ice-cold, angry, but mostly hurt, sad. She wanted her father to be there now, so that she could weep out the hurt and the frustration on his shoulder.

'I love your father, I raised him like I was his mother and sent him out. And he's right, everything he said and says, but it's *different* there, don't you see? There it's words, here it's reality, and dead people, and I for one want no more of it.'

'It'll happen, Aunt Kathy, whether you want no more of it or not.'

'Well, perhaps it just will and all. Perhaps the Brits will leave, tired of their young men going home in coffins. And then perhaps it's like those bloody mad dogs in the Shankhill say. Perhaps then they *will* get out all their guns they've been storing these nineteen years and come hunting the Catholics.'

'A myth. Scaremongering.'

'I pray to the Good God that it's so. But if I lived in the Short Strand or the Markets, hemmed in by those God-fearing sons of the Red Hand, I wouldn't stay to wait on prayers. I'd pack my bags and my kids and I'd be off.'

'Would that happen?'

'It could. Who knows what those Prods would do if they didn't have the British Army to contend with – for they've no love for the Brits either. Disloyal Loyalists, we call them.'

Both women laughed, and it seemed to puncture the sac of poison that had grown between them.

'And who could stand by and see it happen, not the Republic, not America.'

'Then God help us all because there'll be massacres before the Irish Army can fight their way up to Belfast, and then we've got civil war.'

Kathleen felt great tears well up in her eyes, tears of disillusionment and disappointment.

Kathleen Minihan. The name had become a legend with her, and she had been named for it. The woman who had smuggled guns to the boys, helped IRA men shelter when they'd been on the run, who had stayed up in the North, taking the day-to-day abuse of the Protestant B-Specials. The woman who had spent every hard-earned, hard-saved penny to send her ten-year-old brother to America.

For the young Kathleen her namesake aunt had symbolised everything worth fighting for in Ireland, everything that was fierce, independent and uncompromising. Her beliefs had led her to send a frightened child on a cattle-boat destined for an upbringing with distant relatives in Massachusetts.

And those beliefs, that debt and that loyalty had taken that frightened, red-faced Irish kid to high school, to university, to West Point, to Korea and eventually to the Senate.

Senator Patrick Minihan was not a green-beer, Shamrock Day-only politician, playing the Blarney stone, in debt to Tammany Hall – he actually *believed* in one uncompromising principle.

Britain must get out of Ireland, Ireland must be free and united, and if he was asked to condemn violence *before* that happened, then he would not, for what were British troops and guns on Irish soil if not violence against the Irish?

He could have had a government post, had been offered many – especially under the Carter administration – but had always rejected the *quid pro quo*, that he drop his uncompromising position on Ireland. Great Britain was an *ally*, goddammit, and every time Minihan opened his mouth half the British population would have cheerfully chucked every American aircraft and man stationed there into the cold grey waters that surrounded their miserable island.

But Senator Minihan kept his principles and his beliefs, beliefs he had learned at the knee of this very woman, Kathleen Minihan – the *First* as Patrick sometimes called her.

Kathleen said, 'Did you ever tell Dad you felt this way, that you'd –' she paused – 'that you'd changed?'

The old woman gave a quick shake of her head. 'I know what it means to him. I didn't want to disillusion him. If he'd stayed he would have changed too . . . or perhaps he would not.' Her voice was hard. There was silence.

At length the girl said, 'So you don't help any more?'

The old woman shook her head at the futility of trying to explain to this girl from another planet.

'Help to murder thick Prod farmhands on their tractors – so that in twenty-four hours or forty-eight the UDA shoot some innocent Catholic in front of his family? Tit for tat, they call it here . . . sectarian murders. Does that ever make the *Boston Globe*?'

'Yes, it makes the *Boston Globe*. An act of war followed by a murder.'

'And saying will make it so?' Kathleen took a big gulp of Jameson's that made her eyes water as she tried to swallow it.

Her aunt said, 'I just want no part of it any more.

149

How can we tell these people we want to share a united Ireland with them, and then gun them down in their houses, in the fields, on the streets? Christ – and may the Virgin Mary forgive my blasphemy – aren't we all in the Common Market now?'

Kathleen tried to speak, but nothing came. She started again, trying to articulate the anger and hurt she felt, but somewhere between the words forming in her brain and her mouth trying to issue them, her mood began to dissolve like a changing cinema scene, and she spoke with a choking sob of utter sadness.

'And just suppose, Aunt Kathy, that one of these Shamrock Boys you now despise so much came knocking on your door, wounded and hurt. What would you do then, turn him over to the British?'

There was a loud spit and sizzle from the grate that made them both jump with surprise. The intervention seemed to momentarily distract the old woman, but when she looked up, there was fire in her eyes, real or reflected it was hard to tell.

'You do me an injustice, and Ireland too. Never an informer, young Kathleen . . .' The diminutive seemed like a rap over the knuckles now . . . 'never that. There'd be a room, a bed, a bath, food and drink, and nursing if he wanted it, for he'd be a son of Ireland even if he had done wrong.'

'I'm sorry, Aunt Kathy . . . it's just . . . I'm so confused. All my life I've dreamed of Ireland, of you . . . and now it's all different. London was horrible, Belfast strange, disturbing, but when I arrived in Killibrea it was everything I imagined it would be.'

'But I'm not?'

Kathleen shook her head, wretchedly.

'Do you remember that popular song, "You always hurt the one you love, the one you wouldn't hurt at all"?'

Kathleen nodded.

'Well let me tell you something. I reserve my deepest thoughts for the ones I love, and there are precious few of them left, and most of them 3,000 miles across the sea. I've never spoken this to anyone in Killibrea, nor would I. And nor should you.'

'I love you too, Aunt Kathy.'

'Then it's your love I shall take, and not the anger I can see spilling out of you.' She raised her glass. 'Let's see if your da taught you this toast: "Bad luck to the British".'

Kathleen laughed through her tears, lifted her glass and said softly, 'Bad luck to the British.'

She awoke in the large, creaky bed, to a smell of flowers and rain, and the somehow comfy mustiness of the cottage walls.

Her room had flowered wallpaper, cream net curtains, and a jug and bowl on the old dresser. It was not for decoration, as such a combination might have been in some fashionable New England inn; the jug contained water, and there was a tiny sliver of soap. The cottage had a bathroom, but it was an extension tacked on to the rear, through the kitchen. One could wash here and dress if necessary without traipsing through the house.

Kathleen stretched, luxuriously, until the disappointment of the previous evening filtered back to her. But this was a new day, and whatever transpired she was determined to enjoy the rest of her short stay in Killibrea.

Her face peeped like a child's over the enormous quilt, trying to judge by the quality of the light whether the sky was full of rain.

On the walls were two framed pictures, one of her father, small, scared and confused, yet stiff and formal in some anonymous Boston photographer's studio.

The other was of Christ.

Kathleen pushed her head back into the pillow and squinted upwards at the wall-mounted crucifix. Christ crucified gazed piteously down from his plastic cross, the wounded side vivid in a dash of red paint, the loins covered in the carefully draped, plastic-moulded cloth.

Christ on the wall looked older – though that was not possible – than his other crucified image. He looked piteously down at something unknown, his head framed by an enormous, almost solid, halo. His robe was open to reveal a heart exposed and deep red.

Kathleen pushed her head back beneath the quilt and dozed for several minutes. Then she heard kitchen noises, the rattle of crockery, the gush of an ancient tap. Eventually the whistle of a kettle and the tantalising aroma of frying bacon began to drift up the stairs and into her room.

CHAPTER TEN

Outside, the street sounds of an Irish village coming awake, footsteps, the clip-clop of a horse, the slow grind of a bus, the clink of milk bottles taken in from a step.

She heard the slow tread on the ancient stairs, the snap of the metal latch, and Aunt Kathy was standing there, tray in hand, steam rising from an enormous mug of what proved to be Irish-strong tea.

Kathleen sat up, and propped herself upright with the pillows.

'Good morning – Aunt Kathy, bacon and eggs!'

Her aunt plonked the tray down over her lap.

'Get that down you and you'll not come to much harm.'

She sipped the rich brown tea, savouring the bitter smoky taste. 'Mmmmm, it's good.'

Her aunt sat on the edge of the bed, encouraging her. 'Come on before the eggs get cold.' She took a knife and spread the soft, creamy butter on to the brown bread.

Later Kathleen took her wash things, declined the basin, and went downstairs through the kitchen where her aunt was washing up in the sink, to shower in the unheated bathroom extension. The shower was a plastic contraption attached to the bath taps, and a flow of regular heat was difficult to achieve. She emerged shivering and cold, but dried herself briskly on the rough towel her aunt had provided.

After dressing she walked up through the village, out of town on the road that would eventually lead to the Irish Republic, then climbed a turnstile and set off through the fields until the ground began to rise. She cut through a dense bed of ferns – no fear of snakes here, not in St Patrick's land – and climbed a steeper rise to an exposed ridge from which she judged she could get a good view of the village.

She sat alone, until she felt cold and damp from the wet ground, just watching the village, its white cottages, the trails of smoke smudging the air above them.

She walked, half-ran because of the incline, down to the field and the road, and strode back into Killibrea. Stopping outside the parish church, she hesitated, then went inside.

Kathleen had been baptised a Catholic but no longer had religious belief. She had dabbled with Zen at university, flirted with Buddhism, but in truth she felt nothing.

This church was history to her, the place in which her ancestry began, the church to which her father had returned to marry his American bride.

Kathleen recalled the candle-filled cathedrals of her childhood, the mysterious litany of Mass, clasping her father's hand at her mother's funeral, the oak casket heavy and frightening below the altar. The robes of white and purple, the rich Boston-Irish voices, the Latin intonations and incantations, and the heavy, sinister smell of incense.

How she had knelt, the cold of the stone reaching through her woollen tights, her mittened hands clasped together, eyes clenched lest God see her peeping, reciting her silent prayers.

God bless Daddy, God bless Mummy. But God took Mummy, and perhaps it was then, at eleven years old, that suddenly the church became a place of fear, a place they took you when you died.

She had prayed since, in times of crisis, when boyfriends she wanted desperately decided that they did not want her. When she endured a two-day nightmare of terror that she had cancer.

She slipped into one of the rows of wooden pews and sat down, on the hard bench. Ahead was the brightly lit altar with its gold, majestic cross. Below and to one side a cluster of candles flickered in the draughts of the old church.

At the side of the pews the wooden bulk of the confessional, a fabrication that both chilled and attracted her. There was something sensuous in that curtained, grilled box. She'd recognised that as a ten-year-old, feeling the delicious hollowness in her stomach and the warm trembling of her knees as she had slipped into her seat in the semi-darkness.

An old woman came out of the confessional, hobbled slowly to the bottom of the aisle, near the doors, half-kneeled in an agonising movement, made the sign of the cross, and left.

Kathleen stood up, quickly before she could change her mind, crossed to the confessional and went in.

A young voice, but hoarse, said from the other side of the grille, 'Do you wish to make a confession?'

'Yes. Forgive me, Father, for I have sinned.'

'What was your transgression, my child?'

'I have lost faith, Father.'

He must know that she was American, must also know exactly who she was, for the village was a small one, and her arrival would have been awaited and noted. The daughter of the village's most famous son.

The lure of the confessional was confidentiality and anonymity, but how could it be so in a village where the priest must know everyone, would recognise their voices and know of most of their sins before they were confessed? But the darkness and the grille, the partition of separation was part of the sensuous myth that encouraged you to unburden.

'We all have doubts, child, but we can overcome and restore our true faith. Say ten Hail Marys, ten Our Fathers, and recite the rosaries.'

She paused. 'Thank you, Father.'

'Bless you, my child.'

She could see the outline of his face, obscured through the mesh of the grille, hear his breath, fancied she could smell tobacco from his pores. They were like forbidden lovers whispering through the gate of a harem.

'Is that the end of your confession?'

She took a sharp intake of breath. 'Father, is it a mortal sin to support the struggle here? To want Ireland to be free. Is it?'

She sensed the momentary hesitation, heard the slight nervous clearing of the throat.

'It is no sin to want a free Ireland.'

How many men and women had sat in this box and asked his forgiveness for far worse? she wondered.

'To fight for that freedom – kill for it?'

The priest's voice was immediate, piercing like a lance – thrust through the grille, shattering the quasi-religious lovers' tryst.

'Murder is a mortal sin, punishable by eternal damnation. The murderer puts himself beyond God's salvation.'

'Yes, Father.'

'Is that the end of your confession?' The voice was brisk and nervous now.

'Would you help one, Father – one of the boys, if he came here and said he'd killed?'

'The secrets of the confessional are for the priest and for God. And they are not a place for politics. My child, others wish to make their confessions.'

The voice of a frightened man walking quickly, whistling through a dark and dangerous place.

'Thank you, Father.'

'God be with you.'

Kathleen pulled back the curtain and stepped into the grey light of the church. At the end of the aisle she looked back, down towards the flickering candles, the illuminated altar and the gold cross of the crucified Prince of Peace.

Superstitiously she genuflected and made the sign of the cross. Then she left, quickly.

*　　　*　　　*

At seven they went to Killeen's and drank black Irish stout that wore its cream head like a neckscarf.

Kathleen was greeted like a long-lost daughter, her hand shaken until it hurt. Drinks were pushed in front of her by generous hands; more drinks than she could have coped with in a year.

As the evening wore on two men with fiddles struck up a tune and a bearded, red-faced man sang rebel songs, his eyes wet with emotion.

She watched her aunt, heard her sing along, saw her sup the stout, sip at the whiskey, but she was aware of the old woman's detachment.

The Cause was a thing for songs and tears and red-faced, emotional men with memories or imagined memories. Clearly a thing no longer for commitment, not from this old woman who had seen the steel and heard the rifles, who had smelled the blood and listened to the cries.

Aunt Kathy could drink the emotion and memory in gulping draughts and still be left with a sober intellect when she stood up from this table of history. It was all no more to her now than one of the American TV movies; cars, chases, colour and sunshine that she watched so avidly on the small Japanese set in her living room. You switched it off, and it was gone.

Food was put on the bar, pies, sandwiches, a hot dish, too, with baked potatoes, and Kathleen knew it was in her honour, for no bar or pub she had ever experienced gave free food to its customers.

She was hungry and she ate, pummelled with questions between her mouthfuls by the locals in the strange, hard-to-understand accents, until it was time to go, and ones-for-the-road were pushed in front of her. Eventually she and her aunt walked, arms linked, through the soft Irish drizzle, both a little drunk, back to the cottage.

The rest of the days followed a similar pattern, the awakening, the sounds, the breakfast and the walk – although Kathleen never ventured into the church again.

On the second night, a similar performance was enacted for her in Devlin's bar, and she was introduced to a priest in his early thirties, with bad teeth, a shock of red hair and heavily nicotine-stained fingers.

'Father Mullaney.'

'A pleasure, Father.'

It was the same priest. She recognised the tobacco-hoarsened voice, and he would be able to tell her by her accent, instantly. But he did not acknowledge by so much as a flicker of eyelids that words had passed between them, and for her part she said nothing in admission of the dangerous words she had uttered in the dusty darkness the previous day.

Sleep again, breakfast in bed, walks, an evening in. Just the two of them, Aunt Kathy and herself, with the cheap white wine from Yugoslavia that her aunt liked so much.

And on the fourth day Kathleen said, 'I'll leave tomorrow, I've stayed too long, plus I'm eating you out of house and home.'

'Stay as long as you like, a kitten eats more.'

But the old woman's face was neutral at the social lie. There was no plea there, nothing in the eyes that said, Stay. Please stay.

They kissed, lips on cheeks, and Kathleen went to her bedroom, undressed and slid beneath the covers, listening to the soft wind moaning gently in the eaves; like a soul trapped without hope of escape in the cold cottage.

She was everything Kathleen had expected her to be, and nothing. She was Aunt Kathy of the letters and of long nights telling of her, and she was an individual from a foreign land, a stranger.

Kathleen had tried to cross an ocean, a culture, a history and experience of almost fifty years, and she had failed. She had tried to take a dream and make it reality, and she had not succeeded. She had projected her fantasies on to a real person, and then been surprised when her illusion was shattered.

Kathleen hoped it was not some omen, some metaphor for Ireland.

She would leave at dawn, before her aunt was awake; before the kitchen-bustling sounds and the breakfast tray that arrived in her room like a deceitful lover's declaration of fidelity.

Dermot knew he had just minutes.

They would move into the wood and flush him out like a grouse on their 'glorious' 12th. Mad Dog

McGarvey gunned down, but all before the TV crews or the photographers got there.

No Balcombe Street option for Dermot, no coming out hands held high. They meant to finish it this time – and better, he thought bitterly, better than Balcombe Street.

He remembered the humiliation as a schoolkid when an Active Service Unit in London, surprised and chased, were besieged with their hostages in a small flat. And then, after days, surrendering before the live TV cameras of the world. Not that. He burrowed deeper into the undergrowth.

Why had he not killed the inspector? The man had been his target – *legitimate* target – just minutes before. Then the world had suddenly changed. A bullet that should have killed Dermot, a chance to live, then a brave man intent on killing his would-be assassin.

A brave man with a useless gun who stood there, facing his death, accepting it, as some perverted reward for his failure to shoot Dermot.

And at that moment, that split-second from a trigger pull that would have taken off the policeman's head, Dermot had hesitated.

Why? Because . . . ? because . . . ? Dermot's mind had struggled with it . . . because somehow it was pointless, somehow it had – at that precise moment – ceased to have a meaning.

Or maybe, after all the killings, this was simply one too many. He doubted if he could kill now even if he wanted to. He laughed at the bitter irony of it. The Provo who kills his brother cannot kill a Peeler. The man who took the big gun to Cross, who killed the soldiers and the bairn, who brought tears and sorrow to a Christmas home, now he's done with it.

Dermot McGarvey, ex-killer, R.I.P. For within minutes that's what it would be. He tumbled into the stream bed, slipping on the stones. His foot struck a tree root and he cursed from the blow.

Hard. Too hard. He peered down and saw the discoloured rim of curved concrete beneath the overhanging foliage. Kneeling down he saw the dark emptiness of a culvert or a drainage tunnel that emptied into the stream. If it finishes here it must *start* somewhere, and that somewhere might be out of the wood, but just as concealed, somewhere the soldiers did not know existed.

He dropped his rifle and scrabbled full length inside the culvert. Within feet he struck a wall of soft earth and nearly sobbed with disappointment. But he tore at the soil desperately, his hands as shovels, scooping at the earth and hoping, hoping!

More earth and more – he heard voices not far distant – Christ, they were close. And something gave, there was a flatulent hiss, a foul smell that made him gag, then a draught of fresher air.

He wormed in, grazed his head on the culvert's roof, and realised the tunnel was narrow, about twice the width and height of a crawling man.

He could not know where it led. The fresh air might come from a break in the ceiling, or the exit might be too narrow for Dermot to crawl through.

But it was hope, and he scrambled on.

The corporal put down his SLR, slipped off his bulky camouflage jacket and slipped a shiny and lethally sharp knife out of a sheath which he took from inside the back of his trousers.

'Christ, Jimmy,' the soldier with him said. 'Are you going after him?'

'Corporal to you, shit-head, and don't tell the officer I took this.' He waved the knife by its bone handle, and laughed. '*This* means I don't have to read Paddy in there his rules from the little Yellow card . . . this not being my rifle.'

Then he quickly wriggled, snake-like, into the tunnel, the last glimpse of him his boots, waving in some pitiful farewell.

The other soldier said, to himself, 'Rather you than me.'

Dermot heard the sound way back in the tunnel, and some primeval fear began to flicker inside him. Fear of the dark, of confinement, of suffocation, of the unseen hand of the Bogeyman that reached out and touched your face in the night.

Calm yourself, he is a man like you and he gropes and crawls blindly as you do. But the flame of fear was lit, it sputtered, flickered, threatened to grow and consume him if he failed to douse it.

He felt he had come several hundred yards, and now the tunnel was clearly sloping downwards. Perhaps its function had been to drain overflow from the stream to prevent flooding? The wood was on relatively high ground, so the culvert could emerge in some lower field, or the side of a hill. Every few yards now he stopped, ears straining, listening for his pursuer.

And he would hear it: a rat-like scrabbling like the noise one might hear in the dark recesses of an old house. His outstretched hand touched water and recoiled.

Its feel was like the skin of an underground creature whose lair he had violated. Plucking up courage he went into the water, crawling on his belly like a crocodile from a riverbank, and gave an agonised 'Ah . . .' as the icy water met the wound on his back.

First it was inches, then the water covered his neck, and he felt his chin break the water's surface. What if the tunnel floor had broken at this point and the water had found its own natural level forming an underground lake? If it reached from floor to ceiling – and that was a few scant feet – how could he get through it, not knowing how far the water stretched?

Should he take a deep breath and try to crawl through it, not knowing if he could ever reach fresh air? Would he drown there, in the blackness and cold? No funerals or honour guard for Dermot, just a slow rotting, unheralded and unsung, in the bowels of the earth.

Or the Maze Prison, the Kesh? Or death at the hands of the tunnel-rat who scuttled remorselessly after him?

He plunged on.

A gulpful of fetid air, then not swimming, not buoyant, just underwater scrabbling like some doomed human hippo on the bottom of a river-bed.

No panic, for panic meant death, the mouth opening and the black water choking him, filling his lungs.

Strain now, lungs beginning to hurt. Turn back now, turn back while there's still air enough in your lungs to get you back to your starting point.

Better dead from a British bullet than this . . .

Go on . . . on . . .

Impossible, lungs bursting, impossible – can't turn back now, the extra yard has made the difference, too late for that, can only go on to death or . . .

Edge of panic, band of steel across his chest, lungs clamouring to be free of the exhausted remnants of used oxygen, ready to receive anything, even the death-bringing water.

And suddenly air!

The water breaks, an inch, two inches, more.

He felt solid earth, free of water, in front of his hands, and frantically clawed himself forward. He said aloud, 'Hail Mary, Mother of God.'

Then there was a grip like iron on his ankle, a moment of pure undistilled terror, and he was jerked back into the icy darkness of the water, which closed over Dermot and his attacker like an avenged lover.

Kathleen awoke in darkness, programmed by some inner

clock, and dressed by the small bedside lamp. She took the ready-packed suitcase and let herself carefully out of the bedroom, cursing the door's stiff metal latch, and the creaky old panels.

She had reached the bottom of the stairs when she heard the latch on her aunt's door, turned and saw the old woman framed in the doorway, soft in the dim light of her bedside lamp.

'Sorry, Aunt Kathy.'

'You little divil!' the old woman said, kindly.

'I hate goodbyes.'

'As much as clichés?' The old woman's wit had not deserted her, not even at this moment of sadness.

'I avoid *them* like the plague.'

They both laughed at their wordplay.

Then Kathleen dropped the suitcase and dashed back up the stairs and into the warm bed-smell embrace. She felt tears on her cheek, tears not her own, though they fell too.

'I'll come back, before I leave Ireland, I promise.'

'You'll be welcome.'

She pulled herself from her aunt's strong, rough arms, wiry even in age, and went back down the narrow stairs, looking back over her shoulder as she did.

She picked up the suitcase.

'Bye, Aunt Kathy.'

The old woman gave a little wave with her right hand, a small gesture of what seemed very much like hopelessness.

She said, 'I hope you find it.'

'Find it?'

'You know.' There was no question mark behind the words.

'No.' This a lie.

'The Ireland you want – North and South.'

Kathleen walked slowly in the greyer-now darkness to her car. The starter motor was like a harsh invader's cry in the quiet, sleeping village, and, unfamiliar with the gearstick and clutch, she stalled the insufficiently choked engine. She winced as the motor barked into life again, and more carefully extended the choke, eased out the clutch and drove the hired Ford slowly away from the kerb.

She drove out of Killibrea, away from her birthright and her heritage, away from part of her past and a chunk of her belief and her history.

Only her disappointment accompanied her as she drove on, not looking in her rear-view mirror, pointing the bonnet of the car towards the border with the Irish Republic eleven miles away.

The grip was vice-like. Dermot choked on water but kicked out, lunged forward, pulling his attacker with him, and sucked in the life-giving air. He kicked and kicked again, hearing the raw, desperate struggle for breath of his attacker, feeling the grip loosening.

Then he was free. He scuttled forward, into the tunnel, trying to put space between them, and turned to face his unseen attacker.

Here in this Stygian blackness they would have to fight like two subterranean creatures from Greek mythology. The soldier spoke, 'You're fucking dead, mate.'

It calmed Dermot, now the man was human with an imagined form, face and history. Dermot stayed silent, not wishing to betray *his* position, for now he knew the soldier was close, perhaps within feet of him.

There was a swish of air, and a dull clang as something hard and metallic struck the tunnel roof. A knife? Dermot gritted his teeth. How could you defend yourself against a knife in this darkness?

He can only guess, too. Guess and stab and slash, hoping he gets lucky.

Swish!

Dermot cried out as the serrated blade caught his shoulder, cutting through cloth and skin. He thrust out desperately with his left arm, his fist crashing into the other man's bicep. Dermot grabbed out blindly, lost his grip, grabbed again, slid his hand downwards, found the wrist of the knife arm.

Brought his other arm across, slamming the knife arm into the wall. A fist from the darkness exploded into Dermot's face, rattling his teeth; brightly coloured arcs whizzed before his eyes, and the pain spread like spilt ink across his face.

But Dermot's two hands were firm now, one at the elbow joint, one at the wrist. Pushing, pushing, hearing the first, inevitable 'No . . . no . . . no . . .' sounds.

The involuntary, useless protests, then a last desperate attempt at a head-butt in the blackness, and a jarring, cannon-ball collision of heads.

But pushing against the joint, the high-pitched cry, then the sickening snap and ringing scream of agony. Dermot released his grip, feeling the body fall with a soft thud. He hunted frantically, a blind-man's groping, for the fallen knife.

He found it, closed on the handle, searched for the man's head with his free hand, and placed the blade against the neck. The Adam's apple sat beneath Dermot's guillotine like a growth awaiting the surgeon's knife. Dermot was drawing in great breaths of the dark, damp air, waiting for his hand to steady.

After long seconds of thought, he dropped the knife and pushed the unconscious head away. It was done. Done with, over and finished. He would not have the blood of another brave man on his conscience.

Bloody Ireland, crawling with brave men, and it's not enough, Dermot thought. Not nearly enough.

He crawled away from the inert body, on into the darkness until, after what seemed like an eternity, he saw what was both literally, and metaphorically, light at the end of the tunnel.

Dawn came slowly but inexorably, and Kathleen switched off the headlights of the Ford Orion. She was not sure how far she was from the border now, or even if she had crossed into the Republic already, because her aunt had told her that although some crossing points were manned by customs men, by RUC men and British soldiers on this side – Garda Siochana and Irish Army men on the other – there were many minor roads which meandered in and out of the two territories.

She was not sure if this was such a road. It was small, barely wide enough for two cars, and it trailed, serpentine, across the undulating countryside.

To Kathleen the concept of a border – any kind of border – between any parts of what to her was simply *Ireland* was ludicrous.

She accepted it was not the kind of border that split Germany; no towers, or minefields, barbed wire and killing grounds. But it was a border – citizens of one type on this side, citizens of another type on that. Germany's border was its penance for that deadly mortal sin of almost fifty years ago. What had Ireland done to deserve this?

In this field you are an Irishman, in *that* field a subject of the Queen of England.

She turned on the radio and heard some very middle-aged, middle-of-the-road pop music, jockeyed by a man with an accent she remembered all too well from her weeks in Belfast. An Ulster voice, a Protestant voice. The man would be a direct descendant of the Scottish planters who had crossed the short stretch of water at the behest of King James.

A way of taming the wild Irish tribes. Put Protestant settlers in among them, to 'civilise' them. Most had stayed in the North, in the counties of Down and Londonderry – for so they had Anglicised the Irish Derry – of Fermanagh and Tyrone, Armagh and Antrim.

The people who now ran what Kathleen believed to be an artificial rump and Ruritanian state in the North of *her* Ireland, had had it given to them by a cowardly British Government back in the Twenties.

She had heard enough of them in Belfast, hectoring her, telling her how wrong she was about Ireland, about Ulster and the troubles. Suddenly she hated the accent more than anything and switched off the radio.

Kathleen had read her history, as well as taking it in anecdotal bites at her father's knee.

The British Government had at last, after years of bloodshed and executions, recognised the right of the Irish to run their ancient land. An Ireland with its own government in Dublin.

A government for all Irishmen, North and South, for Catholics and Protestants alike. But the bigots of the Orange lodges in the North, weaned on tales of King William of Orange – King Billy – and his defeat of the Catholic armies centuries before in Ireland: they would have none of it.

They were not Irish, they declared, they were men of Ulster, Britain – their loyalties only to the Crown of England. Loyal they were, they called themselves Loyalists with a capital 'L' – and then threatened the government and King to whom they claimed to pledge that loyalty.

Not apparently seeing the irony of their position they claimed that, damn it, they would be loyal whether the British liked it or not. They threatened they would have no truck with an independent Ireland with a government in Dublin. They would fight against anyone, the Nationalists in Ireland or the British Army itself, if it came to that. They weren't too fussy. Anything to stop Ireland ceasing to be part of that United Kingdom that had existed for so long, and which they held so dear.

Had they not given their blood to their King in battles from Sudan to China, and more recently, had their young men not walked bravely to their deaths on that hot June morning on the Somme? Had sturdy Protestant lads from Belfast fallen like scythed corn so that a scant six years later their bereaved would have their country taken from them by a pack of rebel Fenians?

No one in Belfast would forget the dense, small-print lists of casualties in the *Telegraph* in the first two weeks of that terrible June.

And now it was for nothing. Now the beloved Union Flag would be lowered, and the Irish tricolour raised. They would be governed by men whose loyalty was to a Catholic Pope in Rome. Men – many of them so called Irish Republican Army rebels – who for years had murdered policemen and soldiers.

To be ruled by the rebels who had struck at Britain's darkest hour, when she was locked in mortal combat with Germany.

What had these men done then? Taken German agents

and submarines on to the soil of Ireland, cosseted British traitors, planned and fomented rebellion with German arms. Had risen in open rebellion, taking the Dublin Post Office, attempting – and failing – to cause a full-scale insurrection against the British.

Kathleen had heard the bitter litany of so-called betrayal all too often.

'Ulster will fight and Ulster will be right' had been their slogan then, and was still their slogan now – the narrow excuse of their puritanical, yet hypocritical self-interest.

They did not want to lose their privilege, their wealth and their power. Then – *and* now.

It was then, Kathleen fumed inwardly, *then* that the British should have held their nerve. Senator Minihan agreed. The British should have said, We are not welcome in Ireland as conquerors, as oppressors, as subjectors, and the battle has gone on too long. We are quitting Ireland as the majority there – and in Britain too – now seems to wish. If you are Irishmen, you men of Ulster, then stay and work for Ireland. If you are brighter, more prosperous, more hard-working, sober and God-fearing than your Nationalist fellow countrymen, then you will surely prosper and have a major say in the running of this new state.

And if you *are* British, with a loyalty to the Crown that cannot be severed by geography or political change, then come back to the new Britain, the Land Fit for Heroes. Come back as allies and heroes, with resettlement grants provided by the British government.

But do not threaten us with violence, the ones whom you profess to love, if we shall not let you have some absurd state and parliament of your own in the north corner of Ireland. And do not – Senator Minihan could have drafted the document himself in an afternoon – do not threaten rebellion against the Crown or its army.

To the pre-mutinous soldiers in the Curragh Camp, the very *sternest* of warnings. Mutiny is punishable by firing squad.

And some Protestants would have left, most would have stayed (some even *glad* to accept the inevitable, though scared to say so), some might have made feeble rebel gestures. But within a year Ireland would have been free, independent, and united North and South.

Instead, the British panicked, scared by the rantings of Carson and his bully-boys, terrified of the newsreel pictures of the Ulster Volunteer Force drilling in secret fields. And they had bullied the desperate Nationalists into accepting a partitioned Ireland. This or *nothing*. Or worse . . . war! More bloodshed, Catholic against Protestant.

So the Protestants got their Northern state, their toytown parliament high on a hill at Stormont Castle, their border, an armed police force all their own, and now almost seventy years of running their own mini-kingdom.

But for twenty weary years now, that state had been racked by violence. First as the Catholics of the North fought for their rights. Voting rights, housing rights, civil and employment rights so long denied them by the secular state in which a fate of geography had left them. Then as the newly resurgent IRA fought the police and the British troops in a drawn-out urban guerrilla war, with their declared intention of forcing the decision of 1922 to conform with reality.

The Irish Government had at first secretly – passively – backed the rebels, bitter about the injustice inflicted by their Northern Protestant neighbours. But then, Kathleen knew, as the struggle grew more and more bitter and the IRA became the Provisional IRA – men dedicated to getting rid of the British by violence, with bomb attacks on civilians and on the British mainland – government opinion in Dublin began to harden.

This threatened to engulf *all* Ireland; the spectre of 1922 was walking abroad once more. The Protestants had their own para-militaries who came South and planted bombs, killing innocent Irish civilians. And was not the rhetoric of the Provos more Marxist than Nationalist? Was theirs not talk of a thirty-two counties united, *Marxist* Ireland?

So there was co-operation with the British; Irish courts handing back IRA suspects, Irish Special Branch harassment of Sinn Fein workers.

Then there was – in Kathleen's mind – the infamous Anglo-Irish Agreement, co-operation against 'terrorism'. The British Army unofficially allowed to cross the border if in 'hot pursuit' of IRA men, and other tenets. Dublin now wanted nothing to do with the IRA. But were not these politicians the heirs of the cowards who had accepted the compromise of 1922 – and who had warred against their *own* men when they refused to accept that bad-deal treaty?

There could be no peace in Ireland, Kathleen knew – as did her father, and no Marxist was Senator Minihan – until the British left, and North and South were united.

But the Protestants breathed fire at the suggestion – just as they had in 1922 – and there was the wild talk, like that of the man in the London pub, even hinted at by Aunt Kathy: talk of massacres, Protestant uprisings and pitched battles between well-armed Protestant para-militaries and the Irish Army.

Senator Minihan believed, and his daughter too, that the fire-breathing was no more than hot air. A dog on a leash will bark furiously, adopt threatening postures that presage awful doings. But take it off the leash, and things will change. Would the majority in the North want death and devastation when they could have peace and co-operation? Would they choose certain financial ruin and civil war when they knew that by peaceful means they could have prosperity?

Kathleen drummed her fingers on the steering wheel, then flicked on her windscreen wipers as the first drops of rain started to speckle the glass.

After two weeks in Belfast she felt she knew the answer to those questions, and it was as her father and she had always thought. The Protestants were bluffing. There would be peace and accommodation with the men they called 'terrorists'. British colonial history was full of such examples. Yesterday's political prisoners were tomorrow's prime ministers.

The guns would be put away and the talking would start. An end to shootings, bombing and the funerals. The Provisional IRA would lay down their arms and be welcomed as men of peace. Then honoured, as befitted Irishmen who had finally and irrevocably united their country.

Ireland – all Ireland now, with its bigger industrial base in the North, with that Worcester-sauce dash of Protestant work ethic and industrial and business savvy – would become a dynamic presence on the European and world stage. Ireland would be a living example of how dreadful inter-communal strife could be settled, of how harmony *could* prevail.

She had told her Aunt Kathy as much, that night when they had walked back in the soft drizzle, both slightly drunk, Kathleen somehow full of confidence despite her aunt's pessimism.

And Aunt Kathy had said, 'I hope so. I hope to God that it can be so.'

And I hope so, thought Kathleen, I hope it can be.

So *much*.

And *know* it can.

It happened at that precise moment, as she rounded a narrow bend in the road. She was driving automatically, her mind absorbed only in her simple, all-embracing solution to Ireland's problems.

One second the windscreen held only the rain and the rhythmic sweep of the wipers; the next a man, spread-eagled, eyes wide and terrified, hands streaking a trail of blood down the glass. Her ears registering the thunk of the body as it hit the bonnet, then her own voice screaming.

The car braking, screeching to a stop in the wet, and Kathleen aware of a desperate, clawing hand on the wiper and the wiper snapping off and the man sliding away from her, disappearing into the road.

CHAPTER

11

Joe sat in the small office with its aging but highly-polished linoleum, drinking strong tea from a mug, and studied the file.

McGarvey led a charmed life.

The ambush party could not reasonably have expected him to use body armour, nor could they have expected any such body armour to have either deflected or stopped a 7.62 mm high-velocity round fired at a range of less than a couple of hundred yards.

But they *could*, Joe thought angrily, have checked with the local farmers and got an absolutely up-to-date map of the area above and *below* ground. That would have shown the disused drainage tunnel, and the army could have had a stop party waiting for McGarvey to show his face.

Now they had a young corporal in hospital with head and arm injuries – plucky bugger had disobeyed orders and gone into the tunnel after the Provo with a knife – and a lot of egg on a lot of faces.

Joe took out the individual reports and read them slowly, and then read them again.

The corporal's first. He'd fought with McGarvey in the tunnel, pitch black – Joe shuddered – and the corporal had come off worst.

The would-be victim, the RUC inspector. He'd fired twice at McGarvey and missed. The IRA man had shouted something at him, something the policeman either didn't hear or couldn't remember in his shock . . . *but McGarvey had not fired at him!*

A thought came into Joe's head, and he dismissed it as quickly as it had arrived. He went on reading.

The American girl was the wild card. After three days it was assumed to be her.

The Garda disarmed by McGarvey at the Republican roadblock said the car was a red Orion, and Hertz in Belfast confirmed that they had rented such a car to Kathleen Minihan of Boston, Mass.

The shaken Garda had seen pictures of Miss Minihan and confirmed that it was the same girl they had seen in the passenger seat when McGarvey disarmed them.

Her last known port of call was a scant fifteen miles from where the car had turned up, and nothing had been heard of her since.

So no wonder Whitehall was hitting the panic buttons and angry questions were being asked in parliament, the Dail in Dublin, even the United States Senate itself! This Kathleen Minihan was the daughter of the senior senator for Massachusetts, one Patrick Minihan.

Pat Minihan, America's true son of Ireland, arch pontificator on Ulster's problems, and his only child had been hijacked by a Provo killer.

Under other circumstances Joe might have obtained some amusement from that, some *schadenfreude*, that mischievous joy at the misfortune of others.

But not when Mr McGarvey was involved. Joe remembered a hot Gulf night, a crumpled telegram in his pocket, and he could feel no mirth or sense of irony.

He looked at the photographs stapled to the file. The girl's first. Thick, dark hair, strong oval eyes. Her face was laughing, and he could see those white even American teeth sparkling and confident. A New World face, assured, almost arrogant but the pepper-pot dash of freckles over the cheekbone revealing the hint of Irish.

Then McGarvey, a photograph taken after one of his many arrests – all of which, it seemed, had proved fruitless.

He wasn't like some of the other Provos Joe had seen, in person or photographed. There was none of the blankness that spoke of moral void.

McGarvey's face had character, and his mouth was firm and defiant, a compressed line, as though the owner of the lips wanted to make sure they did not betray him. His hair was wild and unkempt, but his eyes had a calm, mocking quality to them.

Joe fixed that camera-held gaze as though interrogating. Was it you? Down at Crossmaglen with the big gun, like Intel suspected. Had David seen his face, or just flashes of fire?

This afternoon he would see the man who'd come in, then he would know definitely. Until then . . . Joe let his fingertips stray to the black and white glossy photograph, tracing across the shiny surface. Then, as though his fingertips had a mind of their own, he could feel his nails draw long tramline tracks across the Provo's face.

'Sarnt Biddle!'

The office door had opened without Joe being aware of it.

'Sir?'

'When you've a moment, Sergeant.'

'Yes, sir.' The new polite army. Nineteen-eighties newspeak for get your arse in here at the double.

Joe went in.

'Well. Any suggestions?'

It was a different one from the man who had greeted Joe to Lisburn just a few brief months before. The Arab-scrapper had not taken the advice he'd given Joe. He'd arranged to meet a contact up in the Whiterock and it was a set-up. He managed to drive off but he had three bullets in him, spent months in the Royal Victoria Hospital, lost two fingers and was now in Colchester waiting to be invalided out.

'Well, I would imagine he's in the Republic, sir.'

'Would you? Wouldn't it be the easiest thing in the world to double back . . . perhaps even on the same road, leading us to think he was in the Republic?'

Joe shrugged. 'Judging by the ease with which he took the guns off the two Gardai I thought he would have preferred to risk the Republic rather than our patrols.'

The officer gave an irritated flutter of his hands.

'Yes, of course, that's possible, but *we* are concerned with Northern Ireland, not the Republic.'

'Then his home here, sir? Relatives, friends, usual haunts, the Republican clubs.'

'They're being done,' the officer said sullenly. 'I'd hoped for some lateral thinking.'

'Lateral, sir?'

'Yes, not on the same line of thought. Solving the problem by not following – have you heard of Edward de Bono?'

'No, sir.'

'Can you activate some contacts? I presume you do *have* some contacts?'

NO! Joe wanted to say. No! I don't have any bloody contacts, I've not been back five minutes.

'Of course, sir.'

'Then get on to them. This McGarvey has nine bloody lives. But that wouldn't be so bad, personally I couldn't give a sod if he stayed down in the Republic for ever. It's this girl, the American angle.'

Joe felt an odd sort of tingling in his hands, and he steadied them against the seams of his trousers.

'I would have thought it could do us nothing but good, sir, given what Minihan's always said about us. Proves what a nasty bunch PIRA is.'

The officer eyed Joe with something approaching contempt.

'May I remind you that this PIRA man *was* fleeing a British Army ambush when this happened. That he *was* wounded, that he *was* set up by an informant. How well do you think that goes down with our allies, Sergeant?

Oh yes, had you forgotten, they *are* our allies.'

'Sir.'

'Minihan is on his way over, and he's coming here with a senior civil servant from Whitehall. I want to be able to assure him when he gets here that if his daughter *is* in the North then it will not be long before we free her.'

'And McGarvey?'

The officer's face set. 'His luck is out. Between you and me and these four walls, we have a strictly unofficial agreement with the people in Dublin who, I can assure you, are as tired of him as we are.'

'Agreement, sir?'

'He's got to surface sooner or later and he is not going to survive the encounter. This has all the makings of a nasty scandal and we don't want McGarvey being splashed all over the American press.'

'Perhaps even a mini-series, sir – if he survived.'

'I don't watch television, Sergeant.'

'Sir. . . ?'

'Yes?

He must know, Joe thought. Either that or he's deaf or stupid or both. The moment Joe got to Lisburn everyone knew in about five minutes.

When the SAS nearly killed McGarvey on the Falls Joe had got quietly and seriously drunk in the Mess.

'Sir. My son was in the patrol of Lancashire Fusiliers ambushed by a PIRA ASU in Crossmaglen on Christmas Eve. He was killed. As you know, Intel believes

McGarvey was the trigger-man on the operation.'

'Yes, I knew that.'

Then you're a bastard. Sir.

The officer continued. 'I also believe that fact might be confirmed – or of course disproved – by the gentleman with whom you'll be speaking this afternoon.'

'Sir, I felt you might feel, I mean . . .'

'I'm not asking you personally to track down McGarvey like some military Sherlock Holmes; I am suggesting you do your job as an Intelligence man, which is to gather information.'

'Sir. '

'Anything else?'

'What made our man come in?'

'Who knows with these people. Perhaps he set up McGarvey, then when he heard of that bloody fiasco he was frightened Mr McGarvey might come back for him. Perhaps it was just the chance of money and a new life.'

'Sir, if he is who he says he is, we've got him bang to rights for shooting some of our lads in the early days.'

The officer smiled viciously. He wondered on what basis they put some NCOs in Intelligence – it certainly wasn't because of their multi-dimensional thinking.

'He will be far more useful to us pardoned, talking and giving us *information* about what is going on *now*, than banged up in the Maze for something that happened when most of us were still at primary school!'

'Yes, sir.'

'Carry on, Sergeant.'

* * *

The two officers were enjoying a pre-prandial gin and tonic. They were both of the same rank, but one was younger and therefore had the psychological advantage. When he reached the other's age he would have gone to Staff College, the only route to senior rank, now denied to his elder who had not been selected for this academy of soldiering skills.

The elder asked, 'You put Biddle on it?'

'Of course.'

'Bit callous that; under the circumstances and all.'

The younger man diluted his drink with more tonic; the gins were big ones in the Lisburn mess.

'I don't believe so. Some of the Ancient Greeks used to put homosexual lovers together in the same regiment so they'd fight better, side by side, with the "other half" to protect.'

'Lost you, old boy.'

'Got any kids?'

'Two . . . you *know* that, Jeremy.'

'What'd you do if anyone harmed them?'

'I'd want to kill the bastard. Oh!'

'Quite. Now what's for dinner?'

It surprised Joe that he could even *look* at the photographs, let alone do so without pain.

Black and white, standard mortuary shots. First the body lying on its back, arms at its side, not crossed for the coffin, head raised, with the neck resting on a small wooden support.

Second the body lying on its face, flat out, with the support removed. Next to the photographs in the blue loose-leaf folder, the pathologist's report with the wounds listed dispassionately.

Joe looked at the corpse of his son and noted, with what he could only describe as a kind of inner greyness, the massive wound to the neck where the heavy bullet had struck.

Then the thigh, with a chunk of flesh the size of a fist missing, and what was exposed reminding Joe of something from a butcher's slab.

The face, eyes closed, mouth drawn in some kind of death rictus, not yet prepared for normal viewing.

You couldn't pretend to be dead. It was not something the best acting school could teach you. That's why war films, gangster films, disaster movies, all of them, were just so much bromide. Because it was pretend dead, play-dead; tick, you're better and up you get. Real corpses were different, like this one, like David's.

Horrible. How could you not be horrified by this vacant, collapsed, deflated shell of a thing that had once contained the spirit of your son?

He closed the folder.

The RUC man looked at him strangely, and Joe realised with a start that he had been crying.

'You OK, mate?'

'Yes.'

'Bit hairy at first. New to this are you?'

'Yes.'

'Here are the other folders you wanted, the three civvies.'

Joe took them and put them in his imitation-leather zip-up case, handing back the file on his son. He wiped his eyes, embarrassed.

'Someone you knew?' the RUC man asked, kindly.

'No,' said Joe. 'No.'

When Joe came out of the room after the interrogation he went straight to his quarters, stripped off his clothes, threw them in a bundle in the corner to be washed or dry-cleaned, and took a shower. Something about the man made him feel unclean. If there was evil, if it existed as something you could touch or *smell*, then the man Joe had interrogated was evil.

How many had died because of him, or at his own hand? And now he sat, sipping British Army tea, eating digestive biscuits, ready for his new life in Canada or wherever his blood money would take him.

But Joe was a professional, whatever that wet-behind-the-ears young officer might think, and Joe had listened.

The thought came back to him, and this time he did not dismiss it. Instead he read the interrogation reports on the McGarvey family.

He had an idea. Something about McGarvey, about his behaviour during the ambush and its aftermath, something that didn't tie in with his history. He didn't know what it was in total . . . it was more a feeling than an idea, and then when he read about McGarvey's sister, the idea branched, formed, took shape.

Perhaps Dermot McGarvey did not want to kill any more, and perhaps Miss Fionulla McGarvey would do anything to see her brother alive. And if he could persuade her that her only hope of the Man surviving to see his days out in prison was to co-operate with Joe Biddle, then just perhaps – and assuming a lot, perhaps the girl could be freed and McGarvey taken.

And not dead as everyone wanted him? Yes, Joe, not dead. And you above all should want him dead after what he's done. And I don't, Joe thought. I don't. I don't care if he lives or dies.

The first girls came out at 3.35, giggling and pushing, happy at their daily dose of freedom.

Knots of them, pretty, almost all long-haired, young – God how young they looked. Most of them would have been toddlers when the gun battles were at their height.

Joe studied the small Intel picture he held in the palm of his hand, then recognised her as she came out of the school gate – not in uniform but in jeans and a leather jacket. Of course, sixth form, no uniform necessary.

There was something in her walk, some hint of realisation that she was different. That because of her brother she was the subject of security force attention – she would call it harassment; that she could never have the peace and innocence her teens should have allowed her.

He got out of the car and intercepted her.

'Miss Fionulla McGarvey?'

Her face hardened instantly like quick-set concrete into a broken, riot-ready paving slab of hostility.

'Who wants to know?'

'My name is Sergeant Joseph Biddle, British Army.'

'Show me some identification, you could *say* you were anybody.'

Joe showed her the plastic, embossed card and she laughed out loud, throwing her head back. Then the smile died and the face closed and set once more.

'You've got a bloody nerve.'

'I wanted to talk to you.'

'You're a bit late – *Sergeant* – I've already been lifted.'

'Just a chat.'

'I *just* have to give one scream now, and you are in big, big trouble, soldier boy.'

'Yes,' said Joe simply. 'If you do, I am.'

'Chat about what?'

'Dermot. Us two, alone, five minutes, in the car.'

She laughed contemptuously this time. 'Get lost. You're crazy if you think I'd get in the car with you. You could still be some Prod nutter. They've forged army identification before now. If you want to shoot me, try it here.'

'I'm British Army, and here . . .' he put his hand out . . . 'you keep the keys.'

Her look did not change, so he said, 'I couldn't try anything here, you know that, even if I was a paramilitary, which you know bloody well from my accent I'm not.'

She said, 'I haven't seen Dermot or spoken to him, and if I had I wouldn't tell you.'

'Five minutes, that's all.'

Joe could sense hostile eyes around them. Telephone calls could be made, everyone knew who the girl was, and dammit all, Joe wasn't even supposed to be here.

She shrugged with affected nonchalance.

'OK – five minutes, and if you try one solitary thing, I'll scream so loud they'll hear it in Dublin.'

'Deal.'

He pressed the keys into her hand, walked to his car and climbed in the passenger seat. After a few moments' hesitation she followed and got in behind the wheel. She looked straight ahead at the oil-smeared windscreen as Joe spoke.

'Some facts. Last Christmas Eve your brother Dermot went down to Crossmaglen with an Active Service Unit of the Provisional IRA.'

'Lie.' Some of her spittle hit the glass.

'The ASU had a Soviet-made machine-gun, a *big* gun. Their target was a patrol of Lancashire Fusiliers.'

'Maybe the ASU was there – Dermot wasn't.'

'. . . The PIRA men opened fire, hit the patrol, but also hit two civilians, a mother and her little girl.'

'I saw the news. My whole family was lifted on account of it. Except it wasn't true, Dermot wasn't there. He doesn't kill children.'

He saw the fury in her face, jaw working with it. But worse, that deep, fanatical belief they all had. How could you beat this?

He continued as though she hadn't spoken. 'One of the PIRA men died from wounds received. Three British soldiers were killed. One of those soldiers was my son.'

Something changed in her face, and her expression was one almost of curiosity, as though she were looking at him properly for the first time.

'Now I see. You want to kill Dermot. And you want me to help.'

And Joe, in turn, felt changed: sitting there with the sister of the man who had killed his only son, he felt an improbable sense of nearness.

He had no link with David now, no tangible bond with anyone who knew him, was close to him. Not Joe's ex-wife, not Joe's own mother, for his wife was estranged from him, now more than ever, and his mother was back in England.

In some perverse way it was as though this girl, blood-tied to David's killer, was a way of giving form to a memory.

He said, 'God knows why but I don't. I want to see him in prison where he can't kill anyone else.'

She laughed in some parody of defiance she must have learned from the movies, curling her lip into a sneer that looked only ludicrous.

'Never!'

'Then they'll kill him.'

'They've tried before.'

'This time they won't fail.'

She gripped the steering wheel with both hands, knuckles clenched white.

'Aye, you bloody killers with your death squads out for any Republican you can find.'

'Are we just . . . ?' Joe could feel the colour draining from his own cheeks. 'And where did we learn it? Car bombs in the streets, men shot down in their own kitchens in front of their toddlers.'

'Get the hell out of Ireland.'

'And when we've gone it'll be all right? What about the Prods and the RUC, they're not Brits . . .'

'Bloody planters . . .'

'Christ, your history's got you all by the throat and it's strangling you.'

The windows of the car began to mist up from their body heat and their hot breath as they argued.

At length she said, 'I think you've had your five minutes.'

Joe looked up from his contemplation of the glove compartment. He had never felt more depressed.

He said, 'He's down in the Republic with this girl, this American. You know that?'

She nodded. 'I read the papers.'

'The first member of the security forces north or south of the border who sets eyes on your brother has orders to shoot him.'

'Even if he's unarmed . . . ?' The words came out

poisoned with cynicism, and it was as though Joe could smell it on her breath.

'He's dead. He just doesn't know it yet.'

'And you'll ride in on your white charger to see he gets typical British justice from a Diplock court?' Again the deep cynicism, appalling in one so young, hanging in the air like CS gas.

'I want to see him on trial. I want to see him admit to killing my son and the other lads at Cross, and to admit killing the little girl . . . and . . .'

'And who?'

'No one. I want you to be there, to sit in that court you hate so much and see your brother admit that he *does* kill children, that's what I want.'

'And then?'

'And then every morning for the rest of my life I'll wake up knowing that your brother is being punished.'

She clicked the door open.

'Then I suggest you find someone else to help you. Because I won't. And when, if you find him . . . Sergeant whateveryourname was . . . he'll probably kill you first.'

He grabbed her wrist, tight like a vice, and he saw her face contort in pain and shock.

'Dermot will never kill anyone, ever again. And do you know why? Because he *can't*, he's finished, past it. He's done with killing. Something's gone in him, like a spring in a clock.'

'You're mad.'

'One minute more . . . *please*.'

'Let go of my wrist.'

Joe did, and the girl gingerly rubbed it with her other hand.

'That hurt. Go on.'

Joe spoke quickly, anxious like a scientist with a new theory.

'After the ambush went wrong Dermot was still going, and he still had his Armalite. He had clear aim at an RUC man, the very man he'd been ready to kill a minute earlier.'

'And?'

'And he didn't fire . . . could've, but didn't.'

'You're putting two and two together and . . .'

'Making four is what I'm making. Next he's in a tunnel and some young lad wanting to make a name for himself goes in after him with a knife. Dermot *disarmed* him. *Disarmed!* This is Dermot McGarvey, the Man. He could've killed that young soldier and he didn't.'

The girl chewed her bottom lip.

'Then he snatches this American girl, or so we think. He busts through a Garda roadblock just over the border. McGarvey could've shot him . . . *didn't*.'

'I'd like to leave now.'

'I'm telling you, he's finished with it. I don't know why now, but he's finished with it. And if you want to keep your brother alive I'm the only chance you've got.'

The girl gave him a long, searching look.

'Maybe I'd prefer my brother dead than in a British prison, locked up like an animal.'

'No you wouldn't. You love him, and you've seen enough IRA funerals to know what it means, that they won't be coming back again, *ever*!'

Her eyes said he spoke the truth.

'And when this is all over – if it ever is – there'll be some sort of amnesty. We all know it, even though our government won't admit it. And one day, in ten years, maybe less, precious Dermot will come walking back. You want that. Don't you?'

'Yes.'

'Then think about it.'

'I will. But, Sergeant . . .'

'What?'

'Your son will never come walking back, will he?'

Joe swallowed, hating himself. 'No, he won't.'

'And you'd still do it – save Dermot's life?'

'On my word. He gives himself up to me and to you, together we take him to the nearest police station with a lawyer. They'd never dare harm him at that stage.'

'Why? Why should you do it?'

'We're the same, Dermot and me, that's why. We've done our share of dirty work for what we both believe in, and now we've both had enough of it.'

'But your son?' Her face looked like that of a concerned teenage girl again.

'Is dead, Miss McGarvey. Call me. Sergeant Biddle at Lisburn. They'll know where to get me.'

She gave him one last look then swung the car door fully open, got out and walked briskly off down the road.

* * *

The man in the green sunglasses had told them everything. Once he knew Dermot had escaped the ambush he'd asked for, and received, amnesty. And from the moment he'd come in, fast, in his own car, once the decision was made, anxious to be done with it, the man had hardly stopped talking.

The Intel men were having a field day, learning more about the Belfast Brigade command structure and order of battle than they could have in a year of hard work. Within hours teams were out, twelve men arrested, and two caches of arms and ammunition uncovered. It was a bad afternoon for the Provisional IRA.

The man in the green sunglasses was sure he'd read somewhere that there is a time in revolution for the revolutionary to retire and let others make the pace – or perhaps it was a maxim he himself had thought up.

Whatever, he had always been a pragmatic man behind the veneer of quotable Machiavelli. Soon he would fly to Lyneham in Wiltshire and spend several weeks at a large country house in Surrey. Then Akrotiri in Cyprus with his Special Branch minders for two or three months, then Seattle. He had no wife, no children, no family, and now he had £150,000 – or would have soon – and a new life away from a struggle that had, he was forced to admit, become tiresome to him.

The man in the green sunglasses had had men shot for far less, and the irony of that amused him.

Joe had been one of the men who'd questioned the renegade, and it was then that the information about

Dermot had come out. The information Joe had *not* told Fionulla McGarvey.

That one of her brothers had killed the other in cold blood.

That information could be saved, like a hungry man's hoarding, for a time when it was sorely needed. Joe hoped, though, that such a moment would never come.

Fionulla lay on her narrow bed, beneath the crucified Christ and the pop posters, like some novitiate of a strange contemporary order in her cell. Hands clasped together, eyes firmly closed, she prayed harder than she had ever prayed before. She prayed to the Virgin Mary, to Christ himself, to God the Father and the Holy Spirit. She prayed for help, for advice, for a guiding path.

She prayed for Dermot's safety and his salvation, and mostly for it not to be true that he was the man behind the machine-gun at Crossmaglen. Please God, she prayed, let him not be the killer of children. Fionulla prayed, too, for the repose of the soul of her dear, departed brother Colm. Let him be at peace, she mouthed through jaws tight with tension.

And though the rhythm and intensity of her prayers beat in her head like a jungle tom-tom, it could not drive away the vision that forced its way into her head, stronger than the power of God or the love of the Virgin Mary.

A vision of Dermot lying in his coffin as Colm had lain, his skin waxen in death, his head framed by the shroud like the halo around the Madonna in the holy pictures Fionulla treasured.

She would always remember the morning the priest called at the RUC's request to tell them Colm was dead. Fionulla had woken to a high wail of unbearable grief, had tumbled barefoot, eyes glued by sleep, into the narrow hall.

Three people were fused into an unforgettable tableau of grief like some statue to commemorate an agonising atrocity. Her mother and father like helpless children, clinging to the priest, the earthly messenger of their religion.

The priest had turned to her, his face white and immovable, sickened but hardened by innumerable errands such as this, and the facts were like nails through the girl's palms, as hard and painful as those endured by the Christ she worshipped.

Colm had been missing for three days, but they prayed he was with a girl, gambling, or drinking in some shebeen. That day, as the grim, grey Belfast light revealed the city, a man walking to work had spotted the crumpled, hooded figure in an alley off the Shankhill Road, deep in Protestant territory. A betting slip in the pocket of the victim's jeans led to a Catholic bookmaker being woken early and given the unenviable task of identifying the dead man as one of his customers, Colm McGarvey.

It merited thirty seconds on the regional BBC TV news; another sectarian murder, presumably by Loyalist paramilitaries. When it was revealed that the victim was the brother of a known Provo gunman, it was put down to a revenge attack, even though the various Protestant organisations denied they had carried out the killing.

Thankfully, and the family took great comfort from this, the victim had not been tortured.

Fionulla's vision broadened cruelly. Next to Colm's headstone in the Milltown cemetery was another. The inscription was for Dermot McGarvey, killed on active service, a martyr for Ireland. She saw the whole family in black, blotched and drawn from weeping. An honour guard of Republicans in black berets, the mournful dirge of the Irish pipes, a volley of pistol shots over the grave, and the British helicopters overhead.

The girl thrust her hands over her ears to blot out the sound of the thump-thump of the rotors, a cacophony of 'told-you-so', 'told-you-so'. She prayed harder, mouthing the words, speaking them, hearing her voice. They were the chants of her young faith, words stumbling over each other, but evaporating in the white heat and glare of the awful visions of past and future.

She gave up the unequal struggle, ceased to pray, and opened her eyes. She would not, *could* not grieve for another brother, not if there was the slightest chance of keeping Dermot alive. Damn the Cause, damn the death and the pain, she only wanted Dermot, alive.

If the Englishman really was trustworthy, perhaps it could work, and they *could* save Dermot. There was something in that sergeant she had not seen in the other

British soldiers who had abused her, arrested her, interrogated her.

It was both a quality of sadness and a hint of madness.

Dermot had not killed the man's son at Crossmaglen, but *someone* had, and perhaps – as the sergeant claimed – that fact had soured him to the point where he was tired of the struggle. Perhaps he was prepared to save Dermot's life. And could it be true, as the Englishman claimed, that Dermot had also tired of the struggle?

They would gun Dermot down like a mad dog, just as the soldier had said. If they got the chance.

Her mind was made up. Others would call it betrayal, but she knew it was a deep love. She would get to Dermot before his killers. She and the crazy sergeant would save her brother's life.

And one day, when Ireland was at peace, when the bitterness was buried with the corpses, when the British had gone, and they could be dealt with as neighbours and not occupiers, perhaps on that day the three of them would sit and talk of their past sorrows and of the bright and possible future.

She closed her eyes and the awful visions departed. She was still young enough to believe in her prayers and her hopes.

The next day Joe's telephone rang.

'Sarnt Biddle? Girl on the line, won't give her name. Wants to talk to you.'

'Put her on.'

'Sergeant Biddle?'

'Yes.'

'You know who I am?'

'Yes.'

'Did you mean what you said?'

'I meant it.'

She gave him an address. 'Can you pick me up in two hours?'

'I'll be there.'

She replaced the receiver.

He knew she could be setting him up in an ambush. She was the sister of a Provisional IRA gunman. He shouldn't go without back-up, without at the very least telling someone exactly *where* he was going, and to meet *whom*.

But he had a gut feeling. This could only work on trust, and if anyone knew *who* he was meeting, then there was no chance for any further secrecy. And if she did agree to help him, it had to be just the two of them. Joe was cynical enough to know that whatever his superiors might promise, this would end up being an SAS job.

They all wanted McGarvey's corpse so bad it hurt.

And why don't you, Joe? he asked himself. Of all the people who *should* want it, Joe Biddle must be Number One.

And I don't. I *really* don't. I want him alive, because I hate him, and I want to go on hating him, and I can only do that if he's alive to hate.

What if he wanted the alternative, Joe? Would you give him the chance you gave the Iranian?

There was no answer, so Joe just drained his cold mug of tea, and shouted to a uniformed corporal, 'Slipping out. Meet a contact.'

At Joe's insistence they left the Republican area and drove out of Belfast towards the airport. The M1 motorway was closed because of a bomb scare, a hijacked lorry abandoned in the slow lane, and RUC men in flak jackets and carrying carbines directed traffic on to minor roads.

It was a security forces master-stroke. They had taken several minor roads that led out to the civilian and military airport at Aldergrove and put permanent road-blocks on them, forbidding them to civilian traffic. So whenever the Provos tried to block main-road traffic to the airport by using suspected lorry bombs, the army simply removed the barricades and set up joint traffic control with the RUC, feeding the diverted traffic through their newly opened 'private' roads.

That way the IRA couldn't continually dislocate travellers into Belfast airport – a surefire way, if they'd succeeded, in ruining regular business and personal travel between Great Britain and Northern Ireland.

The car in which they were travelling was stopped on one such road at an army checkpoint. A soldier with a blackened face stood back, his SLR at the ready, while an RUC man spoke to the occupants. That was the rule now, the police dealt with the public, the army backed them up.

Joe showed the policeman his ID with the Lisburn Intel flash.

The RUC man's eyes flickered suspiciously to the passenger. 'Her?'

'I'll vouch.'

'On your way.'

Joe drove on, left it a couple of miles, found a farm track, turned into it and killed the engine.

The girl said, 'I do psychology at school. That was nice, taking me through the roadblocks and all. Showing me who was in charge.'

Clever girl, Joe thought, but said, 'Wasn't intentional. I was risking my neck up the Falls, and it wasn't *me* who put that lorry bomb on the Ml.'

'OK. Are you in touch by radio?'

'Come on, this isn't James Bond.' But he opened his jacket in a gesture of reassurance and conciliation.

'Right, you want me to find Dermot and you swear he won't be harmed.'

'On my life.'

'He hasn't been in touch.'

Joe could feel the anger surging through him. If this was all a waste of time, after the effort, the *mental* investment, if . . .

'I saw him just before your killers tried to get him, not since then . . .'

'So . . . ?' said Joe, evenly.

'But I know where he *might* be.'

Joe's breath quickened. 'Where?'

'In Clare, on Galway Bay, a place called Ballyvaghan, up towards Black Head.'

'Why?'

'Because when we were kids we had an auntie in the South. Someone left her this place. It's nothing, a ruin practically, a cottage with a stone roof. We used to go there for holidays. It's four miles from the nearest village, and that's only a couple of shops and a pub.'

Isolated, Joe thought, *isolated*. Just what he'd look for. No wagging tongues.

'You think he could be heading there?'

She shrugged. 'Why not, it's the only place he knows for definite.' She had a sudden sense of fear. 'Don't tell them! You promised – just you and me. Then Dermot goes to the nearest Garda station, voluntarily. Not back to the North . . . not unless he's properly extradited.'

Joe was biting his lip. Now that it was real, he was scared. The girl was offering, genuinely offering to take him to where she believed McGarvey was.

They'd have his guts for garters for this. He was a serving soldier in the British Army and he had just been told the location, or suspected location, of *the* most wanted man in the whole of Ireland, North and South.

And it *was* the South. He had no jurisdiction there. If he was stopped, arrested – especially carrying a gun – he would be in deep, deep lumber, and there would be a hell of an international row, all down to Sergeant Joseph Biddle, who would probably become Private Joe Biddle, retired, extremely quickly.

There was a low roar as a British Airways jet passed overhead, climbing on full power for the grey clouds and the normality of England.

'No, I won't tell them.'

Her relief was palpable, and he suddenly realised that she had offered first, she had trusted first.

'So, OK then, when do we go?'

She gave him a little grin, probably more from relief than happiness. '*Now*, you stupid English clot.'

'You'll be having me shot for desertion.'

'It has to be now.'

'OK. But I have to make one telephone call.'

Her eyes were full of suspicion. 'Why?'

'I'm owed leave – if I just disappear they'll be suspicious.'

'I'll be right next to you, and if I hear one strange word or phrase that could be a code you have my word you'll blow the whole thing.'

He said mischievously, 'Don't threaten me – I *know* the location, don't forget.'

'You *think* you do.'

And hell, that was one very good point, Joe thought.

'It'll be a straight call, you have my word.'

She smiled in that innocent, dangerous, teenage way. Well matched, we are, Joe thought. The cynical, devious

English, the innocent, complicated, fiendish Irish. We complement each other.

'How old are you, Miss McGarvey?'

'Fionulla, if we're going to spend time together, and I'm nineteen – well, nearly nineteen.'

Joe shook his head in admiration.

'Nearly nineteen – Christ.'

CHAPTER
12

Dermot remembered little of the going. One moment there was a kind of consciousness, and then nothingness, a roaring waterfall of sleep that drowned him, crushing him to the edge of coma. Then came the terrifying dreams of escape, of the tunnel, of running like the hunted man he was through the cold and lashing rain.

There had been almost no more to give when he heard the sound of a car in the far distance, and clinging to the mossy-green stone wall he had waited.

He caught a glimpse, saw it was not an army vehicle, and felt a distant stab of hope. His right hand gripped the knife he had taken from the British soldier, as the car slowed for the slight bend around which Dermot waited.

At the last safe moment he went out into the road, his free hand outstretched. But as the bonnet of the car appeared, Dermot realised in a split-second of horror that either the driver had not seen him, or planned to deliberately run him down.

He dropped the knife and, with every last ounce of energy, flung himself forward and upwards, desperate to avoid the fearful blow as the car struck him. He crash-landed with a 'thunk' on the bonnet's soft metal, and as the car braked sharply, clutched at a moving wiper-blade to avoid being flung into the road.

It snapped off in his hand and he rolled off, leaving a smear of his own blood to mark his passage. Dermot came to with a girl leaning over him, and he instinctively reached out for, but failed to find, the knife he had dropped before the collision.

The girl helped him sit up, putting a supporting arm around his shoulder, and Dermot realised that he hurt all over, though there was none of the sickening pain that comes with a limb fracture.

The girl was soaked herself, looked upset and was saying over and over, 'I didn't see you, I didn't see you.' She helped him to the car's passenger seat, and offered to drive him to a hospital.

Dermot invented a story that his car had broken down, and suggested a town ten miles further on, where he could seek help. He hoped she put down his bedraggled and injured appearance solely to the accident.

She made noises of agreement as she drove, but he could see that her eyes flickered nervously in his direction. Dermot was almost at the end of his tether now, the pain in his side was excruciating, and he was shivering despite the car's excellent heater. Yet only the shivering fought a rearguard action against his closing eyelids, pressed under the awesome weight of his fatigue. They drove in silence, and Dermot guessed that they must be well into the Republic.

He was just feeling that he had reached sanctuary when he saw in the distance, through the rain-lashed windscreen, a figure standing in the road, waving them to stop.

CHAPTER TWELVE

The man had a peaked cap and cradled a small rifle or submachine-gun of some kind. Dermot was totally awake. Was it the RUC? Was the gun the American Ml carbine, or was it – as the figure got closer he could see that the gun was an Uzi submachine-gun – it was the Garda Siochana, the Guardians of the Peace, the Irish Republic's police force.

Jesus and Mary, but they were co-operating with the British, this was the roadblock that would pick him up and send him back to the North.

He hunched down in his seat. The girl said, 'There's a policeman with a gun standing in the road.' She flashed a look of query to Dermot, and he thought, She *knows*!

'Drive through!' He screamed it.

'No!'

'Drive *through*!'

The figure was looming larger now, and Kathleen had already unwittingly driven into one man that day. It was impossible for her to do so again, this time as a deliberate act.

'Don't stop!' Dermot shouted again.

'No . . .' She screamed and stamped on the brakes, pulling the steering wheel to the right, slewing the car into a skid on the rain-slicked road.

Dermot saw the Garda jump clear, dropping the gun as he fell, then Dermot leapt from the car into the sheeting rain. The Garda was a middle-aged, portly man, and was lifting himself to his knees, struggling to retrieve the Uzi.

Dermot grabbed it first, and shouted, 'Stay back.'

The man shrank back, terrified. Then through the curtain of rain Dermot saw a second policeman clambering out of the passenger seat of the Garda patrol car, which was parked diagonally across half the road. He had an automatic weapon of his own, and was struggling to make it ready to fire. Dermot shouted at the top of his voice, 'Drop it.'

Perhaps it was the noise of the rain that beat a tattoo on the road and surrounding trees, but the Garda either didn't hear the command, or ignored it. He came round the bonnet of the car, the rain shining on his bald scalp, aiming the gun at Dermot. Dermot brought up his own with one hand, setting it to fire. 'Don't be a bloody fool.'

But the other gun was levelled at Dermot and the two men were barely thirty feet away from one another. Please, Dermot thought. Please, put the gun down.

The policeman was terrified, and Dermot realised he could kill the man before he had the time or will to pull the trigger of his own weapon.

But he shouted again, 'Put it down, I won't fire.'

'For God's sake do it, Ferg . . .' Dermot heard the voice of the other frightened Garda. 'It's not our fight.'

Hesitantly the policeman lowered his gun and put it carefully down on the surface of the road. Then he began to sob with relief and shock.

Dermot took the surrendered gun, made it safe, then hurled it with his free hand way off into the trees. He backed slowly towards the Ford Orion where the girl stood, soaked again, shivering with cold and perhaps fear too.

She looked at Dermot quizzically. 'Who *are* you?'

'None of your business, love, get back in the car. You're a hostage now. That's the way it is.'

She ignored him. 'Are you a criminal?'

'No,' he replied bitterly, 'I'm a patriot, that's what I am. Now get back in the bloody car.'

Kathleen got back in under the shadow of the gun. Dermot destroyed the police radio and shot at the tyres of the patrol car before they drove away quickly, leaving the humbled Gardai in the rain. After a while she said, 'You're IRA, you must be.'

He gave her a withering look. 'Well I'm not the Household Cavalry, that's for certain sure.'

She said, 'If you are in the IRA you don't have to worry, I'm on your side.'

He laughed. 'You're an American, I can tell. You wouldn't know the IRA from the YMCA.'

'You're wrong, so stop pointing that gun at me, it might go off.'

The gun stayed pointing at her. 'Didn't you hear what I said? I'm on your side.'

He gave her a bitter glance. 'Actually, love, I don't *have* a side.' And then it was all he could do to stop himself weeping.

As the journey continued, he gave her directions. The cottage was his only chance now. He could rest there, and work out what to do. It would be at least two hours before the two policemen could raise any kind of coherent alarm, and by that time he and the girl could have made it to their destination.

His eyes closed, then he jerked awake again, they closed, he came awake. He thought it was just twice, but he drifted between fitful sleep and rude awakening countless times, and was beyond controlling it. He became aware that the car radio was on and even that someone, a man, had used his name, but it fitted no pattern of the micro-sleep to which he continually succumbed.

Then he was wide awake and feeling wretched as the car stopped. It was the cottage. He clambered out, shepherding the girl at gunpoint, and began to shake again with cold and the onset of fever.

They sat in the musty, long-unused room like two awkward strangers, Kathleen across from him, calm under the muzzle of the gun. She was his prisoner, his hostage, his bankable ace against whatever future hand of cards they would serve him.

She tried to speak, and he told her roughly to be quiet. She remained so. He realised with a kind of futility that he did not know what to do next when he suddenly saw the girl multiply like an amoeba.

There were two of her, then four, eight, sixteen, and he could not keep the gun trained on all of them, so he tried to close his eyes, hoping that when he re-opened them her clones would have vanished and the original girl would remain.

But his eyes did not re-open, and there was just the deep, exhausted sleep, the lungs rising and falling. Down in the well into which he'd plummeted there were monsters and pain and heat, and a puzzling sequence he knew, if only he could thread it together, would solve all of life's contradictions.

Until finally he blinked awake, squinted at the daylight, and closed his eyes again, aware – if that word could be applied in his condition – that not only did he not know *where* he was, he did not know *who* he was.

For ten terrifying seconds he did not even know what *was* was. He was a living organism temporarily – and mercifully briefly – unaware of the meaning of existence. Then he knew, what, who, and last where and why.

He sat bolt upright in the bed.

The girl was sitting by a crackling fire, and for a moment he could not believe it was the same girl, for her hair was cropped short.

The fire!

'Put the bloody fire out, for Christ's sake, it'll bring people.'

Then through the still-hanging mists of his exhaustion he realised the absurdity of that. She was his prisoner – had been. He had been asleep, or unconscious, so if she had wished to flee, she could have. His gun! He looked wildly round the room.

As if reading his mind, she said, 'It's under the bed. Just in case of callers.'

He reached down, felt his body give him a sharp jolt

of pain, but in turn felt the satisfaction as his hand touched the stock of the Uzi.

'How do you feel?'

'Terrible.' He leaned back on the pillow. It had spun out of control again, like Crossmaglen, like the thing with Colm, like the ambush. And he felt too weak and too ill to fight it right at that moment.

He said weakly, 'Please put out the fire.'

'We need it. For warmth, to cook on – and don't worry, no one will come because of the fire.'

'How long have I been out?'

'A day and a half.'

'Christ Almighty.'

'You needed it.'

'Why didn't you go – and what have you done to your hair?'

Instead of answering she took something off the fire, a deep pan, and Dermot smelled an aroma that made his mouth run with saliva.

'Soup.'

She poured some into a big bowl and brought it over to the bed. 'Drink it.'

He did, and burned his tongue. They both blew on the liquid, and then he spooned it down hungrily with the cheap metal spoon she'd given him.

She watched him, and when he'd finished and lay back, exhausted, against the pillow, she said, 'I cut my hair so that I wouldn't be recognised. I went into the village to buy . . .'

'You went into the fucking village?'

'Yes, it was either that or we both starved. There was nothing in here. I doubt if the place has been lived in for years.'

He closed his eyes, feeling weak and nauseous, only the warm soup burning inside him like some revitalising flame.

'I am Veronica and you are Derek. We are from London . . .' she said this in a cut-glass English accent. 'We're on vacation – correction, we're on holiday.'

'In a bog-awful place like this hovel?'

'We just bought it and we intend to renovate it. All the English Yuppies are doing that.'

He opened his eyes again to ensure he wasn't dreaming.

'Why? You were supposed to be my hostage. You could have shot me, run away . . . anything. I . . .' He closed his eyes, and in a few moments he was asleep again, knowing he didn't understand, but realising he didn't bloody care.

He slept soundly and well, his body losing some of its fierce heat, and he was dimly aware that he was being touched, ministered to, and when he finally reawoke, he could feel something soft against his injured side.

It was dark now, and there was only the flickering fire and a small candle to illuminate the room. She was sitting on the floor in front of the fire, her knees drawn up under her chin, peering into the flames.

'Hallo.'

She looked up. 'Feel better?'

Yes.

He tried to swing his feet out of the bed, then stopped when he realised he was naked.

'Sorry, but I had to remove your clothes. They were soaking and you had a bad chill or fever or something.'

'Where are they now?'

'I've dried them out, but if you take my advice you'll leave them until tomorrow. You need at least another night's rest. That is one hell of a burn weal or whatever on your side.'

Dermot realised the bullet must have penetrated the armoured protector, been diverted and by a miracle gouged down his side – leaving the mark the girl was talking about – and then gone *outwards*.

'Well, it sure hurts.'

'Skin has been gouged off, and it could go septic if you aren't careful. I've cleaned it out, put antiseptic ointment on it, and a dressing.'

Dermot groaned, but it wasn't from pain.

'You bought all this bloody stuff in the village?'

'Yes. My beloved Derek has had a nasty Do-It-Yourself accident – stop worrying.'

Dermot propped himself up on his elbow.

'Do you know who I am – why I . . . took you like that?'

'Yes. I didn't think you were just an armed robber. The rest was on the radio in the car, and in the newspaper. Your name is Dermot McGarvey, you're an IRA man, and when you – *met* – me you'd just escaped from a British Army ambush in the North.'

He winced from a stab of pain, then said calmly, 'I was waiting to shoot a policeman, only I was betrayed. I was going to assassinate him for what I believe in, do you understand?'

She nodded grimly. 'Yes.'

'To them . . .' he waved a hand vaguely . . . 'I'm a terrorist. To *me* . . .' he prodded his own chest . . . 'I'm a patriot, fighting for what I believe.'

'I said to you in the car, I'm not your enemy.'

He laughed, almost mockingly. 'You're an American, I don't see that it matters to you, either way.'

'It *does* matter!' Her eyes flashed fire. 'It does. My father was born in Ireland, and he's never wavered in his support of his country since he landed in America.'

'We need all the friends we can get.'

She said boldly, 'My father is a powerful friend . . .' then she stopped short, holding back. If this man was to trust her he had to do so from instinct, not because she poured out a list of qualifications to him, not at this precise moment.

'And this is why you didn't turn me in, while I was out like Sleeping Beauty?' He smiled at her, but deep inside, his own frailty, stupidity, *vulnerability*, burned him. There was a time when the Man would have coped without the kindness of some girl. It had been luck and chance, she was an Irish-American, so he was saved.

She could have been something else, and the Garda

would have been dragging him from the cottage bed and throwing him in jail. Jesus God but he was soft now. Soft like the old men who drank pints and sang of the rattle of a Thompson gun.

You're an old generation now, Dermot, no longer fit to call yourself the Man. The words formed, and he let them, wanting them to sting and hurt. If she was committed, *really* committed, let her learn to what she had given her support, the reality of it.

'I've killed people. Soldiers, policemen, our enemies all of them. There's blood on my hands, girl, can you cope with that? Can you handle the blood as well as the myths and the songs?'

She nodded dumbly, and he felt a stab of pity.

'I did it for what I believe. A free, united Ireland.'

Silence, darkness split only by the crackling wood and the two sources of inadequate light.

'I could do with a drink,' Dermot said.

She got up and stumbled about in the gloom, returning with a bottle and a tin mug.

'Jameson's.'

'Heaven be praised.'

He drank it greedily, feeling the fire and the warmth in his throat. A thought buzzed him.

'Sorry to make you sleep on the floor. Tonight you can have the bed.'

She took a pull of whiskey straight from the bottle. 'Aggh!' She wiped her mouth. 'I slept in there, with you.'

'Jesus.'

'Don't panic. You were feverish, hot one minute, cold the next, I guessed you needed the body warmth. Your virginity is still intact. I had no desire to sleep on the floor.'

He felt genuinely shocked. 'Well, tonight you can have it all to yourself.'

'Tonight is the same arrangement. You're still sick. I still don't want to sleep on the floor. I keep *my* clothes on, and if you're embarrassed you can take your underwear back.'

The conversation had exhausted him and he was too tired to say anything that would have any meaning to this odd, determined girl. His vision was blurring again, perhaps from tiredness or the remains of fever, and the girl suddenly looked very small to him.

But he realised that she was beautiful, in a dark, haunted kind of way. Or is that the delirium, Dermot? He never answered his own question for within a minute he was asleep again.

Swinging in the darkness, trying to clutch on to something firm, something stable, but the darkness just rocked him to and fro.

Dermot was marrying the girl on the Falls, and Colm was there, fresh in his new suit, stepping from the coffin. And the priest was pointing a pistol that began to come apart in his hands, and then they were all in a dark tunnel that was filling with water.

He awoke briefly in the night, suddenly lucid and calm in the pitch blackness. And for that momentary dream of wakening a girl was in his arms, her breasts full and heavy against his ribs, her hair wet and matted against the perspiration of his face.

And in the moment of waking he knew he wanted her, felt his body come alive with desire, but dared not move for fear that the apparition of his fever and his sleep would disappear.

In seconds he was sound asleep again, the fully clothed Kathleen crushed in sleep against him.

They lay that way until daybreak, as she took the heat from him, and returned it in smaller doses when his body chilled, and his teeth rattled in that fugue of sickness.

Biddle and the girl took the main Athlone-Galway road.

They were stopped once at a Garda/Irish Army roadblock, by bored and soaked men who simply checked the car's boot and cast a look inside the vehicle.

Joe and Fionulla had hastily cobbled together a story to explain their presence in the Republic, given that their car had British registration plates. But neither was asked – and the interior of the car was not searched. Joe thanked God for that, because beneath his seat, wrapped in several old newspapers, was his Browning service pistol and two 13-round magazines.

Had the men been more diligent, more professional, Joe's mission – and his career – would have ended there, on a rainswept Irish road. The Irish might be unenthusiastic in general in the fight against the Provos, but they could be *damned* enthusiastic when an armed

British soldier 'strayed' into their territory.

The girl did not know he was armed and he wanted to keep it that way. He intended to keep his word, but he was not going up against Dermot McGarvey without some protection.

They passed Athenry, and Joe pulled in and consulted his map.

'There should be a signpost for Oranmore just up ahead, we take that. The road goes south, then another right to Kinvarra. Then, ah . . .' his finger traced the map . . . 'Kinvarra, into County Clare, and the next stop is Ballvaghan and Black Head.'

He slipped the map into the door pocket, and put the car in gear.

The girl said quietly, 'Keep straight on. Don't turn for Oranmore.'

'The map's clear, through Oranmore . . .'

'Straight on. We're not going to Ballyvaghan.'

'You didn't trust me?'

She shook her head. 'You didn't think I would, did you? We're on different sides.'

He drummed his fingers on the wheel, the windscreen in front of him covered in rainspots now the wipers were switched off.

'If this is going to work we *have* to trust one another, can't you see that? I've kept my word.'

The girl gave him that innocent, dangerous smile.

'Have you? How do I know that half the Irish Army isn't descending on Ballyvaghan at this moment?'

Joe flipped the wipers.

'Read the papers tomorrow,' he said bitterly. 'I gave you my word, for Christ's sake. Doesn't that mean anything any more?'

'The word of an officer and a gentleman?'

'I'm not a sodding officer,' Joe snapped. 'I'm a non-com, do you know what that means? A *non*-commissioned officer. I'm not considered worthy of the Queen's Commission. I know because I applied once. Wrong accent, luv, wrong *look*. I'm not an officer *or* a gentleman.'

He slid the car off the verge and on to the road, the tyres fighting for a grip on the wet tarmac.

'You're an Englishman,' said Fionulla so softly he could hardly make out the words, 'and all our lives we've been betrayed by Englishmen.'

He cast her a quick glance, and saw that look of her brother in her, that wry, cynical look he had seen in the mug shot of Dermot McGarvey. And the thought of that photograph reminded him of another, of his own son lying dead in an army mortuary. And he remembered why he was here, the purpose of this insane trip, which was to put his son's killer behind bars.

Wrapped with the Browning and the ammunition were his other secret weapons. Photographs. Photographs he would not hesitate to use on this girl if she wavered. Three black and white photographs and several Xeroxed, closely handwritten sheets.

He hoped she would never have to see or read what was there.

They drove on towards Galway, the rain coming down like needles, and Joe reflected. *Had* he kept his word, or had he merely been cautious?

He honestly didn't know now, but whichever it was he was glad he hadn't tipped off Lisburn. He had visions of the Garda and the Irish Army, descending mob-handed on to some God-forsaken cottage at Black Head, all at the say-so of one British Army sergeant, Joseph Biddle.

That *would* have been the end of your career, Joe thought.

Dermot was dressing, the girl facing away from him at his insistence.

He said, 'We have to leave.'

'And go where?' She tossed the words over her shoulder.

'Anywhere. Keep moving. I can dump you somewhere on the road, you'll be OK.'

He hoisted the zip of his trousers, and the distinctive sound of it allowed her to turn.

'You're a damn fool. The whole of Ireland, North and South, is hunting for you.'

Dermot allowed himself a little smile. 'I doubt it.'

He felt better. His wound didn't hurt as much, his fever had subsided, and the food and rest had restored him. His initial alarm at being in the isolated cottage had also diminished.

But it *was* time to leave. He desired her, but there was no place for desire, not now.

Perhaps the girl had not been missed yet. She was a tourist, travelling alone. This was an adventure for her, perhaps she had fallen a little bit in love with him. She wouldn't be the first girl who'd been turned on by the thrill of his violence.

But now he must be rid of her, and away. He'd head for Dublin and the Sinn Fein headquarters. Sinn Fein – Ourselves Alone it meant in Gaelic. A legitimate political party with members of Parliament elected to the British House of Commons in London. But no one was under any illusion as to what it *really* was, least of all Dermot. It was the front organisation for the Provisional IRA. Dermot wondered, as they all did, why the Brits didn't simply ban it, in the Republic too. Close its offices and jail its members.

This was a war being fought here, and Dermot and the others believed in no quarter asked, none given. The Brits argued that by banning Sinn Fein they'd drive it underground and make it harder to keep tabs on. Dermot thought the Brits were crazy.

In Dublin – Dundalk if he could get there – he'd be found shelter and hidden away for as long as it took for the clamour to die down. Then he would have to think seriously about his future.

Suddenly he cried out, a piercing 'Agh!' like a man in pain.

'Are you OK?'

She came towards him, but he waved her away.

His sickness had played tricks on him, blotted out

his memory. There could be no going to Sinn Fein any more. His own comrades had betrayed him to the British. If they took him now it was Colm's fate for him. Some anonymous garage or wasteland, the hood and the pistol-shot.

The grief of it twisted inside him like real pain.

There was nowhere now. Nowhere and nothing. Everybody wanted to kill him, no one to save him. He looked to the future and saw only a blank brick wall. His exclamation of pain had been real. Everything he had believed in was now nothing. The Movement would dispose of him as it had policemen, soldiers, informants, petty criminals. All that he had done would count for nothing. And worse than anything, he would never know why he had been written off, betrayed, sentenced to death.

The girl said, 'You've got nowhere to go.'

He nodded his head in agreement.

She handed him a rolled-up copy of the *Irish Times*.

'Read this.'

He unrolled the newspaper, dimpled from the damp of the cottage, and read with increasing horror. When he'd finished he let the paper drop to his feet.

'So now you see. In my own inherited way I'm just as well-known as you are, Dermot. My father has clout. "Ireland's biggest-ever manhunt". You saw the headline.'

He was like a man sliding down a steep, shaley slope. Every time he tried to grip, to make a handhold, he lost that grip and plunged further down.

And each time his momentum increased and the chance to stop himself became more remote. His mind went round like a wheel at a fairground, too fast for him to put anything into focus.

'So you see, we can't go, not yet.'

Dermot looked up, dimly, his mind clutching at the mere fragment of a something. 'Your father – he's spoken for us, in America.'

'Yes, he's on Ireland's side.'

'We *are* fucking Ireland.'

'Are you, Dermot? Before I came here I thought you were – now . . . now I'm not so sure.'

He got up from the bed, gripped her arms.

'Aren't you? You could have fled to the Garda, could've shot me with me own gun. But you didn't. I'm a mad-dog killer, it says so in the bloody paper. You could have shopped me.'

She brought up her hands and gently prised his fingers off her arms.

'Do *you* still believe in it, Dermot? It says in the newspaper that your own people betrayed you to the British.'

The intensity of his eyes frightened her.

'I'll always believe it, *always*! Maybe my part's over now, maybe it's time for the younger men. The people who betrayed me are scum, criminals. They'll be dealt with. I'll stay in the Republic, join Sinn Fein, I'll do *something*.'

'Would you – would you kill again?'

She saw the eyes' intensity dim, like a blazing fire doused with water, saw the flicker of the eyelids, the firm set of the jaw suddenly slacken.

'You said things in your sleep.'

'Things?' His heart was beating faster now.

'You spoke of "Nulla" . . .'

'She's my sister – what things?'

She disturbed him, this girl, he felt as though he was *her* prisoner now, not she his.

'You kept saying "I can't". Over and over again, "I can't".'

He sketched a bad outline of a laugh.

' "I can't"? Doesn't seem to mean much.'

He could smell her now. She'd bathed somehow, while he was asleep, had washed her clothes. She smelled of soap and shampoo, foreign, forgotten smells to him.

How long was it since he'd had a woman? And he had never in his life made love to a woman as beautiful – as powerful? – as this.

'Back at the roadblock, after you took the machine-gun, you didn't fire at the other policeman.'

So close he could see her heart beating, her breasts rising and falling to the rhythm of her breathing.

'You just didn't fire – or was it couldn't, Dermot?'

'You're bloody mad, woman.'

'So "can't" what, Dermot? What is it you can't do any more – kill?'

She touched him, gripped *his* arm, and it was different

229

from his gripping of her, it was like an electric shock through him.

Desire and confusion raged through him like competing flames licking at some combustible arsenal at the core of him.

'There's a chance.'

'What the fuck are you talking about?'

'A chance for you.'

Kathleen couldn't be sure if she wasn't totally crazy even *thinking* about it. She knew how she felt about Ireland, although that was changing, weather-beaten by the climate of the country.

But this was a self-confessed killer. Perhaps he was a psychopath like the British propaganda always said about the Provisionals. Despite her half-baked psycho-social theory perhaps he would not hesitate to kill *her* if he had to.

Yet she was steeped in Ireland now, dyed in it as surely as if she was a blank sheet immersed in a tub of green. She had become part of it the moment that terrifying spectre of a face had confronted her through the windshield of her car.

She had not made a rational or conscious decision at that moment, to be part of it. In Massachusetts or any other American state she might have reversed away as quickly as possible. Then she would have driven past the man in the road and contacted the Highway Patrol.

There – in America – the intruder would have spelled fear, here, in Ireland, he spelled something else; a possibility, an adventure, perhaps a commitment.

CHAPTER TWELVE

Perhaps this strange young man still believed he had kidnapped her, but she doubted it. She could, had she been so minded, have killed him in the road by driving over him. But she had not, nor had she considered driving off. This was another draught of Ireland, and she wished to drink of it. And after the Garda roadblock and the news bulletin she knew he was an IRA man.

This was the struggle incarnate. This bloodied, unsophisticated man was the terrorist or the freedom fighter, depending on where you lived or which news bulletin you viewed.

Kathleen had been made unsure by what her aunt had said; the picture had become blurred and indistinct.

But one thing was sure. She would not betray him.

She had bathed his wounds and tended him while he slept an exhausted sleep, and she had no thought of flight or of contacting the authorities. Then, after her shopping expedition to the village, after her purchases and her fictitious explanation of their presence at the cottage, she read the newspaper and knew there could be no easy resolution of the matter.

Listening to his talk as he slept, snuggling alongside him, their bodies wet against each other in the narrow bed, her mind had raced far and wide in search of possible solutions. She knew – absolutely – that she would do everything in her power to stop him being shot down, or spending the rest of his life in prison.

Now she said, 'Have you ever been to America, Dermot?'

'No – what kind of bloody fool guessing game are we playing?'

'Would you like to go?'

'Yer mad, woman. I'm on the run; the Brits, the Garda – even the Provies want my blood and you're talking about trips to America.'

Her nails were in his arms. She was moist, and knew it; couldn't separate passion from desire, anger from lust.

Her closeness disturbed him. He hated his own lack of control, his stupid male desire at such a dangerous moment.

She said through clenched teeth, 'To live – to settle, you stupid bastard. My father could get you out of this. Political asylum, it's your only chance . . .'

'You're my fucking *hostage*!'

She released her hand and slapped him sharply across the face so hard his ears sang with the force of it.

'Jesus Christ, woman!'

'Listen to me, Dermot, listen hard. I'm your only chance. I'm not your *hostage*. I'm your safe conduct, if you'll let me be. I could have shot you while you were asleep, I've used a gun since I was eight. I could have driven my car over you at the beginning.'

Dermot was red from humiliation and anger and desire.

It was true, and that meant everything was out of control again. What seemed like a lifetime ago he'd been in charge. He'd been the Man. They sang about his exploits in the Republican clubs of Derry and West Belfast.

Then he'd taken the big Russian gun to Cross, and from that moment someone seemed to have pulled the bones out of his life until he flopped around without form or structure. The SAS trying to get him on the Falls; Colm's body slapping like dead abattoir meat on to the concrete floor of the garage; the phoney ambush, the policeman's white face in his sights, Dermot unable to fire.

Then the girl. God Almighty, how could he get in control again?

He felt his cheek stinging from the blow. And now some bloody Yankee politician's daughter slaps me and gets away with it. You've gone soft, Dermot, soft to the core.

He said bitterly, 'Well, it's a nice idea, but I doubt if it'll work since every soldier and policeman North and South wants to blow my head off.'

He could see the girl's eyes blazing now.

Dermot had seen that before in Americans. In Belfast they called it the NORAID look. Those Americans from the fund-raising clubs of Boston and New York. They came to Belfast flushed with the fanaticism of distant adherents on a personal pilgrimage.

It was their Lourdes, their Vatican City. The waters were the crack of an Armalite and the smell of cordite, their St Peter's Square the Catholic ghettoes of the Bogside and Andersonstown. Or was it _ the thought touched him briefly – something else, something far more dangerous, in this girl?

Her sheer physical presence disturbed and excited him. Now, at this precise moment, they wanted each other in an animalness they both understood with their bodies but could not rationalise.

She said, 'I'll telephone the US Embassy in Dublin, there must be one, a consulate at least. I'll tell them we're coming in, and that I am your safe conduct, not your *hostage*. If they try and harm you, then they'll harm me.'

Dermot shook his head. 'They'll take us out. An ambush. They won't care about you. The bloody Branch down here are more ruthless than the Brits.'

'They won't . . .' she said fiercely, tightening her clawing grip on his arm . . . 'not if I'm not a *hostage*. The consulate will make it clear to them *who* I am, and *where* we're going. Dermot, do you know how the networks operate in the States?'

Dermot shook his head. He didn't really know what the girl was driving at.

'I'll call CBS too. They have an office in either London or Belfast. If the cameras are on us we have a better chance.'

And a thought pierced her brain like light. And cousin goddamned Michael. They wouldn't dare, wouldn't, *couldn't*.

He said, 'What's the joke?'

'No joke. I just remembered something. Believe me, with me riding next to you the police are not going to touch you. I'm Senator Patrick Minihan's daughter and take my word, that is going to mean everything.'

CHAPTER TWELVE

'OK!'

'You'll do it?'

'Sure, but after we get to the consulate they'll never let us leave, you know that?'

'We'll get to that.'

'You think so. I know better. They've bloody extradited our Volunteers from America to stand trial in England.'

'Those Volunteers didn't have the connections you now have.'

Dermot put his hand on the girl's face. The desire was deeper now. 'And what makes you think your precious father will go along with this? It's one thing drinking green beer and singing rebel songs in Boston. It's another when a bloody IRA man drops on your doorstep.'

She took his hand, brought it down to her breast. He could feel the full swell of it, and the nipple, rock-hard.

'Because I *know* him, and if I want it, he'll do it. He's a conviction politician.'

Some hope flickered within him. We'll go to America, the two of us, away from this mad island that I love. To the world of big cars and new houses, of steaks and swimming pools. And she'll fall in love with me and we'll live in one of those wooden houses like on *The Waltons*, and we'll marry and have kids.

And the Pope's a Jew, Dermot. He shrugged, his hand still on her breast.

'It's worth a try.'

She said, 'I want you.'

She kissed him on the lips, and he pulled his free arm around her, crushing her into his hardness.

It was then they heard the sound of the vehicle coming down the narrow track leading to the cottage.

He moved like a phantom, flat against the wall, back from the window, peering through the raggedy curtains. It was a small green van, the kind tradesmen used.

It pulled up outside the cottage, and a middle-aged man in a white smock was climbing out of the driver's seat.

Kathleen remained where she had been, standing in the middle of the room, like one half of a fading image that had been their embrace.

'Get rid of him.' Dermot's voice was low but it had a deathly quality to it. Two pairs of eyes went as one to the base of the bed where the butt of the Uzi protruded.

He moved, kicking it quickly back beneath the bed.

Then their eyes met, and she said, 'Don't, Dermot. Not now.'

She saw some kind of assent in his eyes, heard the rap on the door, took a deep breath and slipped the latch.

'It's a soft day –' The man doffed a trilby hat.

'Yes? I'm sorry, I don't know who . . .'

'Mr Kelly. The village yesterday. You came into my shop to buy groceries, tins, that sort of thing.'

'Yes, I'm sorry. What can I do for you, Mr Kelly?' Remember the English accent, Kathleen, she tried to remind herself.

'I was talking with Bridie – my wife, Bridie – and she was saying, what with you and your husband being new to the district, if there was anything we could, you know . . . if we could help at all . . .'

'No . . . no thank you. But it was kind . . .' She tried to close the door.

'I deliver, you know, in the van and all. Give me a list, I'll be only too happy to drop it off.'

Out of the corner of her eye Kathleen could see Dermot. Silent, but poised, like some deadly snake.

'Well, perhaps. Of course, we'll bear it in mind, thank you . .'

Go! Kathleen was pleading, go! Go or I'll scream.

'It's been a soft morning, but they're forecasting sun later.'

'Soft? I . . .'

'Raining, miss – missus I mean, you'll forgive me.'

'Thank you, Mr Kelly. Perhaps next week . . . next week you and Mrs Kelly will come for dinner? When we're settled.'

Go, you old fool. Go!

'That would be nice.'

'I hope you'll excuse me . . .' Kathleen lowered her eyes in what she hoped would look like polite embarrassment. 'My husband and I were just . . .' she deliberately hesitated . . . 'resting . . . '

She saw the man go deeply red.

'Oh . . . yes . . . I'll be off. Good-day to you both.'

She closed the door and watched through the window

as the man climbed into the van, did a three-point turn and drove off up the bumpy, rocky track.

'Jesus.'

Dermot came away from the window and put his arm round her, but his eyes followed the retreating green square of the van's rear doors.

'*Did* you see him yesterday?'

'Yes, he runs the little general store.'

'Sure it was the same man?'

'Yes, it was him. He was just being kind.'

'Maybe.'

They both sat down on the bed, their arms around each other, more for comfort and security than passion, now.

'Could you make the call tonight?'

She looked up. 'Yes! *Yes!* Oh, Dermot . . .'

'He didn't sound or look too bright, our Mr Kelly, and types like him don't normally pay too much attention to the papers or the telly, but you never know. Never underestimate a stupid Irishman.'

CHAPTER

13

'Stop the car.'

Joe did as Fionulla asked, pulling over.

She pointed through the windscreen. 'About half a mile on – I think – you'll see a sign, a small one, to a village called Ballypool. Take it.'

By Joe's estimation they were not far from Lake Carrib now. They'd passed Oughterard ten minutes before and were well out on the road to Connemara.

He drove on, found the signpost, and soon they were on a narrow, hedged road. In the distance he caught a glimpse of the lake, two or three miles away, the tiny waves glimmering in the darkness.

The girl said, 'Go on through Ballypool.' Joe did, driving through a hamlet with a few cottages, a telephone kiosk, a tiny provisions shop, and what might have been a bar or simply a counter for off-licence sales.

Half a mile farther, Fionulla pointed again. 'There.' She indicated a lane, little more than a track. 'It leads down to the lake. A dead end. The cottage is at the end, about a mile and a half.'

Joe drove down a little way, and the hedges gave way to grass and woodland bordering the road. He saw a firm-looking piece of ground and drove off the track into a widely spread clump of trees lit up by the headlights.

'Why are we stopping?'

Joe killed the engine. 'Simply, if we drive any nearer he might hear us – if he's here, that is.' He looked carefully at the girl. 'We could be on a wild goose chase.'

'I never once said that wasn't a possibility.'

They both got out and stood in the shade, stretching their legs after the long drive.

She stirred her foot in some loose soil, and looked up at him. 'We can just drive down there. He won't shoot at me.'

Joe remembered she was only nineteen – nearly.

'He might not wait to find out *who* it is.'

'You said he was done with violence.'

Touché, thought Joe, but said, 'I did . . . I *do*. But I'd rather not test it until I'm absolutely sure.'

Joe moved back towards the driver's seat, keeping the car between himself and the girl, and muttered, 'Bloody shoelaces.' He knelt down and took the package from beneath the driver's seat.

'I love him, Joe . . .' It was the first time she had ever used his first name. 'If you try and harm him, I'll – I'll harm you.'

'Don't worry . . .' he continued the pantomime, tucking the parcel beneath his shirt, and standing up . . . 'I gave you my word.'

'And you'll keep it?'

He said that yes, he would keep his word. He would take Dermot McGarvey to the North – somehow. And one fine day Dermot would stand up in that dock in Belfast Crown Court, and Joe would be there, and he hoped Fionulla McGarvey would be there with him.

And she would learn – Joe knew it was cruelty, sadism almost, but he *wanted* her to know, *everyone* to know – that McGarvey was no run-of-the-mill Provo killer, he had the mark of Cain on him.

She said, 'Swear it on your mother's life.' It was childlike but somehow touching.

My old housebound mother, bowed by the weight of her diseased legs and her personal Irish tragedy. Alone with her fears and her memories in that damp Lancashire town that looks so much like Belfast. On her life.

'On my mother's life, Miss McGarvey.'

When it was dark Kathleen gathered up all the coins she and Dermot possessed, and took the keys to her car.

Turning to Dermot, she said, 'I'll get back as quickly as I can. How efficient are your telephones – not like the ones in England, I hope?'

Dermot shrugged. 'Public telephones don't exist in Belfast, we have a habit of setting them on fire. Here it could be different.'

She reached up and kissed him. Her body ached from their lovemaking, and she was suffused with some immense feeling of completeness. It frightened her more than a little, and she dared not try to analyse it, but for now it was enough that it existed.

When he broke their embrace he gave her a wry look.

'How do I know you'll come back – or that you won't just call the Garda?'

'Because . . .' she said, without a hint of humour . . . 'sex is not a recreation with me. It's a commitment. Does that satisfy you?'

He had been a passionate lover, a little clumsy, but what bothered her most was that he seemed to keep something back, some secret part of himself.

Their lovemaking had been protracted, and afterwards he had not wanted to pull away, he had clung to her for long minutes, their bodies glued by the temper of their passion.

He put his hand into her cropped hair, but didn't reply. Instead he pulled her face towards him, kissed her, then bowed her head to his chest.

When she pulled away, he said, 'Come back to me, Kathleen.'

Tom and Bridie Kelly ate their dinner, watched a little TV including the RTE news, then each took a cup of cocoa up to the small bedroom above the store.

Mr Kelly had to be up at five to drive to the whole-salers' at Galway, but that night he found it difficult to sleep.

A thought kept buzzing around his head like a winter fly in the living room, until – with Bridie snoring beside him – he could stand the irritation no longer. It was like lying in a bed with crumbs in it, or trying to sleep when you were hungry or needed to pee. Until you did something about it you could never rest.

He stepped into his slippers at the side of the bed and padded quietly, so as not to wake his sleeping wife, downstairs to the big, black telephone on the stand in the hallway.

Thumbing slowly through the telephone directory, he located a number. Then he picked up the receiver and carefully dialled. It rang for a long time and he was on the point of giving up when a voice he recognised answered.

Mr Kelly said, 'Is that you, Billy?'

'This is Garda McBride, who is that?'

'Tommy – Tommy Kelly from Ballypool.'

The policeman's voice brightened. 'Tommy Kelly! And how are you, Tommy? I've not seen you since the wake when your cousin left his life on the road to Killarney.'

'I'm well, Billy, well . . .'

'Bridie?'

'Like a young one . . . Billy, I know you'll be thinking I've taken leave of my senses, but . . .'

Joe and the girl had walked less than half a mile down the track when they heard the sound of a car coming towards them.

'Get into the trees.'

They scrambled into cover as the twin headlight beams, rising and falling on the bumpy track, approached them. The car was in low gear as it ground past them, but they could hardly catch a glimpse of the driver or occupants. Their night vision had not adjusted after the glare of the light and the interior of the car was dark.

The girl said, 'Who was it? Did you see? Was it Dermot?'

Joe watched the red lights disappear.

'I don't know. Somehow I think he wouldn't move at night if he could avoid it. In some ways it would be more dangerous. Fewer cars, fewer people, more chance of being caught in a random Garda check.'

And if it wasn't Dermot it couldn't be the girl, Joe concluded. Not on her own, anyway. Not unless McGarvey had terrorised her into driving out for food, or maybe into ferrying him to some location, her driving, him hidden in the boot or somehow beneath the back seat.

He would soon know; they would both soon know.

Ballypool was deserted, and Kathleen stopped her car outside the single, green-painted telephone kiosk. There were no directories, and she groaned. Come back, Ma Bell, all is forgiven.

She dialled the operator, waited what seemed an age, and then a sleepy woman's voice came on the line. Kathleen asked her for the telephone number of the United States Consulate in Dublin.

The sleepy voice told Kathleen she would have to dial *another* number for that information, and Kathleen did, again waiting a seemingly interminable time for a reply.

Kathleen repeated her request. There was silence for a minute, then the enquiry operator said: 'Will that be the US Consulate in Elgin Road?'

Kathleen wanted to scream: 'How many goddamn US Consulates are there in Dublin?' But she merely said, 'I'm sure it must be.' And was rewarded like a child who has answered a question correctly, with the number as a prize.

She dialled it urgently, made a mistake in her haste, dialled again, her coins stacked ready.

It started to ring. Two rings. Three. Four.

God please, there must be a duty man.

Five rings. Six.

It's eleven o'clock at night, Kathleen. Maybe they shut the consulate totally. But please, *please*. Someone. Anyone.

Seven. Eight.

'United States Consulate.'

A beautiful male American voice; a voice of confidence and strength. Kathleen spoke urgently but with assurance. She established who she was and what she needed. The official was first suspicious, then bemused, eventually brisk and businesslike.

Kathleen said, 'My father *must* be by the telephone there in eight hours from now. He's in Belfast, I know, because it was in the newspaper. You must get him down to Dublin.'

The voice said he would move heaven and earth.

'Talk to these Irish government people, whomever,

you know that my father's cousin runs the goddamn country. This is not the North, and the fugitive's crimes are political. I am an American citizen and I am seeking refuge in my consulate with a political refugee who needs asylum.'

She put down the telephone and realised she was sweating heavily. It all had to work. The sheer power and influence of the United States in the person of her father and his senatorial rank had to work. But it could hinge on Dad's cousin Michael. Praise God for family ties. Perhaps that could load the dice in their favour.

It was a massive gamble, she was acting instinctively and intuitively. If it failed it wouldn't only be Dermot in trouble.

She was planning – she, Kathleen Minihan of Boston, Massachusetts – to drive the breadth of Ireland with a wanted IRA gunman. Then she planned to lead him into the church-like sanctuary of the United States Consulate.

The official put down the telephone and examined his hand-written notes. He wished he'd forsaken the third martini before dinner. He felt sure it was not a hoax, the girl knew too much about Senator Minihan for that – and there were always the names she had said would ensure Minihan realised it really was her.

But perhaps she was acting under duress. She was *supposed* to be a kidnap victim, after all. Perhaps this boy McGarvey had a gun to her throat? Perhaps it was the Stockholm Hostage Syndrome, where hostage falls in love with, and under the influence of, captor.

Who knew? The official's last Foreign Service posting had been Beirut, and when he landed in Dublin he'd thought, what could possibly happen here?

The cottage sat on a slope that led down to the lake's rocky shore. It looked isolated, and very deserted.

Joe whispered, 'That the one?'

'Yes.'

No lights, no smoke from the brick chimney. Perhaps the car that passed them on the lane had contained lovers using the location for courtship.

Or worse. Perhaps McGarvey *had* been there, and was now gone, in *that* car, just an arm's length or more from Joe. So many 'ifs'.

Now that she was here Fionulla was desperately worried. From the day of her first awakening to knowledge she knew that you did not betray; not to the British, not to the Peelers.

Tout. It was the worst word you could use about a person. Was she a tout now? And if she was not, if it was honourable to want to save the life of your brother – the other lying dead in his grave – could it work? Could she persuade Dermot that this sergeant – Dermot's sworn enemy – was here to save him? Would Dermot *prefer* the inevitable prospect of death to years of imprisonment?

Above all, was she doing it for Dermot – or for herself?

The cottage was bathed in a half light that came from a sliver of moon peeping from behind the clouds. It was as it had been when they were younger – how many years ago, just ten, just a decade? Colm a gangly teenager, Dermot still at school, she an eight-year-old, hero-worshipping her older brothers. The three of them splashing in the water at the lake's edge, skimming flat stones over the calm surface, a whoop of joy if you got a five-bounce.

Picnics with Mam and Dad, away from the claustrophobia of the Divis, of Belfast, the bomb scares, the gun-battles and the aggressive, ill-mannered soldiers and their body searches.

It was like returning to a favourite dream, that now was a nightmare. Colm in his grave, Mam and Dad old beyond their years, Dermot a famous Volunteer, with a death sentence hanging over him.

And she, Fionulla McGarvey, bringing a British soldier to find her brother. She'd had a poem once on her damp bedroom wall. Omar Khayyam. 'The moving finger writes, and having writ moves on. Nor all thy piety nor wit shall lure it back to cancel half a line; nor all thy tears wash out a word of it.'

She turned to the sergeant. 'What should I do?'

There was no easy answer. If McGarvey *was* there and armed, he might be nervous and instinctively shoot at the first person he saw or heard.

'Wait five minutes. Go to the door, knock and quickly shout your name.'

You're copping out, Joe, he thought. Copping out because you're scared of McGarvey and scared of yourself. Scared that he might shoot *you*, and worse, scared that you might shoot him, out of hand, without a thought; promises thrown to the wind.

The girl said, 'What will you do?'

'Stay hidden,' Joe lied. 'Wait for you to talk him round. Then bring him out.'

He held his breath. She had proved herself smart; how could she be so naive as to believe he would sit and wait for some peace parley?

But she believed him, desperate as she was now to lay sight on Dermot, hold him once again, to tell him she had come not to betray but to save.

'Five minutes.'

He moved away from her, deeper into the trees. Safely out of her vision he took the Browning out of the package beneath his shirt.

So close now.

Fionulla looked at her cheap plastic watch, got up and crossed to the cottage.

She was frightened of the dark, scared of the brooding presence of the cottage and its memories. She crossed herself and said a silent prayer that Dermot would be there.

She knocked on the wooden door. 'Dermot! It's me, Nulla. Nulla!'

Her voice seemed to echo down to the water, and across the lake. Then there was just silence and a slight wind stroking the trees and ruffling the lake.

'It's Nulla . . . please God, Dermot, it's me, Nulla.'

The door opened with an agonised groan and she started, her hand up to her mouth in terror.

'Dermot?'

Silence and darkness from the cottage.

'It's only me, Dermot. Just Nulla.'

Darkness and silence and the ghostly breath of the wind. She was on the verge of flight.

A soft voice said, 'Christ, girl, but you shouldn't be here.'

'Dermot!

'He became a shadow, a shape, then form, and she flung herself into his arms as his face showed like a silver orb in the moonlight.

'Dermot, oh, Dermot.'

'Easy, Nulla.'

'God, Dermot, I never thought . . .'

'Will you be careful, girl, if you're not after getting us both shot, that's a gun I'm holding there.'

Then a deeper voice said, 'One move, McGarvey, just one, and I'll spread your brains over the lake.'

And Dermot felt the barrel, hard steel pressed against his scalp. He felt no fear, just deep disappointment. Was there no end to the potential of this family for betraying its own?

He said, 'You should have known, Nulla. Never trust a Brit. What lie did they tell you – surely not money with you, girl?'

She was sobbing, and saying over and over, 'He promised – he *promised*.'

CHAPTER THIRTEEN

Garda Billy McBride helped himself to another glass of Jameson's. His boots were off, his tunic hung over the back of the chair, and he had his stockinged feet up on the desk.

Soaked twice that day, kicked in the leg by Conor Spence drunk on Guinness, and now his bloody fool brother-in-law seeing IRA kidnap victims all over the place.

And what on earth would this Provisional and his hostage be doing here in the West of Ireland at some God-forsaken cottage buying groceries from Tommy Kelly, and himself saying that the girl was *English* not American.

Billy was off duty in ten minutes and if he started raising alarms and suspicions he'd be there all night. There was a regular hue and cry over this man McGarvey, and you could bet he'd be out chasing shadows. Not to mention the trouble he'd be in when it all turned out to be some fever of Tommy's imagination.

Garda McBride looked at the telephone. Then, of course, it was also true that if he *didn't* mention it to Galway, and *if* it did turn out that . . .

Could they kick you out for that? Billy wondered. Only two years to the pension. Stupid to risk it. He picked up the telephone direct link to the Galway Garda Siochana barracks.

'It's McBride at Dynamoor . . . this IRA man from the North. I just had a call . . .'

Kathleen pulled the car in front of the cottage, got out and rapped lightly on the door.

'It's me – Kathleen.'

Dermot opened the door and she embraced him. She was hot and he seemed very cold.

'It's fixed. They're going to have Dad there at eight . . .'

'Run . . . run . . .' Dermot's voice was a sibilant whisper.

'What . . .? Dermot . . .?'

Then a deep English voice came from the darkness.

'Step in. Both of you. Dermot, tell her I have a pistol.'

'Come in, Kathleen, he's armed.'

He pulled her in and closed the door. Then the man stepped away from the oil lamp whose light he had been blocking, and she saw him, and the gun that was pointing at them both. His hair was close-cropped, receding at the temples. He looked so . . . ordinary.

Kathleen saw another figure off to one side, but still in front of the man with the pistol.

The English accent, unlike any she had ever heard before, said, 'Miss McGarvey, light another lamp, then pull the curtains.'

The girl did as she was bid.

Kathleen said, 'Who is he, Dermot – and her? She has your name. Your wife?'

'Sister,' Dermot said flatly. 'And this man is a British soldier. He's come down from the North to take me back.'

The soldier said, 'You're supposed to be a hostage, Miss Minihan. It doesn't much look like it.'

She tried to make out more of his features in the

unnatural light, but all she could think was . . . ordinary. If she never saw him again from this moment she would be unable to describe him.

There were millions of such faces in the Western world. She presumed the armies of the nations were full of them. Faces that seemed to have suited their shape to anonymity, to a uniform pattern.

Kathleen directed her voice at the girl.

'You brought him here?'

'Yes.'

'How could you do it – betray your brother?'

Joe said, 'You –' at Kathleen '– sit down. There . . .' The pistol pointed at an upright chair. 'McGarvey, back to your place. Miss McGarvey, the chair there.'

Fionulla sat down dejectedly, afraid to meet anyone's eyes. She had really thought the Englishman would not betray her. She made one last vow. The moment the sergeant tried to kill Dermot she would fling herself in front of his gun. That would be her atonement.

McGarvey sat back on the bed, relaxed, poised, deadly as a curled cobra, and Joe never let his eyes leave the sitting man.

'He promised to help. We'd all go to the Garda together. You promised, Joe.'

'Joe, is it?' Dermot said softly. 'I never believed my little sister would get so cosy with the Brits.'

She was in tears. 'It was to help you, Dermot. They want to gun you down, all of them, North and South, gun you down like a mad dog.'

She looked imploringly at Joe. 'Tell him . . . tell him it's the truth.'

Joe said, 'You killed my son at Crossmaglen. He was a Lancashire Fusilier. He was in the patrol you fired at in the market square last Christmas Eve. The same night you shot the other two soldiers. And the mother.' He paused. 'And the little girl.'

Dermot spread his hands. 'Sorry, soldier boy. Wrong man.'

'I *told* him, Dermot . . .' Fionulla cried. 'I told him you'd never kill a child.'

'Oh, he'd kill kids all right, wouldn't you, Dermot? There really is no limit to who Dermot might kill.'

McGarvey felt the threat of the dangerous knowledge across the room, deadlier than a bullet. Surely no lone-wolf British sergeant could know about Colm. No one but a chosen few knew that, and no one would be telling the Brits. But if the sergeant suspected, and voiced his suspicions, he could lose Kathleen.

She was his passport to a new life, perhaps to a new love, the two of them. But if she knew he'd executed his own brother, supporter of the Cause or no, she'd not be able to understand or stomach it.

Surely the soldier would try to kill him soon. Only a fool would even *think* about taking him back to Belfast, or turning him in to the Garda, because Dermot would allow neither.

No Kesh for the Man, no Mountjoy and extradition either. No Diplock court and a wasted life with the

Volunteers in the Republican compounds. Dermot knew what his options – nay, his only choices – were now. Death or America.

'You were *there*,' Joe said. 'I *know*.'

You cannot *know*, Dermot thought, unless . . . and if you know that, then you can also *know* about Colm.

'Know, is it?'

'Yes, McGarvey, *know*. O'Connell came over to us.'

'Liar.' Dermot was going cold, his bowels chilled.

'He came over, green sunglasses and all. Half the Belfast Brigade's lifted.'

'Liar!'

'He betrayed you. Set you up in the ambush, thought we'd do his job for you. Thinks you're a mad dog.'

'Fucking tout.'

'He's frightened of you.'

'He's a dead man.'

Joe shifted the pistol to his other hand, saw the figures move then settle again. The American girl was watching him intently.

'So I *know* you killed my son.'

Dermot shrugged, wondering when the Brit would use his other, far more dangerous piece of information. Dermot knew he must try to delay that moment if he could.

He said, 'I'm sorry. He was a soldier, and it is a war.'

'The woman? The little girl? Were they soldiers?'

Nulla and the American girl looked at Dermot.

'An accident . . .'

Joe laughed bitterly.

Dermot said, 'It's the truth.'

Kathleen remembered the moment back in her home on Christmas Eve when they'd heard the news. Her stepmother saying, 'How do you support the killing of a child?'

Dermot. Dermot. Dermot. Dermot.

'What happened, Dermot?' she asked.

He looked at her. 'Would you believe me if I told you – or would you prefer British lies?'

'Yes, yes I'll believe you – tell me. A *child,* Dermot.'

Fionulla was shaking her head as her world fragmented like an impacting meteorite.

'And you, Nulla . . . do you want to hear why your brother had to lie to you?'

She steadied herself and nodded dumbly.

'Cross is one hundred per cent Republican. The locals don't want the British soldiers. The British have stuck a bloody great fortified base down one street. They come in and out by helicopter – daren't risk the roads. So much for the United Kingdom and the consent of the governed.'

Joe watched him, gun steady. The devil voice said, shoot him now, Joe, shoot him before he poisons it, before he lies his way out, before he demeans the death of your son, diminishes what he did to that mother and child. He breathed deeply to calm himself.

Dermot had stopped speaking, looking at Joe. Joe realised his gun hand was shaking.

'The Brits kill us, we kill them. We planned an ambush. Something went wrong with the gun, it fired wide. That's when the woman and her child were killed. A Volunteer lost his life to a British bullet. No one regrets the death of that mother and child more than I.'

Dermot said to Kathleen, 'It's the truth, girl, but I don't expect you to stomach it. It's easy to be for the Cause when you're 3,000 miles away putting dollars into a hat. This is our *reality*. It's corpses, and British bullets, and the Milltown the only way out for most of us.'

When Joe had imagined his son's killer he had worked him up into a monster, a clearly evil thing, demonstrably vile and sick. But this man, this Dermot McGarvey, the feared killer they had called 'the Man', he was so nondescript, so *banal*.

Kathleen said slowly, 'Nothing's changed, Dermot. I swear, nothing has changed.'

'Nulla?'

She looked at her brother.

'A *child*, Dermot?'

'The British have been starving and killing our children for ever. They gunned down our people in Derry in 1971, they massacred them centuries before at Drogheda. Read your history, girl.'

Joe felt his head swim. It was all too convincing; potted social history to justify murder. There were thirteen rounds in the magazine of the Browning, enough to wipe out Dermot McGarvey, to erase his history, his view of history, his poisonous lies and his propaganda.

Enough to avenge David, to avenge all those who had died at this killer's hands, to . . .

'Joe . . . please . . .'

He heard Fionulla's voice as though it were waking him from a trance.

'Don't fire, please. Don't kill him.'

He laughed bitterly.

'I *promised*, didn't I? We're going to the Garda, the four of us neatly packed together, and you, McGarvey . . . you're going to surrender.'

Dermot said, 'Never.'

'You've no choice. You push your head outside there alone – or even with your tame "hostage" here – and you'll have that head blown off your shoulders.'

'I'll take my chances.'

'Dermot, please . . .' Fionulla was pleading. 'It's your only chance.'

Kathleen said incisively, 'It's not his only chance. Listen to me – Joe – you know who my father is?'

Joe said sarcastically, 'He's our favourite American politician.'

She ignored the sarcasm. 'My father has arranged asylum at the US Consulate for Dermot. He is a political refugee and he is seeking asylum from what he – and I and my father – believe is political vengeance which could lead to his death.'

Joe said grimly, 'Jesus, but you Yanks have got a fucking nerve.'

'Nerve or not, that asylum is granted and arrangements are being made with the Irish Government *at this moment* for that asylum to be effected.'

Joe could feel a sort of unhealthy heat creeping over him. Asylum? This wasn't Russia, or the Middle sodding Ages. And after asylum, what then? McGarvey sitting in the US Consulate the rest of his life? No, then it would be . . .

He said, 'And then you spirit him to America? Is that it . . . IS IT?' Neither Dermot nor the American girl replied.

The heat was choking him. It was like the prelude to tears or terrible anger.

'And then you parade him on the TV, like some fucking Irish hero singing "Danny Boy". Is that it? Oh no. Oh no you don't, you bastards.'

Kathleen said quietly, 'Joe, you are a British soldier, and you are armed and on the land of a foreign power. They don't take kindly to armed British soldiers in Ireland – so I'd guess.'

Joe could see only Dermot, see only the killer of his son, the man who was going to walk away, laughing.

'You risk a long term of imprisonment. I think you should put your gun away, and let us leave in peace. We wish you no harm.'

So clean and American, Joe thought. Just like the GIs when he was a kid. Good-looking, tall, beautiful uniforms, powerful and clean-cut, everything technicolour and simple. America was strong, America was beautiful, America was always *right*, and so fucking *sure*! Well, not this time. Because grubby Joe, short, snotty-nosed Joe from old, out-on-its-feet England, the lad from the back-to-backs, would see to that.

He thought of the mortuary pictures. Of David, and the woman, and the little girl in pigtails.

Make that right, America, he thought viciously. Pour some billions into *that* and make them climb off the slab like your rockets off the pad.

He said calmly, 'Here's your choices, McGarvey. You get up right now, and we drive to the nearest Garda station. That's one.'

Dermot smiled lazily. 'And the other?'

'I shoot you dead.'

Kathleen said, 'You wouldn't dare, and you know it.'

Joe said, still calm, 'Five minutes ago you would have been right, I was through with it all. I thought he was too. Now I know I'm not and neither really is he.'

Kathleen was tensed and afraid. The soldier was clearly unstable, unhinged by his son's death. It was a deadly dangerous situation. She would have to defuse it – or act.

She said, 'You have my word that Dermot will take part in no more acts of violence. He is no longer part of the armed struggle.'

'Sorry, love.' Joe was fixed on McGarvey now, who watched Joe calmly. 'It's not like British bloody Railways. You don't retire with a gold watch. It's the prison or the grave for boyos, eh, Dermot? Tell them that's the way of things.'

Dermot gave his infuriating casual shrug.

'You have all the answers, soldier boy.'

'I'm getting impatient, McGarvey.'

'They say us Irish are mad.' Dermot laughed.

'Please Joe . . . please . . .' Nulla was pleading.

'Don't plead, Miss McGarvey . . . *tell him*! I've kept my word up to now, you keep yours. Make him surrender to the police.'

'Dermot . . . do it. He'll kill you . . .'

'He'll have to.'

'You've run out of time. On your feet.'

Dermot remained sitting.

'I'll do it.'

'Sure you will.'

The American girl got up from her chair.

'Sit down!'

'To him, perhaps, but not to me.' She put herself between the gun and Dermot.

'Get out of the bloody way or I'll shoot him through you. I've got thirteen rounds to do it with.'

'You won't do that. You have no quarrel with me.'

Kathleen was quivering with fright, holding herself as rigid as she could to hold it in. She had fired a gun, and seen what it could do to a bottle or a can, to a snake or vermin. She had been told never to point a gun at someone unless she intended to kill them, and never, *ever* to put herself in front of the barrel of a loaded gun.

What she was doing went against every instinct she possessed. But she believed – she was gambling everything on her instinct – that although the soldier might, in his grief and anger, shoot Dermot, he would not shoot her.

She realised her life would depend on her judgement.

Joe spoke through gritted teeth. 'Get out of the way. Automatics are unreliable.'

'I know, I've fired one.'

'This is not Hollywood, get out of the fucking *way*!'

She was level with him, the gun at her chest. She brought her hand up slowly, slowly, and with her palm gently pushed the barrel to one side.

Joe punched her viciously in the midriff, driving the air from her, and she collapsed in agony.

McGarvey was motionless.

It happened in a split second. The American girl was getting groggily to her feet. Joe was aware that Fionulla was not in her place, there was a hint of a shadow, movement, the swish of air, then the awful, agonising hammer-blow as the whiskey bottle caught him with full force on his left temple.

There was a blinding light, his head seemed to explode, his legs turn to water and he was sliding into a black lake, without time for anger or regret at his own stupidity.

'Good girl, Nulla.'

She leant over him, feeling his skull. 'I think I've killed him, Dermot.'

Kathleen knelt down, practical, lifted the soldier's wrist, felt his pulse.

'Don't worry, he's alive.'

'Nulla? Where's his car, the Brit's car, where is it?'

Fionulla looked up, dazed. '. . . The top of the lane, in the trees . . . Dermot, he needs to go to a hospital.'

'Keys, Kathleen, find his keys. They won't be looking for his car. It'll give us breathing space.'

She rummaged in his anorak, found the keys and handed them to Dermot. 'Right.' He retrieved the Uzi from beneath the sink, where Joe had chucked it, then rummaged on the floor for the magazine. He found it underneath one of the chairs, and slipped it into his trouser pocket.

Kathleen was rubbing her stomach where the Englishman had struck her. 'You won't need it,' she said groggily, 'you've got a safe conduct.'

'Perhaps. But if I've got this they won't know whether you're my hostage or not.'

And *am* I? She wondered. Aren't I *really* your hostage, Dermot? A hostage to Ireland, too, to my father, to history and to someone else's memories.

The sergeant was white, his breathing shallow. Fionulla was on her knees, next to him, rubbing his hands, his wrists. She looked up at Dermot and this strange foreigner who seemed to have so much power and control.

'I can't come with you.'

Kathleen said nothing. She was pleased beyond relief. The girl was an extra factor, a complication they didn't need.

Dermot said, 'I'll send for you.'

'Please do, Dermot. *Please!*'

He found the keys to the Orion, and tossed them to his sister. 'Can you drive yet?'

'I've taken lessons.'

'If he's not awake in the hour, drive him somewhere, a hospital, a Garda station. Could be his skull is fractured.'

Kathleen remembered the pistol.

'He would have killed you.'

'Sure he would, it's all a game with us and the Brits. Don't want it on Nulla's conscience, do we?'

Or yours, Kathleen thought. There's too much weighing there already, and who knows what the last straw could be for that camel's back of guilt.

She spoke to Fonulla. 'Think you can do it – it's stick shift?'

Seeing the girl's uncomprehending face, Dermot said, 'Means a gear lever, Nulla,' and to Kathleen, 'It's all "stick shift" around here, Kathleen. It's what Nulla learned on.'

Fionulla said, 'Yes, I can drive it, I'm sure.'

'We need to go,' said Kathleen. 'Get as near to Dublin as we can.'

Dermot lifted his sister from the prone Englishman, and hugged her very close.

'I'm the same person, Nulla. We're fighting a war.'

'For you. In the name of Colm's memory, be safe.'

The spear in the side. The wound of your own betrayal. He put his fingers to her lips, took the moisture to his own, and returned it.

'Be safe.'

CHAPTER THIRTEEN

Then he and Kathleen were gone, and there was just the pale light, the cottage, the silence, and the injured sergeant.

She realised what she had done. But she knew that if she had not done it the sergeant would have killed Dermot. The American girl had intervened, and though Joe was unwilling or unable to use the firearm on her, he had punched her out of his firing line.

Fionulla realised that had it not been for her own intervention, then Joe might have pulled the trigger. And she was a Republican, and Joe was her enemy.

Dermot would be safe now, not gunned down without mercy, or locked into some British internment camp for the rest of his life. Thanks to the American girl he would go to America and live in peace. Perhaps he would even settle down with Kathleen, marry and have children.

She went back to Joe, noting the massive swelling over his temple, praying she had not injured him severely. His face was still white but his breathing seemed more even, so she found a bare pillow and gently lifted his head, placing the pillow beneath it. Then she loosened his shirt collar and felt his pulse once again. She heard a rustle from beneath his shirt, and touched with her fingers around his chest and armpit, the artificial bulk that began to show there.

It felt like an exercise book or a bundle of papers. Curious, she unbuttoned the shirt, and felt next to his skin. She found a newspaper folded around several photographs and some mimeographed sheets of handwriting on lined paper.

She took the photographs by finger and thumb, held them up to catch the meagre light and gave a small gasp of shock. She recoiled in horror. It was a photograph of a dead, naked woman, her face mutilated.

She repressed a desire to vomit, dropped the first picture, but held on to the second. She waited three long seconds, then, unable to stop herself, she held that one up to the light.

It was a naked, dead child, with pigtails; horribly disfigured. She let that picture flutter down to the sergeant's gently rising chest.

There was one last picture, and she held it away from her like some evil Tarot. Like a card that might spell a gambler's doom or his salvation. In the end she was powerless to resist the temptation.

She turned it.

It was her brother Colm. Naked, and dead on a mortuary slab.

She screamed.

She awoke cold and still, unaware whether she had fainted or simply slept, hoping that it had been a nightmare, realising instantly that it had not. The photographs lay, mercifully, on their exposed faces, and she brushed them further away as the squeamish will brush a dead insect.

On the still-unconscious body of the sergeant lay the sheets of mimeographed paper. She picked them up, ensuring that they were not photographs, and that they contained no image. They were glossy Xeroxes of an RUC statement form, stamped at Castlereagh, the interrogation centre to which she knew Republican prisoners and known IRA men were taken.

She narrowed her eyes and read in the gloom. It was the statement of one Donald O'Connell. That name, O'Connell? The sergeant had used it when he spoke of the Crossmaglen ambush.

She started to read. The man was clearly confessing to having been a member of the Belfast Brigade of the Provisional IRA. At the foot of page two, Fionulla stopped, gave a strangled sob, bit her lip and read on, the words like nails in her coffin lid.

Reasons. Location. Witnesses. Weapon. Fionulla was weeping, the tears dropping on to the Xeroxed sheet as she took each word like a tiny dart of pain. Then she dropped the paper and lay down against the unconscious form of the sergeant, praying they could both die together, that some unseen hand would pass them into the next world.

The sergeant's gun lay where it had fallen when she struck him, just feet from his body, and she stretched a hand to retrieve it. Clumsily she placed the barrel to her head and closed her eyes, remembering the waxen oval of Colm's face peeping from the shroud. She thought of the Biblical sin.

She opened her eyes, lowered the gun and wept quietly; and carried on weeping until she was drained and cold.

CHAPTER
14

The man in Whitehall uniform of black jacket, grey waistcoat, black tie, white shirt and grey striped trousers came into the room of leather armchairs and oil portraits.

'Senator Minihan?'

He turned from the fire, coffee cup poised over the saucer. The civil servant announced, 'The Secretary of State will see you now.'

Senator Minihan put cup in saucer, and both on to a polished table, then strode quickly through an opened door into an office similarly decorated.

A man as tall as himself, only stouter, with big red-veined cheeks, came out from behind a massive desk to shake his hand.

'A pleasure, Senator Minihan,' said Her Majesty's Secretary of State for Northern Ireland, although the exact reverse was true.

'News?' asked Senator Minihan, anxious to get to the point.

'Ah . . . well, yes.'

'She's safe?'

'Bear with me, Senator. One hour ago a girl who claimed to be your daughter telephoned the US Consulate in Dublin. They, in turn, and quite properly, contacted the Northern Ireland office . . .'

'*Claimed* to be . . . !'

The Secretary of State coughed his polite little politician's cough, and consulted a piece of paper.

'Do the words Washington, Jefferson, Lincoln and Harding mean anything to you? American presidents, of course, but . . .'

'Dogs, goddamnit, our spaniels when Kathleen was a kid. It's her! What did she say, where is she?'

The Secretary of State gave a small nod of his head and the civil servant left the room.

'Can we speak frankly?'

There's just the two of us, thought the Senator, why not?

'Sure.'

'It's highly embarrassing. For me, my government, perhaps for you and *your* government.'

'But Kathleen *is* safe?'

'As far as we know.' The minister lifted a silver coffee pot. 'You?'

'No thank you. What's the problem?'

'The problem is . . .' The minister with the most difficult job in the United Kingdom government's portfolio added cream, despite his doctor's advice.

'. . . she is not . . . repeat NOT, a hostage.'

'Thank God.'

'On the contrary. She seems to be acting as agent for this PIRA man McGarvey. She wishes him to enter your consulate in Dublin as a political refugee. She's seeking asylum for him.'

The Secretary of State swallowed his high-cholesterol coffee and sniffed his disapproval.

'My God,' said Senator Minihan.

'Quite. She wants to speak to you at the consulate in . . .' the minister consulted his affectation, a Timex watch he'd bought ten years before . . . 'at eight o'clock tomorrow morning.'

'I'll never make it.'

'We have a helicopter standing by in the grounds. It is at your disposal. The Irish Government has cleared it to fly into its Eire-space.' The Secretary of State laughed. 'Eire-space.'

The Senator missed the joke but understood the gesture. 'You have my gratitude, Mr Secretary.'

Minister, thought the Secretary of State. Actually, you should address me as minister, but I suppose in this situation one should not stand on the finer points of protocol.

He went back behind his desk and assumed his House of Commons stance, hands clasped behind his back, chin jutting forward. Some parliamentarians had said he looked like the young Churchill.

'You will have Her Majesty's Government's every cooperation in this matter, notwithstanding that sovereignty lies with the Irish Republic.'

There had to be more. The Senator fidgeted. 'As I've stated, my gratitude is immense. My only daughter's welfare is paramount in my wishes.'

'Quite. Absolutely. Yet I would be failing in my duty

as the minister responsible for this province of the United Kingdom if I did not point out that the man for whom your daughter seeks asylum is wanted for several murders in Northern Ireland.'

'I am aware of that.'

'And under normal circumstances, if he was arrested by the Irish Republic . . or –' the Secretary of State paused for effect – 'in the United States of America, then Her Majesty's Government would institute legal proceedings for his extradition.'

'I'm familiar with your procedures. You will be familiar with my views.'

The Secretary of State sat down behind the safety of his massive desk, and cleared his throat.

'I am authorised to say that Her Majesty's Government would take the most serious view of any decision by the US Consulate to provide asylum. We feel it would be an event without precedent.'

'I can think of many precedents.'

'May I continue, Senator? An unfriendly act by an ally, and one contrary in spirit and practice to our joint stand against international terrorism. If such asylum was granted, we would lodge the strongest possible objections in both Dublin and Washington.'

The Senator made for the door.

'If it meant saving my daughter's life or securing her safety, the IRA could have Vermont *and* Scotland.'

'Understandable sentiments, Senator Minihan. But you will not be unaware that our prime minister is on the most excellent personal terms with your president.'

Senator Minihan gripped the polished brass door knob.

'They can kiss each other's ass from here to Shanghai for all I care.'

The Secretary of State spilled his coffee, and stood up.

'There is, of course, the matter of your daughter's apparent collusion in this matter. Her extradition could also be sought.'

The Senator flung open the door.

'Try it. Do I get the helicopter?'

The Secretary of State came out from behind his desk, wondering if this Senator had any idea what it was like trying to run this place. Two sets of warm, witty, articulate, idealistic – murderous – people at loggerheads with each other.

'Above all we want no bloodshed. We are aware of your views on Northern Ireland – but we pray for your daughter's safety.'

He put out his hand; the grip was firm, and the smile genuine.

Minihan took it.

Within minutes he was launching his weary frame – he had hardly slept for three days – into the helicopter, strapping himself in and gratefully accepting the ear-defenders to blot out the din.

It was a big old Westland. Pat Minihan had first flown in one in Korea, 1951. The British were still flying them.

* * *

She heard the sergeant groan, move and groan again; saw him vainly trying to open his eyes, failing and closing them tighter, face contorted with pain.

She stroked his face gently. 'I'm sorry. I didn't mean to hurt you.'

His eyes became slits, and his mouth bared in another rictus of pain. His head bounced and echoed with a rhythmic throbbing.

'Christ, my head.'

'Lie still.'

He tried to get her into focus and his vision swam. He made a vain effort to sit up but his whole body revolted against it, and he lay back exhausted and sick. There was a deep, dark swelling across his left temple where she had struck him with the bottle, and Joe brought a hand up to feel it, winced and withdrew his searching fingers.

She was terrified that she might have fractured his skull and that he might die. Now she knew what drove him – now her loyalties had been turned topsy-turvy.

His eyes opened again.

'You were going to kill him. That's why I hit you . . .'

It all came flooding back to Joe through the blinding pain in his head. He had had McGarvey at his mercy, and now his son's killer was gone. He groaned, not from the pain this time but from inner agony, and opened his eyes to the acid light that burned his pupils.

'Where is he? Where's your brother and the girl?'

'Gone, Joe. To Dublin, I suppose.'

She had a strange look on her face; mystical, faraway,

as though some tenuous hold on reality had been relinquished. Instinctively Joe put a hand to his chest, to where the papers and pictures had been. Nothing.

She knew.

Her eyes met his, and he saw the dreadful knowledge in her eyes like the symptom of a disease. Joe felt dirty and bad. He felt he had infected her.

'I'm sorry.'

She had aged in hours, crossed from youth to adulthood like a girl expelled against her will across a frontier.

'Are you?'

'I hadn't wanted you to know.'

She shook her head. 'Why bring them? Those awful pictures and the RUC statement?'

Joe couldn't hide the guilt. It was true, he *hadn't* wanted her to know, *unless* all else failed. He had carried the package like a secret weapon, not for use on Dermot . . . but on *her*.

And she knew.

'Do you have a brother, Joe?'

'I had a son.'

She turned away and walked to the far wall, and he could see from her shoulders that she was weeping quietly. Joe groaned from his splitting head, rolled to one side and forced himself up to his knees, right hand gripping at a chair for support.

He got to his feet unsteadily.

'I must follow him – must stop him going to the consulate!'

She turned and her face terrified him: it was a rage at life.

'Let him go. Let him be gone from Ireland and his family, and may he never return.'

'No!' Joe was surprised at his own determination. 'No!'

The Irish Justice Minister and the Irish Prime Minister – the Taoiseach – stood together in the grey, silent room.

The Taoiseach was older, a convinced Republican in his younger days, an ardent supporter of overturning Union rule in the North and returning the Six Counties to Eire.

He'd done a little gun-running during the IRA campaign in the Fifties, and been a member of Sinn Fein for years, before, as he wryly put it, 'going into politics'. Age and political compromise, added to the increasing bloodshed in the North, had matured and altered him. He no longer believed it was possible – as the phrase put it – 'to bomb the Protestants into a united Ireland'.

The old songs and the old wrongs were irrelevant now. Ireland and the United Kingdom were fellow members of the European Economic Community – the so-called 'Common Market'. It was the age of the farming subsidy and the Easter Rising meant nothing to an inter-European group of parliamentarians at Strasbourg or Luxembourg.

He believed it was butter, not guns, that would solve Ireland's problems, prosperity not protest. Who would care about being out of – or in – a united Ireland if they were prosperous? He favoured *links* with the North, and closer co-operation with the British. The Taoiseach didn't understand the Provos. They weren't like the old Official IRA. There was a nasty streak of Marxism unhealthily allied with South American-style Fascism in the Provos.

Shooting Protestants in front of their families or walking home from church smacked too much of death squads in El Salvador or Argentina for the Taoiseach's liking. Down South, and thank God for it, he breathed, we've got them by the balls. They can drink and shout in Dundalk but any nonsense out of them and the Special Branch don't let their feet touch the ground.

But they were dangerous. Not for their killings and their military threat – he believed if they ever tried that in the Republic they'd be crushed. The Taoiseach knew that Ireland didn't have the moral bags and baggage the British carried. We could deal with them brutally and the world wouldn't turn a hair – just chastising our own.

No, it was the passions they were capable of unleashing. There is no steel fence between us and the North, he would tell the young TDs. If it spilled over into fire and blood up there we wouldn't be immune. The Provos were like some delinquent child of Ireland. But if the worst of all scenarios happened and the Brits *did* leave before a proper political settlement, he felt sure the South would be dragged in.

The Taoiseach had no doubt some Catholics in the North would be massacred, and no government of whatever political hue in Dublin could stand by and watch that happen. He would have to either urge quick UN intervention or order the army to cross the border. Then, unless the Protestants backed off, it would be civil war in Ireland – bloody and religious war fought with all the murderous fervour of such wars.

Like Spain, he thought, just like Spain. It haunted his dreams. Even without that worst-case scenario, the passions were dangerous enough. The Protestant para-militaries had come South on occasions, trading bomb for bomb, and innocent Catholic kids had been killed and maimed in Dublin itself.

All the beautiful, dangerous passion of Ireland threatened to boil like an unwatched cauldron, and overflow, drowning them all in its torrent of fire. And always the threat of a McGarvey to embarrass us. It was a bloody fine mess they were in now, and him the Taoiseach plonked by blood ties in the middle of it. Minihan's daughter asking for asylum for herself and a Provo. The British Minister for the North screaming blue murder down the telephone.

The Taoiseach turned.

'A monkey puzzle, Sean.'

'It is that.'

'We're sure the girl is not under duress?'

'As sure as we can be, and of course, if she was, when they got in the consulate the Marines would just chuck him out into the street.'

The Irish Prime Minister stroked his chin.

'What were Garda instructions in the matter of McGarvey?'

The Justice Minister blushed.

'As always, Taoiseach, to capture him, unhurt if possible.'

The Taoiseach saw the lowered eyes, the red cheeks. Shot during capture, was it? Who could blame them? They were all demoralised and fed up to the back teeth with these bloody Provos. McGarvey had humiliated their men at the roadblock, and he was a known killer. They would have shot him first, and explained it afterwards.

Bad for the Garda, bad for Ireland. The man McGarvey was like poison.

'What time will Minihan arrive in Dublin?'

'Any time now, Taoiseach. Coming in a British helicopter. Goes first to the consulate to speak on the telephone with his daughter, then I've asked the consul to bring him here as you requested.'

'Good.' A sudden nagging thought burst into life in the Irish Prime Minister's mind.

'Better tell the Garda to stay well away from McGarvey now until we sort this thing out one way or another.'

The Justice Minister felt that colour drain from his cheeks as quickly as it had arrived. Christ, if the bloody Garda came across him now, and if McGarvey was – shot resisting arrest – then there *would* be hell to pay.

'I'll see to it.' He left the room.

The Taoiseach sat down and thought. Can't capture him, not with the girl in tow. Can't kill him. Can't send him back over the border to the Brits – not in election year.

McGarvey was a hero in the North again. Some IRA man had gone over to the British and shopped half the Provos in Belfast. And he was the man, it now seemed, who'd betrayed McGarvey – so now the Provo was rehabilitated. All the more difficult then to send him back.

The US State Department had moved quickly – at lightning speed by its standards – and McGarvey *could* be received in the consulate.

The Taoiseach lit his pipe and sucked on it noisily. Then we *do* have a problem. It could end up like that East European cardinal who sought refuge in the American Embassy for God alone knows how many years.

The Brits would be over with their extradition papers neatly signed and everything in order – they'd learned their lessons the hard way on that. Sinn Fein would picket the consulate in support, half the world's press would be there.

A viper held close to the bosom.

Best to be rid of him, somehow, get shot altogether and damn the future political consequences. The opposition would never forgive the blood tie, but what could he have done anyway?

They called Minihan 'Ireland's Best Friend', and

dammit all, hadn't he been just that over the years? There was heavy American investment in the offing, Common Market or no, and they *needed* Minihan's support and influence.

The Taoiseach blew instead of sucked, and the pipe bubbled and smoked. He cursed gently. Can't keep McGarvey, but can't seem to be rid of him. The thought of him riding in triumph through Dublin to the Elgin Street consultate, TV crews monitoring every mile. God, it's more than I can bear.

The Justice Minister came in and wrinkled his nose at the pungent wet smell of the boss's pipe.

'It's going out to all units.'

'Sean, I've had a thought. Get the head of Aer Lingus over here.'

'Taoiseach, at *this* time?' He lifted his wristwatch.

'Wake him up if you have to – send a car, I want him *here*.'

Aer Lingus was the Irish international airline. It owned or leased several Boeing 747s, and ran a scheduled service between Shannon on the west coast of Ireland, and the east coast of the United States.

'Ah . . .' The Justice Minister was beginning to see.

The Taoiseach said, 'Mr McGarvey is Belfast-born, am I right?' The Justice Minister nodded. 'Which makes him a citizen of the United Kingdom of Great Britain and Northern Ireland.'

'And the girl,' proffered the Justice Minister, 'is a United States' citizen.' He followed the Taoiseach's eyes. Which meant they were both aliens. They were also both guilty, *prima facie*, of several criminal offences. So if the Irish Government wanted neither in its country it had a perfect right to . . .

'We deport them, Taoiseach!'

'We do indeed, we do indeed. And I think the logical place to deport them *to*, under the circumstances and all, would be the United States of America. Wouldn't you say so, Sean?'

The Justice Minister agreed, and began to realise why this man had the top job, and he did not.

It was a windswept country road with little traffic, just the odd car or tractor-pulled farm cart. The telephone kiosk with its Gaelic sign – Telefon – stood out like a Martian intruder.

Kathleen dialled the number, coins clunking in her hand as she shook them nervously, aware of the press of Dermot's body beside her, their breaths misting the panes of glass.

'United States Consulate.'

'This is Kathleen Minihan for Senator Minihan.'

'Hold please, Miss Minihan.'

'Kathleen!'

Her father. Relief flooded through her, a gush of it, a release from the anxiety and stress of the tumultuous events of recent days.

Dad would make it right.

'You OK, Kathleen?'

'Dad, I'm great. Just the sound of your voice . . .'

'Not hurt? Not sick?'

'No, Dad, I swear I'm fine.'

'Where are you?'

'Just the other side of –' She felt Dermot's fingers pressing into her and saw his shaking head.

'Dad, I don't want to say. Your line might not be secure, there are people who want to kill Dermot.'

Senator Minihan asked firmly, 'Don't want to – or can't? Are you held against your will, Kathleen?'

'I'm here because I *want* to be here. You have my word.'

'This man you're with is a killer.'

'He's a patriot. How many times have you said that to me back home?'

And she was right, Senator Minihan thought. But back home it was all so – damn, he hated to say it, but – *glamorous*. Here it was grubby and real.

He got down to business.

'The consulate will take this man . . .'

He heard the amplified whoops of joy. My God, how deep was she in with this man? Were they lovers? My daughter sleeping with a – he felt 'killer', but had to concede 'patriot'.

'Don't move for the time being. The Irish Prime Minister is seeing me in half an hour. He thinks he has an easier solution to this.'

'Hold a second, Dad.' Kathleen put her hand over the mouthpiece. Dermot said, 'He wouldn't stitch us, would he?' She shook her head. 'Not Dad. It'll be OK, believe me.'

'OK, Dad, sorry.'

'The Irish police have been told to *leave you completely alone*. Do you understand that? I need the licence plates, colour and make of your car, that way there can be no slip-ups.'

Dermot, who had his ear next to Kathleen's on the telephone, put his hand over the mouthpiece, and said, 'Or with that information they could take us out. Take *me* out.'

Kathleen pushed his hand away. 'Dad. Can you *trust* them?'

'I'm telling you they wouldn't dare.'

She wiped away condensation from one of the small panes of glass with the palm of her hand and read off a letter, three numbers, and three more letters.

'Got it.'

'It's a – what the hell is it, Dermot?' He whispered in her ear, she repeated, 'a Maxi made by Austin. It's pale blue, kind of turquoise.'

'Got it.'

'What now, Dad?'

'Call me on this number –' he read out a direct line number – 'two hours from now, after I've seen the Prime Minister. And *don't* move!'

Two hours and one minute later she emerged from the same kiosk and got in the car.

'Well?'

'Do you know where Shannon Airport is?'

'Sure I do, about two hours' drive from here, we'd

have to go back part of the way we've already come.'

She smiled. It was so, so simple.

'Dermot, we're being deported. Both of us. We have a safe conduct to Shannon Airport, a guarantee that we will not be impeded in any way. And we have two tickets on the 5 p.m. Aer Lingus 747 to Kennedy.'

'New York!' Dermot let out a whoop. 'Christ, but I don't have a passport – a visa, anything.'

'Forget it, Dad has squared it. We're being *deported* and you'll be issued with a temporary stay visa when we arrive in New York.'

It was breathtaking, and breathtakingly simple. Dermot looked out at Ireland. He was leaving it, but it was like a fairy tale come true. No more killing now, no more running and hiding, sleeping in different beds, looking over your shoulder for the Brits.

'America.' He said the word like a prayer.

And when he was there he could send for Nulla, Mum and Dad, for . . . No, he couldn't send for Colm.

Just as long as Nulla came. He could make it all up to her, and one day she would understand. And if she was in America, that dreadful germ of knowledge, the truth of Colm's death, could never reach her. He looked wonderingly at Kathleen.

'I'm bloody well going to America.'

The man with the long rifle in its leather carrying case joined the others at the edge of the trees where they had been keeping watch on the cottage.

The car parked outside was the one the American girl had been driving when she'd disappeared, and that was enough for them to have their Uzis ready. McGarvey was a known killer and if he *was* still in the cottage he was coming out feet first. The men in the Garda Siochana were fed up with being humiliated by the Provos – running free in Dundalk like they owned the town – and they weren't standing for it any more.

The oldest of the men there had been in the Garda for twenty-odd years and he'd never known it at such a low ebb. What the Provos did up North was their business, but when they came South, taking hostages and stealing Garda weapons at checkpoints, well that was *our* business, thought the man.

He's in there, *if* he is – with a fully loaded sub machinegun capable of cutting a man into two pieces.

The marksman asked, 'Any movement?'

The veteran shook his head. 'Quiet as the grave. They could be sleeping, only came light . . .' he glanced at his watch . . . 'about half an hour ago. Bring the radio?'

The marksman nodded and slipped the personal radio out of his waterproof jacket. The veteran cradled his own Uzi, took the radio, set its frequency and switched on, careful to keep the volume at its lowest point.

The rifleman settled down, took his gun out of its case. The weapon was a lovingly polished thing of wood and dark gun-metal, oiled and shining. He fixed on a telescopic sight and started making adjustments.

'Girl there as well . . . ?' He spoke out of the corner

of his mouth, his eye on the lens of the scope.

'Don't know.'

'He's got a weapon, right?'

'Uzi. Took it off that stupid sod near the border.'

'Don't worry . . .' The man looked up from the scope, one eye closed, squinted with the other, then put it back on the ground glass. 'Won't get near enough to use it.'

'What did they tell you when you left Galway?'

The marksman didn't reply.

'Hit him?' the veteran asked.

The man looked up from his scope, as though annoyed at being interrupted in an engrossing card game.

'Unless you'd prefer him to get close enough to use that little tommy gun of his?'

The veteran Garda pulled his face in comprehension, and said, 'Fine by me, I don't want to play Gunfight at the OK Corral.'

At his side the radio crackled softly like subdued applause at the cynicism of the decision and his easy acquiescence.

Joe felt very groggy.

'Did he take my pistol?'

She shook her head numbly. 'No. He still has the machine gun.'

Joe swung round, feeling the room tilt and some kind of spirit bubble race to one side of his head. He put out a hand to steady himself and Fionulla took it.

'Are you OK?'

'I'm fine – there . . .' He saw the gun lying beneath the table where it must have fallen when the girl struck him.

He lowered himself clumsily to his knees and retrieved it.

She said, 'You don't need it. He and the girl will be half way to Dublin by now.'

Joe ignored her, put the gun in his waistband – and realised his foolishness. A gun like that should be holstered, but tucked as it was, if there *was* an accident, it would blow his balls and appendage off!

He looked at the girl, and her image was fuzzy.

'Remember what I said, before you tried to bash my bloody brains in? His options are, either he goes to Belfast for trial – or the nearest Garda station, I'm not fussy – or he's dead. I don't bloody care any more.'

She looked unbearably sad.

'I don't believe you'd do it.'

'Watch me.' He swayed, buckled, and she caught him, supporting his sagging body. He felt awful.

'You're hurt, Joe, please go to a hospital. You'll never catch Dermot now.'

Joe regained his feet and said, 'Yes – I *will*. He's not going to go to the consulate and sneak off to bloody Yank-land. He's for trial. For David, for all of them – all the innocents he's slaughtered.'

The impact of his words was magnified a thousand times in her mind now she knew the dreadful truth, and he saw the deep wince of pain as he spoke.

Somehow he couldn't bring himself to feel pity for

her at that moment. If Dermot escaped into sanctuary *she'd* be to blame. He only wished now that he'd gone for the jugular straight away, taken off the gloves, shown her the pictures and the damning police statement *before* they confronted McGarvey.

He glanced out of the window. The hire car the girl had been driving, the Ford Orion, was still there. But that would be no use because although McGarvey would have taken Joe's car – less easy for the Garda to identify – he could have either immobilised the Orion, or taken the keys.

Joe said, 'How can we get to Dublin? Quickly! How?'

She found her bag and rummaged in it, producing the keys.

Joe was astonished. 'Why?'

She shrugged. 'It was so I could take you to hospital – if you were badly injured.'

Joe thought, McGarvey is going soft. It's a wonder he didn't put a bullet in me while he had the chance.

He took the keys from Fionulla's hand, feeling the babylike instinctive touch of the fingers, grasping for some human support in the alien world of treachery and death into which she had suddenly been plunged. He held on to the fingers.

'Miss McGarvey, the nuns taught you right from wrong?'

'Yes.'

'Then come with me. *Help* me, properly this time, now that you know.'

She started to weep. 'Why, Joe? How could he do it?

His own brother.'

He pulled her towards him.

'I don't know, little girl, I don't know.'

She looked up, face streaked with tears. 'You'll kill him, though. Deep down that's what you want to do.'

And perhaps deep down it was. Perhaps it was what he *had* always wanted to do. Perhaps the rest was some veneer of civilisation he had hastily and psychologically painted over his real self's surface.

'Perhaps I do. Perhaps *you* do now?'

She wrapped her arms around him, like a little girl to her father, just as David had done when he was a little boy and Joe had come home on leave and David had seen him at the end of the street and run, leaping into his father's arms and holding on tight, tight.

Joe closed his eyes, seeing David run down the broken pavements of the council estate.

The whole thing was *unbearable*.

He pushed her back gently. 'Come on, love, let's go and find him. I don't think I could kill anybody now.'

'Movement inside.'

The marksman said it without taking his eye from the telescopic sight.

The men all tensed and reached for their weapons, or clung more tightly to the ones they held.

'A figure, could've been a man. Yes. See him. Man. Talking to . . . see his mouth working . . . ah . . . ah . . . girl . . .'

There was a tiny burst from the radio, a voice, giving their call sign. The men ignored it, transfixed by the potential danger from the cottage.

The radio crackled. 'Come in.'

'Door opening . . .'

'Ready, lads.'

'Come in.' The tiny, tinny, insistent voice of the radio.

'Fucking thing...' The Uzi man put the radio up to his ear. 'Can't read you. Over.'

A man's face emerged from the cottage and into the circle and cross-hairs of the telescopic sight.

'Here he is . . .' Everyone was stiff and tense. 'Girl's blocking a clear shot – he's armed – pistol, see the butt sticking out of his jacket.'

The radio's insistent voice burst against the veteran Garda man's ears. He took the 'over' and whispered urgently, 'We have McGarvey and the girl coming out. I repeat, *coming out*. Do you read me? Over.'

The marksman was totally relaxed. Once the girl went to her car door, it was a clear shot to McGarvey.

'Moving to the car. She's still blocking him.'

The man said to the radio, '*Affirmative*. McGarvey. Repeat the message, you are not clear. Over.'

The marksman saw the girl move out of the scope's vision, and the man come round the body of the car, to the bonnet, one second, two, three, and he was a clear torso shot . . . Hairlines centred on his victim's chest, the marksman's finger tightened on the trigger.

Clear shot. Now!

'No . . . !' The policeman dropped the radio and dived at his colleague. 'No . . . !'

The sound of the shot was like an axe hitting bark, a crisp crack shattering the woodland silence.

The Taoiseach shook Senator Minihan's hand, and the American said, 'You have my eternal and deep gratitude.'

The Irishman smiled. 'You've been a true friend to us over the years.'

'I see a "but" there in your eyes.'

The Taoiseach acknowledged it. '. . . *But* I will also have the wrath of the British minister responsible for the Northern counties. He has – even as your helicopter was in the air – telephoned me to ask for my assurance that this man will not be given asylum.'

The Taoiseach beckoned Senator Minihan to a seat, which the American took gratefully.

'I hope you told him to keep the hell out of Irish affairs.'

'Senator,' the Taoiseach's face was stern, 'Ireland is a part of the British Isles. We don't have the *cordon sanitaire* of the Atlantic to protect us from the madness that sometimes goes on here.'

'So what *did* you tell him?'

'I told him that I had every respect for Her Majesty's Government's point of view in this matter, but that I had *not* repeat *not* committed the government of the

Irish Republic to any course of action on this matter.'

'Although you have . . . ?' said Minihan, quizzically.

'Not on the matter of asylum – in a manner of speaking.'

The Senator thought, you crafty old fox.

'But I did more than hint to the minister that I felt it unlikely McGarvey would get asylum, and that the man would not be welcome to stay.'

Minihan smiled broadly. 'Which he will think means you'll drive this IRA man up to the border and hand him over to the Royal Ulster Constabulary.' The smiled clouded a fraction. 'Because, of course, you've done it before.'

The Taoiseach met his eyes. 'With good reason – and will do so again when the occasion and the law demands it. On this occasion the British – who already think us a little stupid – will forgive us if we don't make our meaning fully clear.'

Minihan said, 'We've had our differences in the past, over the North . . .'

'You don't live here, Pat . . .' The Senator noted the familiar. 'You might feel differently.'

'Perhaps, Michael, but I've always respected you.'

The Taoiseach thought, just let it end peacefully, this bad, shameful, dirty business, and with some good for Ireland.

'And it was for you, Pat, you and Kathleen and your family – not for this man McGarvey. You and America are welcome to him.'

The Senator got up and hugged him, a big, bear-like,

crushing hug. 'Michael, I promise you. We'll never forget it, Kathleen or me.'

The Taoiseach was red with embarrassment and lack of breath. 'Will you be after breaking my ribs, Pat? It was nothing. Was your father not my father's brother?'

Joe felt the heat of the bullet's passage, its air displacement, and heard the whiplash sound, in one simultaneous shock of the senses.

Down, Joe, down. Where's the girl? Confusion, wondering who and why. Not McGarvey, surely, long gone?

'Down . . . get bloody down.'

It was madness, why would he come back? Brain coming together. That was a rifle shot, a deep, distinctive crack. An Uzi firer would let go a burst, or at least a series of rapid shots.

He could see Fionulla crouching near the back wheel, white and terrified. Joe tried to peer round the front of the bonnet without exposing any of his head or body for another bullet. He didn't know what the hell was going on.

There was a movement at the edge of the woods, the fluttering of something white, a handkerchief perhaps? And a man's voice shouting. Joe cupped a hand to his ear. The man called again.

'Hold your fire.'

Joe waited. He saw the figure grow larger, frantically waving the handkerchief with one hand, his other arm held wide from his body, presumably to show he was not holding a weapon.

When Joe felt he was near enough he shouted, 'Hold it there.'

The Browning was in Joe's hand, his palm felt sweaty on the butt, and his head was throbbing with pain. He knew his eyesight was normally good, but he could not make out the man's features distinctively.

The man shouted, and Joe could make out the words distinctly. 'I'm Detective Superintendent Michael Collins of the Garda Siochana.'

Joe felt a cold shiver pass over him. In deep trouble now. Couldn't shoot or talk your way out of this one. Irish fucking police, him a British soldier, armed, on their territory; political ructions, Joe kicked out of the army. But worst of all that murdering bastard McGarvey with his feet up in the consulate. Shit. Shit. He looked around. No way out. The Irish police . . . Christ and double Christ.

'Can you hear me?'

'I hear you,' Joe shouted.

'Listen carefully, Mr McGarvey.'

McGarvey? McGarvey! He thinks I'm McGarvey, and the girl is . . . Good God, no wonder they fired at me.

And a voice in his head said, Keep it shut, Joe, keep your lip buttoned tight until you know what is going on.

He looked quickly, saw the incomprehension on the girl's face, and put a finger from his gun-free hand to his lips. She nodded.

'The shot was an accident. Do you understand me – an *accident*! We have orders not, I repeat not, to molest or interfere with you in any way. That comes from the Prime Minister of Ireland. Do you understand?'

Joe grimaced at the treachery and the devious delight of it all. He shouted back in as neutral a voice as he could muster, 'Yes, I understand.'

'You have safe passage to Shannon Airport, I repeat Shannon Airport, for your flight to the United States . . .'

Shannon *Airport*. Shannon, flight to America, not the consulate and a series of diplomatic and political wrangles. No, you crafty Irish bastards, get them out of the country quickly. He felt the anger surge in him.

The man turned and walked quickly back to the woods, and Joe waited. The girl was looking at him. It couldn't be a trap, the Garda were known to be trigger-happy, and no Ford Orion would stop bullets for very long.

Joe put a hand to his head and squeezed, trying to somehow ease the pain that raged through him. Now all they had to do was get to Shannon before McGarvey and the girl.

It was pride now. The sodding Micks and the Yanks thought they'd got it nicely sorted out between them, and McGarvey thought he was going to live happily ever after with the American bird in Never-Never Land. And they were all wrong, Joe thought. Fuck Washington and our allies, fuck the Micks in Dublin, fuck them in Westminster and Lisburn, fuck the army, and . . . the pain seared the back of his eyes.

Because I don't care any more. The Man, the sodding puky little Man was going back.

Joe had never been more sure of *anything*. The awful

pain that seemed to split his skull gave him a feeling of incredible euphoria. And he had a free passage to Shannon, courtesy of the Garda Siochana.

The Lynx helicopter of the Irish Army whopp-whopped over the green countryside with its two passengers, United States Senator Patrick Minihan, and Republic of Ireland Justice Minister Cathal Davies.

It amused them in the Dail, that, an Irishman called Davies, and he would laboriously trace his ancestry to the Gower Peninsula of Wales and proclaim, 'And aren't we all Celts, the lot of us?'

It was a mess, the Justice Minister knew that. The whole of bloody Ireland was compromised by its history, the strands of the tragic past wrapping them in some Celtic Gordian knot that was impossible to unravel. And when some tried – as they frequently did – to cut through it Alexander the Great style, there was just bloodshed and corpses.

McGarvey should be in a prison, confined for what he'd done, not sitting in the first-class cabin of an Aer Lingus 747 sipping champagne, which is where they'd allow him to be in a few hours' time.

He had no love for the dour-faced Protestants of the North, but he was no Marxist either, and he was pretty sure he knew what the Provos were about. If they got their way in the North it would be the South's turn after that.

Cathal Davies wondered what his own position was. McGarvey had made an ass of the Garda.

The last thing that dispirited, under-paid, under-budgeted force needed was some folk hero from the North coming down and taking their guns from under their very noses. But then to see him spirited away in style with the Justice Minister's connivance, God, it was all too awful to think about.

The Taoiseach owes me for this, the Justice Minister thought fiercely. If we win, damn it, *when* we win the election I'll have another portfolio – Agriculture – then perhaps I'll get some of those trips to Strasbourg and Brussels.

He was lost in his thoughts, and beside him Senator Minihan watched the countryside of his birth and of his blood flow beneath him like an unfolding carpet. He'd had to make some anxious telephone calls; call in debts, badger, plead, cajole, pull strings, and make rash promises, using every ounce of his political pull and reputation to get the State Department approval for McGarvey's entry.

The British were fanatical about IRA men taking refuge in the US and the Brits had more pull on Capitol Hill than they deserved given their reduced power, influence, and economic status in the world.

Thank God for the primaries. He and the President were on opposite sides, but the old man would never risk losing millions of Irish-American votes, and he *wanted* that second term.

The Senator was quite clear now why *he'd* done it. Not for Ireland, not for memories, not for political allegiances or long-held beliefs. He'd done it for his daughter. He did not know, did not even want to know what might be happening between her and McGarvey. It was enough that this was her crisis, and her life had been – whatever she might think in the future – in danger. She was playing with vipers right down there in the pit, and he had hauled her out before she was bitten. That simple.

He'd shackled her with *his* history, and *his* beliefs. If he hadn't, she wouldn't be in Ireland now, wouldn't be helping this IRA man. He had reared her on his shamrock tales, and now she had found herself a Shamrock Boy to bring them alive.

That's what they'd called them when he was a lad. Shamrock Boys, or Blarney Boys. Irish lads with their heads full of myth and romance, their hearts filled with a love of Ireland and a hatred of those they thought had done Ireland wrong.

He'd been a Shamrock Boy himself once, that's what his sister Kathleen had said. A hooligan from the street corner anxious only to be a martyr for his country. She had seen it, seen the green on him like a rash, and sent him away so the Shamrock Boy could *live* for his former country, not *die* for it.

Now the seed of his body was made flesh, grown and beautiful, and she'd inherited the germ from him, and found her own Shamrock Boy.

It seemed like a divine and cruel justice.

CHAPTER

15

For Joe there was just the road now.

He no longer felt the presence of Fionulla in the seat next to him, couldn't sense or hear her tiny gasps of fear as he drove and cornered at alarming speeds.

Everything in him was focused like a laser, the beam fuelled by a pain that pressed down on his skull and emerged white hot from his eyes.

All his life and purpose was in these moments. There was the road, the wheel, the determination and the gripping pain, vice-like on his skull, and those things circumscribed his shrunken world.

To Fionulla McGarvey Joe's face looked distorted, almost demonic, and it terrified her. She felt in some way that she had unleashed him. She could have hidden the keys, or lied, or shouted to the policeman that Joe was not her brother, that he was a British soldier.

In the latter case he would have been arrested, she could have seen that there was no bloodshed, and Joe would have been sent back to the North.

But in her grief and confusion she had done nothing; just followed. She felt like the prisoner of some wild roller-coaster, powerless to do anything but hang on and pray for survival.

The Orion groaned and screamed as Joe thrashed

through the gears, breasted a small rise, with a heavy thunk as the car sank on its suspension, and then a screech of rubber as he threw it protesting through a tight 'S' bend.

If her world had been shattered into fragments, the only thing to do seemed to be to hang on to what was left. And strangely now the only thing that seemed to be left was the crazed, injured British sergeant.

Kathleen climbed back in the car.

'Managed to call three. Two have got crews within striking distance, who can be at Shannon within the hour, the other will try and get a crew over by private plane from London.'

'It's the right thing?'

'Believe me, I know what I'm doing. Plus I called the British Press Association. When I was in London I met the editor of *The Times*, and I got a little rundown on newspapers. This Press Association is like the UPI or AP in America, they'll put it out on the wires to all the British Isles' newspapers.'

'So . . . ?' asked Dermot.

'So, when we finally get to Shannon the world media will be there.'

'Who gives a fuck for the press?' Dermot said with unnecessary harshness.

'You do. Look, my Dad wouldn't be party to any trick, I said that, right? But just in case anyone in the Irish Government or police tries to take the law into their own hands . . . well, we have a lot of witnesses.'

Dermot started the engine of the Maxi. 'I hope you're right.'

'I *know* I'm right. You're going to be on prime-time television.'

Dermot knew the power of TV. In the early days when he was just a kid, he knew how to get the cameras there by throwing a few stones or telling the journalists there was going to be a riot. That way the crews came, and the lads obliged with an orgy of stone-throwing and one or two Molotov cocktails. The crew got their film, the Brits got a hammering, and the lads got their riot.

Everyone happy.

If the media could stop someone taking a pot-shot at him at Shannon, then that was fine by Dermot, but somehow the thought of being visible, *exposed*, frightened him.

She said, 'How far now?'

'About twenty-five miles.'

'Well, when you find some clear countryside, pull over for a while. We've got hours yet, and I'd sooner the TV people and reporters get there before we do.'

He found a piece of open road, a farm track, and a spot along it where they could not be seen from the road. He stopped the car.

Kathleen began to fiddle about beneath her seat.

'Do the seats on these British cars recline?' She found a lever. 'Yes they do.'

He looked at her in astonishment. 'Are you tired?'

She gave him a my-God-you're-naive-look and replied, 'No, Dermot, I'm not sleepy.'

She put both her hands behind his neck and pulled him down on top of her, kissing him fiercely, her tongue seeking his.

'Christ, Kathleen, suppose a farmer comes or something?'

'Then he'll wonder what he's been missing all his life.'

She pulled her sweater over her head and peeled it off. Beneath the cups of the bodice, Dermot could see her full breasts, and the sensuality of the moment stiffened him.

He said, 'This is a crazy bloody time to be doing this.'

Her voice was husky with desire. 'It's just the beginning.'

Dermot slipped the thin straps from her shoulders and began to fully undress her. Then she pulled at his clothes, urgently, tugging impatiently, him helping, all the awkwardness of undressing in a confined space, with the imperative of needed sex at the end of it.

He was surprised at his own desire. They kissed again, and he climbed awkwardly from the driver's seat until he was astride her. He kissed her, his head on the back of her seat, his hands stroking and kneading her breasts.

'No, Dermot. Do it – please! Do it now. I want you inside me.'

He entered her, silky smooth, a moment of calm as she gave a deep sigh of satisfaction, then he was thrusting into her, and she moved wildly but rhythmically beneath him.

Her nails dug into his back until he had to bite his lip not to cry out. He glimpsed her face, saw a passion and a look of desire and pain that frightened him.

She clung to him as he made love to her, and he felt as though he were being swallowed. He felt bound in a spider's web, entrapped and entombed. There was a nightmare moment of claustrophobia like he had experienced escaping through the drainage tunnel. He felt she might consume him like a tarantula devouring its mate.

Before – with the women who had shared his bed – Dermot had been the master. They lay beneath the Man, grateful and submissive, and took what was on offer, asked for no more, and pleasured him when he felt the moment had come.

But this was different, so different from anything that had gone before. Dermot had been summoned to the royal court, and was being used, the scent of death and danger that hung about him was like some perfumed aphrodisiac for his mistress.

He closed his eyes, wondering how his body could feel so much desire, his mind so little.

At length it was over, and the girl subsided beneath him like an angry sea quieted. Dermot closed his eyes and tried to look into the future.

But could see only blackness.

*   *   *

It was genuine now, Dermot knew that. He had seen several Garda patrol cars parked discreetly off the road, and none had made any attempt to follow or intercept him. No doubt they had radioed the car's progress, and Dermot wondered idly if they would realise it was a vehicle owned by the British Army.

There was a nice irony in that for him, that his transport to freedom should have been provided by his enemies.

He slowed to a crawl as the car came up behind a farm tractor on the outskirts of a moderate-sized village, the giant tyres leaving clods of earth like a snail's track behind it. A roundabout came up – left for Shannon, Dermot noted – and he breathed a sigh of relief as the tractor moved its dirty trail off to the road heading right.

He signalled left, moved off, instinctively checking his mirror, and saw it, like some avenging fighter diving from the sun.

A Ford Orion, headlights blazing, growing larger by the second in the mirror's small frame. Dermot swore under his breath.

So it wasn't over yet.

Joe saw the car, and felt the exultation rise in him. His head was splitting, his forehead throbbing like an extra heart, but he knew that there was no going back on what he had to do. It was him or it was McGarvey, it had come to that now, and the women were irrelevant bystanders.

He punched the gear lever into third with an

answering scream of revs, roared past a delivery van, and slid the car left around the roundabout after McGarvey.

Joe knew the Maxi; it was a typical family car, no guts, no punch, and it was clapped-out from abuse by service drivers who didn't give a toss how it was when they left it.

The Orion, on the other hand, was more powerful, regularly serviced – and newer. But McGarvey was trying, flattening the accelerator, a plume of blue smoke curling from the exhaust.

Joe gripped the steering wheel viciously. It was no contest, he knew that.

Dermot said, 'We've got the Brit with us.'

Kathleen whipped her head round to peer through the rear window.

'How? How! That's *my* car.'

Dermot was grim-faced.

'I'm going bloody soft. Nulla was supposed to take the bastard to hospital. I should've made sure of him when I had the chance.'

His foot was flat on the floor, whipping every ounce of speed from the Maxi. Christ, Dermot, will you be after killing yourself with your foolishness?

They never give up, these Brits, never know when they're bloody beaten. Their whole history is littered with it. Bulldog is right for them, they get their teeth in, and never let go. But when they were dead, then . . .

'Can't you lose him?'

'Not in this junk.'

Dermot put his hand under his seat, feeling for the Uzi. Kathleen saw the movement and cried out, 'No . . . Dermot. You'll ruin everything. You can't do it, you know you can't.'

'And how am I supposed to be stopping him?'

She didn't have time to answer because as Dermot glanced back over his shoulder, momentarily taking his eyes off the road, suddenly a figure was stepping from the pavement, oblivious to the danger.

An old man, flat cap, stick . . . dog on a piece of string.

Kathleen screamed short. Dermot whipped round, saw the man, and braked. There was a squeal of brakes, a stench of scorched rubber, but there was no time.

He jerked the wheel, there was a bang as they hit the kerb and the tyres exploded, then a crunch of metal and a splintering of glass.

Joe saw it happen, heard Fionulla's gasp of horror, then slid the Orion into a skidding stop.

Men were spilling out of a nearby pub, alarmed by the sound, glasses in hand, rough, red-cheeked and weatherbeaten men in collarless shirts.

A group of men came out from a partly finished house, still holding the tools of their trade: hammers, saws, a mortar trowel.

Joe saw first McGarvey, then the American girl, stagger groggily from the crashed car. Joe was out in an instant, the

Browning up and cocked, levelled at the IRA man.

Nulla screamed, 'Joe – don't – *please*!'

'McGarvey!' Joe's voice was rock steady.

The drinkers took a pace back, frightened by the gun, but the building workers just watched, quietly.

'You're going back, McGarvey.'

The IRA man was bleeding, a splash of red on his forehead; the American girl was holding her left arm, and her face was white.

McGarvey shook his head.

'It's America I'm going to . . . Brit!'

'Lie down on your face . . . DO IT!'

And again that urge, to press the trigger, one, two, three, four, feel the automatic buck, see the gouts erupt on McGarvey's chest, this killer of his son.

'Lie down!'

McGarvey turned to the crowd.

'I'm a Republican, I've been given safe conduct to Shannon by the Irish Government . . .'

'Shut up . . .'

'He's a British agent, an SAS killer.'

Joe heard the crowd growl like some animal, and he swivelled the pistol, first to the drinkers, back to McGarvey, and on to the building workers.

'Stay back. I have enough here for all of you.'

And the voice, the Englishness of it, echoed back to him through the steam-hammer noises in his skull. Why couldn't they understand? It was not their fight. None of them, just him and McGarvey.

But the IRA man was shouting to the crowd.

'I'm from the North, a Volunteer. Done with it now. I'm going to America with the girl. Don't let him take me.'

The crowd's growl was deeper, and a man shouted something Joe couldn't make out.

One of the building workers, a man with a claw hammer, moved several paces closer. Joe swivelled, feeling the brains rock in his head.

'Not one more.' The man stopped, but made no attempt to retreat.

The pistol back on McGarvey.

'He's a killer,' Joe shouted, 'he killed my son.'

'A British lie,' McGarvey addressed the crowd.

'Not a patriot – a killer.'

Joe heard voices and feet hitting the road behind him to his left. He turned and saw the advancing men stop and shrink back.

'I'm *telling* you – stay back.'

He saw Fionulla at the corner of his now-blurred vision.

'Get back in the car, Joe, they'll kill you.'

Joe wavered, felt the pain and the danger, then steadied himself. 'Your last warning, McGarvey.'

The IRA man shouted back, 'Use it, Brit – gun down an unarmed man, it's your style.'

Joe's skull was crushing him, snapping like pincers at his eyes. He knew he was losing it, all of it.

He heard the American girl's voice, trembling with pain. She was talking, not to Joe, but to the crowd. 'He's through with violence, it's true what he says. He had a gun, but he would not use it.'

The man with the claw hammer took two steps. Joe raised the gun skywards and fired. Everyone ducked, there were cries of fear, and some of the crowd scattered for cover. But those who had moved a few paces reformed and straightened their backs.

Fionulla screamed, 'Please, Joe, in the name of God.'

But Joe was in his own world, a world of sharks circling his lonely raft, and all he could see were the predators, their fins, and he clung to his weapon like a saviour.

'Just a warning shot,' he shouted. 'This man is a fugitive, wanted for murder in Northern Ireland.'

One of the drinkers called out, 'We know about British justice – shoot to kill is it, now?'

Joe knew that if McGarvey didn't move soon, the chance was gone, and the mob would probably beat him to a pulp.

'*Now*, McGarvey –'

Joe gave a long, agonising scream as the claw hammer shattered his arm and the pistol clattered to the pavement. Then they were on him like merciless baboons.

A fist flush in his face, eyes exploding, skull seeming to stretch with the vicious tear of pain. Kicks, punches, hands pulling and gouging at his clothes and his flesh; unbearable agony from his arm.

He screamed again as a hand grabbed his shattered

arm. Kicks and a burst of agony in his legs. He was going under, swamped by a human sea, an ocean of a thousand vengeful hands and feet.

For a split second he glimpsed Fionulla's terrified face on the edge of the mob, pulling at a man, then Joe was down, plunging into the cavern they had dug for him.

There was a sickening crack as a boot hit his nose, he choked on blood, spat it out in a glutinous red-black gob . . . then there was a flash of intense red and yellow as a boot stamped hard on his head. He glimpsed something metal and shiny come through the waving sea of disjointed hands, through the stench of beer and sweat, through the morass of soiled clothes and drink-sodden faces.

The edge of the mortar trowel caught his skull and he felt as though the top of his head had been sliced off like a boiled egg. He clawed with his good hand, in some vain belief that if only he could put a hand on the car door, he could hoist himself into the driver's seat and somehow escape the mob.

A nailed boot came down and crushed the fingers of his left hand, and he felt them break like some distant event. There was the sound of someone crying and pleading for mercy, and Joe realised with astonishment that it was he. But nothing stopped.

Something hit him viciously in the groin, and the desperate pain seemed to flee from his other extremities and concentrate in some joyless celebration of agony there, between his legs.

Hams of knuckles crashing into him. He saw a patch of blue sky, and watched it turn to black as a pick-axe handle lifted, and fell, smashing his kneecap.

After that he was more of a spectator to it all. The blows fell with increasing rapidity like a shower of rain that has turned into a torrent.

Joe could feel them, but eventually they landed with no more pain. All his nerve endings, the receptacles of agony, seemed to be concentrated in his head now.

Through the forest of faces Joe saw that of McGarvey, the face of his nightmares. Joe knew what he must do. He must get up, shrug off his attackers, take McGarvey by the scruff of the neck, and walk him back to Belfast.

But his body seemed to belong to someone else now, and although he tried to concentrate all his efforts on standing, nothing seemed to obey. And then the fuse that had been slowly burning in his skull reached the powder keg, and the explosion gave birth to a new universe.

Joe was a planet, a projectile hurled out into the blackness, soaring with amazing speed into infinity.

And at last the pain stopped.

The Justice Minister took Senator Minihan to one side in the small office that belonged to the Shannon Airport Operations Manager.

'There's been an incident . . .'

Minihan gripped his arm. 'What?'

'We've just got the first Garda report in. Someone

tried to arrest McGarvey at gunpoint – it seems this was a British undercover agent.'

'Good Christ.'

'Your daughter is unhurt apart from a bruised arm – their car crashed – she and McGarvey are on their way here *now* in a patrol car.'

Senator Minihan ran a hand through his hair.

'The British have got a bloody nerve. Was he armed, this man?'

The Justice Minister nodded. 'Yes he was – a serious business.'

'Put the sonofabitch on trial.'

The Justice Minister shook his head.

'He'll be going back to the North. You can't put a dead man on trial.'

Fionulla sat in the small chapel of rest at the rear of the undertaker's office, her body drained of weeping.

Joe's body lay beyond the glass window, covered in a white sheet, below the crucifix, flanked by burning candles.

It seemed that all her life it had been funerals and wakes, graveyards and masses for the departed.

She had grown to like the sergeant. He had seemed to be honest and decent by his own lights, and for a while he had seemed to offer the only hope of saving Dermot.

Fionulla blamed herself. She must have hurt him grievously when she struck him, and she had allowed him to follow his crazed pursuit of her brother. She had been powerless to stop the mob. Perhaps if he had not had the gun, perhaps if he had not fired it, perhaps if he had not been English.

Ireland was sensitive and afraid: of agents, of assassination squads and sectarian killers.

She looked through the glass at the covered shape. Holy Mother. Is this what it meant to be Irish? To kill in hate and hot blood? Are our passions incapable of taming?

The sergeant's belongings, including his pistol and wallet, lay – the bloodied, torn clothes neatly folded – in a pile on a chair near the door.

She took the wallet, a cheap imitation-leather affair, and removed the snapshots that poked from a folded driver's licence. A young man in uniform, smiling, that must surely be Joe's son, the Fusilier killed – by Dermot, she thought.

Killed by Dermot – at Crossmaglen. A picture of Joe himself, bare-chested and sunburnt, in some foreign location, judging by the palm tree. An older black and white snapshot of a stout, thick-legged woman in an old-fashioned dress, holding a little boy in her arms.

She shuffled the pictures into line and slid them back into the fold of the licence.

The sergeant was dead, but he had left his bacillus to incubate within her. He had carried the dreadful knowledge with him, and by accident she had stumbled across it. She had drunk of it as accidentally and innocently as a child might drink from an abandoned bottle of poisonous adult medicine, or a lab technician contaminate himself with an infectious organism.

Joe had given her his plague, and now the plague was taking hold. She looked again at the shrouded body.

Colm dead, the sergeant dead, the dead of Crossmaglen, the horribly dead mother and child. Soldiers and policemen, Provos and Catholics and Protestants. Innocents murdered by mistake. How many more bodies before Ireland – the whole of Ireland – could be at peace?

And Dermot away in America, his sins wiped clean by 3,000 miles.

There seemed to be no life left now for Fionulla. She was one of Ireland's walking dead, those who live but have nothing left within them. She knew she could never return to Belfast, to school, to a grieving Mum and Dad in that flat in the sky.

She had become the plague carrier now, and there seemed to be only one cure. The cure of fire.

Fionulla spoke to the thing under the shroud. 'I'm sorry, Joe.'

CHAPTER
16

The Irish Justice Minister gave interviews.

Word of the Englishman's death had reached the media at Shannon and they clamoured for more details.

This deportee – McGarvey – had he been the one responsible for the Englishman's death?

And Davies could say truthfully that that was not the case. The man, whose identity had not yet been fully established, had opened fire on the crowd. He had been injured in the ensuing melee and had died later from what doctors believed (and the Justice Minister fervently hoped would be proved by pathologists later) to be a compressed fracture of the skull suffered earlier.

No, the Justice Minister said, he did not know whether the dead man was a British SAS soldier. But how he prayed that the man was. Killed by a mob or no, Westminster would have a hard time justifying the presence of an armed SAS man so deep in the Republic.

But dammit all, he thought, McGarvey seemed to trail death behind him like some vampire.

Then it was Senator Minihan's turn with the media, and it was a rough twenty or so minutes – the British being the toughest on him.

What pressure had he put on the Irish Government and his *cousin* the Taoiseach through Washington, or *personally*, to deport McGarvey, rather than let them go ahead and co-operate with Great Britain under the tenets of the Anglo-Irish agreement on security and the North?

He denied all this. He also denied that he had become involved as some stunt to get himself re-elected in the fall. Yes, he agreed irritably, he *had* sponsored McGarvey's entry into the United States. He did not believe, he told the reporters, that the man could possibly receive fair treatment at the hands of the British. He had irrefutable evidence, he told them, that an attempt to assassinate Dermot McGarvey had already been made in Belfast itself. It sounded deep and considered, a product of meticulous research, but it had come rather from his daughter's remarks about Dermot's plight that early morning on the Falls Road.

A bitter-sounding bloated man, from one of the British tabloids, referred to Senator Joe Kennedy's disastrous tour of Ulster when he had clashed with British soldiers, Ulster loyalists, *even* Sinn Fein councillors.

'How,' the man asked, 'would you like it if British members of Parliament visited El Paso and talked about your treatment of Mexican immigrants?'

Senator Minihan knew an opportunity when he saw it, and gave a five-minute historical account dispelling any possible comparisons between the two areas, or the two possibilities, successfully boring the pants off everyone waiting to ask more relevant questions.

Very well, asked a slightly more august figure with

the BBC, how did he justify sponsoring the entry into the US of a wanted man, sought for several killings?

Minihan replied that the French Resistance fought against what was then regarded – even by Britain – as the legal government of France at Vichy. Those men committed murders but were frequently given sanctuary in Britain. In short, it was a question of the legality of British rule in the North, and of the resistance to that.

The reporter affected to look puzzled and asked was the Senator comparing Westminster with Vichy France: a government installed under severe moral pressure of a Nazi occupying power – and the mother of parliaments?

Senator Minihan refused to answer more questions, and the angry reporters and TV crews went out to the airport approach roads to await the arrival of the celebrated would-be deportee.

But that was a pictorial disappointment. The IRA man and the Senator's daughter were crouched down in the back of a patrol car, blankets over their heads. Within minutes, Kathleen, her bruised arm dressed, was in her father's arms, sobbing.

'It's OK now, baby, it's all going to be OK.'

She looked up at him.

'He's not what you think, you have to believe. All that stuff from the past is over.'

Senator Minihan gently released his daughter and walked across to Dermot, who sat with a cup of tea in the corner of the office, a plaster across his gashed forehead.

The tea had been generously laced with whiskey, and

it warmed and calmed him. The mob's behaviour had chilled him, although he knew that he had incited it.

He had tried to get through to the Englishman, to try to save him, but by then the crowd's blood was up, and it was too late. He cursed the man, even in death, for being so *stupid*, so *stubborn*. Why could he have not just let the two of them go? He was a soldier, couldn't he understand that it wasn't personal?

In an hour or so Dermot would be free of it all, but this had soured it. He could see it in the girl's face. That frisson of fear and danger had passed, leaving just some post-coital-like tristesse, and a heaviness at wasted life.

He looked up at the girl's father, and climbed slowly to his feet, his fist still wrapped firmly around the cheering cup.

'Sir.'

'You're McGarvey.' The Senator did not proffer a hand, and Dermot did not think to put out his.

'Dermot McGarvey, sir. And I'm very grateful.'

'This is all a bloody mess, McGarvey.' He pointed an accusing finger in Dermot's face. 'I'm doing this for Kathleen, not you, do you understand that?'

Dermot nodded.

'It's what she wants, and she says you're worth it. Are you?'

'Yes,' Dermot said, 'I'm worth it.' And what the hell else can I say? The girl's put everything into this, she's committed her belief and her *soul*. After the mob she knows now what she's involved in, what she's become *part* of. So all she has left is this stupid obsession with me. The least I can do is not rob her of that.

'You'd better be. I'm going to be in seven kinds of shit over this. So you had better be Mr Perfect in the States, do you hear me? The model citizen, or we'll kick your ass back over here and they can do what they want with you.'

Dermot looked into his eyes, saw the bitter rage, but above all the *jealousy*. He knows I've screwed his daughter, and he hates it.

'I'll be the perfect citizen, sir.'

It seemed like some strange new blood oath. The fraternity of the normal and the civilised opening up to Dermot McGarvey.

'And if you ever . . .' Minihan's voice was quavering . . . 'hurt that girl, in any way . . .'

Dermot could see the girl's eyes on him, blazing with some evangelical belief.

'. . . I'll kill you personally.'

And he knew that he couldn't ever hurt her. She was taking him to America, her personal trophy, her adventure, the badge of her commitment to the Cause.

Well, the girl had earned it. So he would go and be friend, lover, husband, whatever she wanted. And he'd live out that lie for the rest of his life. The fraternity of the normal and the civilised required some sacrifice, and in Dermot's case it would be his soul.

It belonged to the girl now.

He said, 'You'll have nothing to fear from me and

you'll not regret what you've done. And as for your daughter, sir, I'd never hurt her.'

Her eyes pinned him like a butterfly to a board. She was the mistress of the rest of his days.

'I don't know what will become of us. That will be for Kathleen to decide −' he looked at her, steeled himself − 'for myself, I know I love her. But I will let what will be, be . . .'

Her eyes claimed her prize.

The Senator turned.

'Kathleen?'

'Amen, Dad.'

The radio in the big Peugeot diesel taxi was turned to the RTE live broadcast coming from Shannon, and Fionulla heard every rumour straight from the reporter's lips.

An SAS assassination squad had tried to gun down McGarvey in the village of Brayduran on the road to Shannon, having already kidnapped his sister in West Belfast to use as a hostage.

Irish Army detachments were at that moment moving to Shannon to guard against a British Entebbe-style attempt to snatch Dermot McGarvey.

The Irish Justice Minister had threatened to resign unless McGarvey was arrested and charged with assault on the Garda. The Garda had threatened to resign en masse if McGarvey was allowed to leave the country.

The authorities at John F. Kennedy airport in New York had refused landing permission for the Aer Lingus jumbo if McGarvey was a passenger. The American senator, Minihan, had guaranteed the building of a vehicle parts factory, an investment of 50 million punts, and 4,000 jobs, in return for the Taoiseach's co-operation in spiriting McGarvey and the girl out of Ireland.

The American girl had been on a money-running mission for the Provos when she and McGarvey had fallen foul of bitter inter-factional Provo rivalries.

Kathleen Minihan was carrying the IRA man's child. A caller with a Belfast accent had threatened that there was a bomb on board the 747. Aer Lingus pilots were talking about striking if they were made to carry McGarvey as a passenger.

None of it was true: Shannon was a rumour factory, the vacuum left by the absence of anything concrete being filled by a whistling rush of 'facts' as insubstantial as air.

RTE was live, and every station in the United Kingdom was taking its broadcast. An estimated 20 million people were watching, and the hungry minutes demanded fact-fuel.

All that Fionulla knew to be true was that an Englishman was dead at the hands of an angry mob. But more. Because she knew the look of his face, the feel of his hand, the smell of him, his history and his humanity. And that now he was cold beneath the crucifix, covered in a shroud in an air-conditioned funeral parlour.

As the taxi laboured noisily through the countryside, she checked her watch. It was four-fifteen and the man on the radio said the 747 was scheduled to depart at five.

Perhaps she was already too late.

The Justice Minister held two envelopes bearing the seal of the Irish Republic and he handed one to McGarvey, the other to Kathleen Minihan.

He said, 'Open them if you wish. Each contains a letter signed by me stating that your presence is not considered conducive to the peace and order of the Irish Republic and that you are to be deported by the first available transport.'

Kathleen said, 'Thank you.'

Dermot was silent, fingering his envelope thoughtfully.

The Justice Minister continued, 'Under normal circumstances you will be refused entry if you try to return to the Republic of Ireland. Do you understand?'

Kathleen nodded.

'Mr McGarvey, I would further advise you that if you ever return you will be liable to arrest.'

'I understand,' Dermot replied.

The man became brisk now.

'The passengers are being boarded at this moment. We understand several reporters and at least one TV crew have purchased tickets for the flight. That is something you will have to deal with yourselves, we have no power in that matter.'

'The hell you don't,' Senator Minihan said angrily. 'It's a goddamned state airline, you needn't have *sold* them the tickets. Rescind it, refund their money, get 'em off the plane.'

The Justice Minister's voice was ice. 'You listen to me, *Senator*. This is *not* the United States and you have no power or rights here. We do not take orders from the United Kingdom and we do not take orders from you.'

Senator Minihan swallowed hastily. 'Forgive me. I was out of line.'

The door opened and a hard-looking man in civilian clothes raised the fingers of both hands to the minister. The politician acknowledged him, and turned back to his charges.

'We'll take you out in ten minutes.'

'What about the press *here*?' This time it was McGarvey. He was nervous. Nervous of being exposed, of lights and strange faces. He was used to darkness, and secrecy, people he knew and trusted – though not for long – to anonymity.

Suddenly he had become a celebrity, and his whole being was like an exposed nerve that could not bear touch.

'They have an airside facility but don't worry, it's well back from the aeroplane. We've changed the boarding practice. We've parked the 747 away from the terminal. We'll drive you out straight to the steps. *That* way you don't have to go through passport control or customs, or clash with any cameramen who may be in the departure lounge. Does that meet with your satisfaction?'

The politician made no attempt to hide his anger and the sarcasm.

The atmosphere in the small room suddenly seemed hot and oppressive.

The Justice Minister looked at his watch.

'Nine minutes.'

Fionulla walked through the crowded concourse clutching her handbag. She saw a man festooned with Nikon cameras talking to a woman who carried a massive tape recorder and microphone.

She walked up and said boldly, 'Has he gone yet – Dermot McGarvey?'

The photographer looked around, irritated to be disturbed in making plans for the evening ahead. But when he saw Fionulla his mind registered that she was pretty.

'Nah, not yet. About half an hour they're taking us airside. They couldn't organise a piss-up in a brewery.'

He looked her up and down, noting once again that she was pretty and *young* – but nervous.

Bloody provincials are bad enough. Bloody *Irish* provincials, Christ.

He asked, 'You local?'

She nodded, anxious to affirm anything he said. Half an hour, there was still time. She had to see him and she knew that if she approached the authorities they'd just hold her until Dermot and the girl had left.

'Which one?' the photographer said, suddenly

beginning to realise that this Irish bird was really not a bad bit of stuff. If he couldn't make it with the radio reporter, then perhaps this scribbler from the bog would do as a substitute. He got lonely in hotels.

'One?' she said, bewildered, realising that the woman with the tape recorder was giving her hostile looks.

'Which paper? That bloody rag at Galway?'

He was from London and he didn't know a paper other than the *Irish Times* over here. She quickly understood that the man thought she was a journalist.

'Yes . . .' she plucked a name from her mind . . . 'the *Advertiser.*'

'Bit late, aren't you? I've come from London.'

The radio girl knew the photographer was losing interest in her, and said with an injection of bile, 'I might see you later then, when the farce is over . . .'

'Yeh, right love . . .' He turned back to Fionulla, feeling his heartbeat quicken. She was actually quite sensational, and so young. Dennis was forty-five, and he didn't consider himself past it by any means. And if he could make this chick – God Almighty, she was eighteen if she was that . . .

'This is your first big one, isn't it, I can tell.'

She nodded.

'Don't worry, stick with Dennis and you'll be OK. Bloody small fry this. Done Belfast for years, Beirut, Vietnam, this is a poxy little story by comparison.'

She said, 'Thank you. I'm grateful.'

'Don't thank me, have a drink with me once laughing

boy's on his way to New York and I've got my film away.'

'That would be nice.'

'I'm at the Strathmore. Piss-poor food, but the rooms are OK. We'll have a drink, then find a decent restaurant.'

She asked hesitantly, 'They're letting . . . us . . . out on to the Tarmac?'

'How quaint – Tarmac. Airside, darling, we're going airside. Got your press card?'

She stuttered, 'No . . . no, I left it at home.'

He winked, lasciviously. 'Don't worry about that. Press cards are for wankers anyway. Never shown one in *ten* fucking years. You're with Dennis.'

She was begging for it, he always knew the signs did Dennis. She had this bit of sweat on her upper lip, and he could see her heart going boom-de-boom boom under the left boob. Help her out on this crap; few drinks, bottle of shampoo with dinner, give her a few tales, impress the shit out of her, stop the car on the way back.

Roll on tonight.

The airport director had the assembled journalists, more than one hundred and fifty of them, grouped in the departure lounge.

'OK. Now listen to me, I'm not going to repeat it. We'll take you airside to a line marked off by my personnel . . .'

'Who'll get in the bloody way of a clear shot –' shouted a young photographer.

'Who will *then* allow you a clear view for your pictures,' the director said with heavy stress.

'What about questions?' a TV man shouted from the centre of the pack.

'Just like that – you'll have to shout.' The director laughed, good-natured, and though the TV man cursed, his colleagues laughed and cat-called him.

'Right. This is self-policing. You *don't* move over that line – if you do one of my lads has orders to push you back again and they're *big* lads.'

A reporter wolf-whistled. Someone said, 'Seems like a nice boy,' and there was more laughter.

'Anybody you don't know, point them out, this is press only, no sightseers.'

Everyone looked self-consciously around, winking, making jokes to the effect that several well-known Fleet Street journalists could only possibly qualify as amateur sightseers.

Fionulla saw one man gaze suspiciously at her, and mouth to the photographer Dennis, 'Who's she?'

Instinctively, she moved closer and linked Dennis's arm.

He said, 'Nice one,' and kept his body close. The man who had raised the issue winked in admiration at the photographer's renowned bird-pulling power, and looked away, satisfied.

Fionulla hated herself. Hated what she was doing, and what she had become. But the world had changed, and it was the only way. She had to see Dermot before it was too late.

They filed after the airport director to a door, jostling and pushing to be at the head of the queue and, once through, descended a set of metal stairs and stepped out into the sunshine on the concrete apron of one of the airport docking bays.

Fionulla could smell heat and aviation fuel, then saw, about one hundred and fifty yards away, the Boeing 747 in its Aer Lingus livery of green and white, with the giant shamrock on its tail.

A line of airport security men at two-yard intervals formed a diagonal barrier behind which the director stopped.

'Right, this is it.'

There were protests, and cries of 'Not near enough', but eventually the protests subsided, and the cameramen began to unpack portable step-ladders and tripods, jostling for position. They knew they were lucky even to be this close.

The director was happy. He did not give a fig for politics, especially not that bloody mess in the North. But he knew that a lot of people didn't realise Shannon Airport even *existed*. And those that had heard of it did not know it had scheduled and charter services to America's East Coast. Now a departure would be seen live by millions!

Fionulla stayed close to Dennis, who was reassuring.

'Don't worry, love. What you miss you can get from the others, see on TV later or read in the dailies tomorrow. By the time your rag comes out it will be old history anyway.'

She nodded dumbly, still clutching her handbag, like a shipwreck survivor on to a piece of floating wreckage. The photograper busied himself with his preparation, and Fionulla had time to think. Now that the moment had come she felt frozen, her motivation paralysed by an ice-pack of fear. What would she say to him?

Two ghostly images haunted her. Colm, framed by the shroud, his face waxen in death; the anonymous form of the sergeant beneath the sheet.

And crazily she thought, I wonder what America would be like?

The hard-looking man came in through the door again.

'Sir. Time to go.'

The Justice Minister shook the Senator, the girl – and reluctantly, McGarvey – by the hand.

The Senator said, 'I shall not forget.'

The security man handed each of the passengers a boarding pass and said brusquely, 'Follow me.'

They did, down a set of stairs to an open door, where a white Ford Transit estate waited with its engine running, and a man behind the wheel.

'In.'

They climbed in and Dermot noticed that Kathleen held on to her father with her uninjured arm.

The 747 was one hundred yards away and Dermot could see the blobs of curious faces peering from the windows. To the van's left, perhaps twice the plane's distance away, a line of photographers and TV cameramen.

It's happening, Dermot thought. It's really happening. Crossmaglen, the ambush on the Falls, Colm, the betrayal, the terror of the tunnel and the death of the Englishman. None of it matters now.

The pack saw the white Transit, the blurred distant figures climbing in, and the cry went up.

'It's them!'

Motor drives clack-clacked, TV lights came on and reporters whipped up binoculars, thoughtfully brought, or strained to see. Voices spoke breathlessly into microphones.

Fionulla saw it all too.

She brushed past a photographer, who swore at her.

And she ran.

A security guard spotted her running, her handbag swinging on her arm, and he shouted. When she ignored him he gave chase, but he was fifty and pot-bellied and had no chance of catching her.

She was almost half-way to the aircraft now, and the lenses were switching to her as the Transit came to rest at the foot of the aircraft steps.

As he got out of the Transit the Senator was the first to spot the running figure.

'What the hell is that?' He jabbed a finger in the girl's direction.

The security man said, 'Shit,' as he too got out, going for the gun in his shoulder holster.

Kathleen screamed, 'Dermot – it's your sister!'

'Nulla?' Dermot leapt out of the Transit.

She was thirty yards from them, running as hard as she could, and the security man, scared and uncertain, had his pistol half out of his holster.

No one had briefed him for this eventuality. Perhaps it was just some crazy reporter going for a scoop, but how could he be sure, half of the British Isles wanted to get even with Dermot McGarvey.

He kept his hand on the butt of his gun and shouted, 'Stop! Stop right there.'

The girl kept running.

'No,' McGarvey shouted, 'it's my sister, that's all. It's my little sister.'

But the man had the gun out, not aimed, but up and ready. Unsure what to do, nobody had told him this would happen. And it *was* a girl.

Dermot came level with the man, seeing the uncertain, terrified look in his eyes, noting the closeness of the finger to the trigger. He put a hand on the man's steadying arm, gently, anxious not to make him fire a shot accidentally.

'It's OK, she's no danger, God's honour. Just my stupid little sister.'

The security man seemed to come out of some trance, and lowered the pistol.

'It's OK now,' Dermot said, 'really. Everything's OK.'

Then Fionulla stopped before them, her lungs heaving from the run.

Dermot said, 'Bit late in the day, Nulla. You could have come with us back there. You chose to stay with the Brit.'

'He's dead.'

'I'm sorry, and that is the truth, but it was his choice, and I tried to stop those lads, you saw me yourself.'

Kathleen came up and joined him, touching his arm, while the Senator watched curiously.

'We have to get on the plane, Dermot. Tell her she can come with us if that's what she wants – Dad?'

Kathleen looked to her father for his approval, and got it in a terse nod. He said, 'But hurry it, Kathleen, this is turning into a bloody circus.'

'Hear that, Nulla? America! You and me in America.'

He took a step towards her, and she started back, pushing her hand out to ward him off as though some invisible part of him, some spectre, had already reached and touched her.

'Get away!'

'Nulla? What the hell is it?'

Her face twisted in a kind of terrible and bitter-sweet anguish.

'Why did you kill Colm?'

Dermot felt the pain like the spear in Christ's side; the final anguish.

He said slowly, 'You'd never understand, Nulla.'

Kathleen's face was a mask of horror. 'Dermot! She's lying, isn't she? Colm was killed by a sectarian assassin – you told me so. What's she saying?'

He gave her only a sideways glance.

'Shut up. This is me and her.'

Kathleen staggered back as though struck by the rebuke.

Fionulla said, '*Tell* me, Dermot. I must know *why*. *How* you could.'

He shook his head with resignation, bowed by the terrible knowledge and years and experience that he could never share. Not with her, not with anyone, least of all now with the empty-headed girl who wished to whisk him to America.

He said, 'I killed him, Nulla, because . . .' He heard her stifled sob, and tried to measure the words like the articles of an impossible-to-understand faith to an unbeliever. 'I killed Colm because I loved him.'

He paused. 'As I love you.'

She gave a terrible, high-pitched animal cry of sheer agony, then she pulled something from her handbag, letting the bag fall with a soft thud to the concrete. She held a pistol in both hands.

Cocking the gun the way she had seen the sergeant do, she pointed it at Dermot.

It was a waxwork tableau. No one moved, no one spoke, there was only the sound of their breathing and the distant airport noises.

Her face was screwed up, peering at Dermot as though seeing him in a different way. The silence hung like an eternity.

She said, 'As I love you, Dermot.'

And fired once, twice, three and four times, quickly.

The bullets took Dermot in the chest and he went back hard on to the concrete, already oblivious to Kathleen's scream as the blood from the killing wounds splashed across her and Senator Minihan.

Fionulla McGarvey lowered the gun, and said, so softly that only she herself could hear, 'As I loved you, Dermot.'

Epilogue

The shooting of IRA man Dermot McGarvey by his sister at Shannon Airport was shown on the major TV news bulletins through the Western world.

Fionulla McGarvey suffered a mental breakdown in custody while awaiting trial, and was eventually confined for an indefinite period in a psychiatric hospital.

Kathleen Minihan and her father returned to the United States where Senator Minihan announced that he would not run for the Senate in the fall elections.

His daughter disappeared to Central America, met and fell in love with a doctor working at a jungle clinic. The couple eventually married and eighteen months later Kathleen gave birth to a baby boy. She called the boy Patrick.

The Taoiseach and the Justice Minister lost their jobs when their party failed to regain power in the Irish elections.

No one was ever prosecuted over the death of Joe Biddle, it being deemed that the individuals involved – more than thirty of them – had acted to protect their lives.

The British Government at Westminster, acutely embarrassed that an armed British soldier had been discovered in the Republic, let the matter rest.

Joe was buried next to his son in the cemetery outside the Northern town in which they had both been born. It was a private funeral, not a military one, so there was no guard or firing party, just a handful of black-clad relatives huddled in the cold.

Joe's mother lives on in her tiny terrace house.

The Divis flats are being demolished, section by section, and Mr and Mrs McGarvey will soon be re-housed in a neat, modern house with all modern conveniences.

Dermot McGarvey received the traditional IRA funeral, with a lone, mournful piper, a slow-stepping cortege, and a coffin flanked by black-bereted youths in dark sunglasses.

The coffin itself was draped in the Irish tricolour, and a symbolic black beret and a pair of black gloves lay atop it. It was the lowest funeral turnout for a dead IRA volunteer in the short, troubled history of the modern conflict.

Newspapers wrote learned stories saying that at last the Catholic community were rejecting the 'men of violence'.

A week later two British soldiers were shot dead by a sniper in the Ballymurphy district. The IRA man who fired the shot was eighteen years old.

Another Shamrock Boy lives.

If you have enjoyed this book you will enjoy these great titles from Blake Publishing:

STUART WHITE   **'TIL THE FAT LADY SINGS**
From the author of The Shamrock Boy comes the devastating story of a darkly beautiful woman called Bianca and of Nick Carter, the international journalist who knows her deadly secret.

"Stuart White is one of the few writers around whose books you just cannot bear to put down." *Evening Standard*.
ISBN: 185782-004-5   **£4.99**

JENNIFER HULLAND   **BLOOD RELATIONS**
Sandra... A lost little girl whose life changes for ever when Tom, her strict, religious foster father persuades her to go into the attic. Beth, the friend with a terrible secret. A secret that will end in murder...

"Well written, sensitive, restrained, sexually overtoned."
The Times
ISBN: 185782-050-9   **£4.99**

ED GORMAN   **SHADOW GAMES**
Cobey Daniels has it all – he's rich, young and the hottest star in the country. But the messy business with 14 year old Kimberley means change for Cobey. Now the bad times are coming and, if Cobey wants to live, he will have to learn to play... Shadow Games.

"Gorman's writing is strong, fast and sleek as a bullet. He's one of the best!" *Dean Koontz*
ISBN: 185782-031-2   **£4.99**

JOHN SHIRLEY   **WETBONES**
It's just a book, it won't hurt you badly... A killer is on the loose. An ancient evil is destroying women... A shattering, memorable novel from one of America's finest young writers.

"Wetbones is a wild and giddy ride." *Clive Barker*
ISBN: 185782-032-0   **£4.99**

All Blake Books are available at your local bookshop or can be ordered direct from the publisher.